Not For Keeps

LAKE CITY BOOK TWO

JASMINE AHMAD

Author's Note

Dear Reader,

Thank you for picking up this book. While I hope this story brings you joy, connection, and maybe even a few tears, I also want to acknowledge that certain topics in this book may be difficult for some readers.

Content Warning:

- Grief & Loss - Death of a loved one, discussions of past loss.
- Disaster Trauma - Fire and traumatic emergency situations.
- Mental Health: Trauma responses.

I encourage readers to take care of themselves while reading. My goal is to tell stories that honor both the joy and hardship of life, holding space for healing, love, and resilience. From the bottom of my heart, thank you for being here.

Con mucho amor,

Jasmine

Playlist

1. Work Song - Hozier
2. The Smallest Man Who Ever Lived - Taylor Swift
3. Running Up That Hill - Kate Bush
4. Eternity - Alex Warren
5. Skin - Rihanna
6. Back To Friends - Sombr
7. Drunk In Love - Beyonce
8. Feels Like - Gracie Abrams
9. That's How Strong My Love Is - Alicia Keys

Dedication

For the dreamers who had to let go of their first map, the right destination is still waiting. Vienna waits for you.

Chapter One

ANALYSE

"Would you believe me if I told you the husband wasn't the killer this time?"

I snort into my coffee. "Doubt it."

Taking a slow sip, I let the warmth spread through me as the host continues unraveling the case. Nothing like a little murder with my morning routine. The house is quiet—just me, my coffee, and the soft crackle of my earbuds. In about twenty minutes, Maya will wake up, and I'll have to trade cold cases for cartoons. But for now, it's just me and the mystery.

I take another sip, savoring the few peaceful minutes I have left. The kitchen is dim, lit only by the glow of the range hood light, and the sky outside is still an inky blue. The whole house is quiet—no tiny footsteps yet, no cartoons blaring from the TV.

I glance at the clock. Any minute now.

The podcast continues playing in my earbuds as I lean against the counter, but my mind drifts. Today is—what? Thursday? No, Friday. The end of the week, not that it makes much difference. Lately, all my days blur together into a mess of work, getting us both out the door for school, and reheated coffee.

"Authorities now believe the timeline is off by at least two hours, which changes everything."

I hum under my breath, tapping my nails against the ceramic mug. Changing a timeline is huge. If the time of death is wrong, then the alibi—

A soft sound pulls me from my thoughts—the shuffle of blankets, a tiny sigh. Just like that, my alone time is over. I set my mug down as I hear the familiar creak of Maya's bedroom door. Light footsteps tap down the stairs, slow and steady, the rhythm of a little girl who isn't quite awake yet.

I glance up just as she peeks around the banister. First, the mess of brown curls—wild and unruly like mine. Then, those big brown eyes, blinking sleepily, and her round cheeks, still warm from sleep. She clutches her stuffed frog to her chest, studying me like she's deciding whether she's ready to fully commit to being awake—although I know she doesn't really have a choice. Then, without a word, she crosses the room and tugs at the hem of my sweater.

I look down, smiling. "Morning, mija."

She rubs her eyes, her voice still thick with sleep. "I had a dream that I won the pie-eating contest."

"Oh yeah?" I reach for the frying pan, setting it on the stove. "Did you finally beat Alejandro?"

She lets out a long, dramatic sigh, which I'm going to take as a no. "I *almost* did. But then I started laughing and got pie up my nose."

I chuckle, shaking my head. "Maya, that's *exactly* what happened last year."

"I *know*, Mami. But this time, I was *so close!*" She slides onto one of the chairs at the table, her little hands animated. "I had a whole strategy—no laughing, no looking at Alejandro, just *pie*."

I nod seriously. "That sounds like a foolproof plan, mamita."

"I know, right?" She swings her legs back and forth. "Ahora tengo hambre."

I smirk. "Let me guess—pie for breakfast?"

She gasps. "Can I?!"

I give her a look.

"Fine." She sighs like she's suffering. "Salchichas con huevos?"

I nod. "Deal."

She grins. "Ooh! And maduros! *Please, Mami?*"

I shake my head, already standing. "Fine. Go get dressed. It'll be ready when you come back down."

She squeals and runs back up the stairs, her curls bouncing behind her.

I pause for a moment, watching her go. She looks so much like me, and her attitude matches mine, too—sharp, stubborn, and full of fire. Sometimes it's hard to believe she'll be seven soon. It feels like just yesterday she fit perfectly in my arms, this tiny, perfect human. I remember the first time I looked into her eyes, the way love crashed over me so completely it almost knocked the breath from my lungs. I knew right then —I would tear the world apart for her.

What I *still* don't understand is how anyone could know of her existence and not want to be in her life. How someone could walk away from something so pure, so beautiful, and not realize how privileged we are to love her.

The thought lingers as I turn back to the stove, stirring the eggs absentmindedly. I take a deep breath, glancing toward the window. The trees outside are at their peak, deep reds and golds stretching down the street. The air smells like change— sharp and cool, but still touched with warmth.

October in Lake City means the Fall Festival, the one event that makes this town feel bigger than it is. The whole place comes alive—hayrides rolling down Main Street, kids painting pumpkins on the sidewalks, the scent of roasted nuts and cider thick in the air. The chili cook-off will bring in the entire town, and the sack race will get too competitive, as always. And then there's the pie-eating contest, where Maya will do her best to beat Alejandro, and I'll pretend I don't already know how it's going to end. My girl is competitive, but she does not have the stomach for all that pie—I wonder if I can get away with bribing a six-year-old. No, no, it's okay—losing builds character.

The Fall Festival is one of those traditions that reminds me of how much I have. And how much *he* has missed out on. Nico. I hate that man. I loved that man. Maya's dad walked away before she was even born. One conversation. That's all it took for him to decide fatherhood wasn't for him. We were twenty-four. He said it was too much. And just like that, he was gone. A fucking joke, really.

For a moment, I hoped he would change his mind. For weeks, I convinced myself that he would call me and say he made a huge mistake and that he would be there for me, for our baby. This was a man I loved. A man I had a relationship with, someone I thought I'd spend my life with. Sure, things weren't perfect, but are relationships ever everything you want them to be? What mattered was that I cared for him, and I thought he cared for me, too. I wasn't naive to think he'd be ecstatic about the pregnancy, but never in a million years did I think he would just walk out on me, on us.

It was at my eight-week appointment, when I heard her heart for the very first time, that realization set in—Nico would not be coming back, and I had to be okay with that. But I was furious. I was so damn angry and so damn sad. My heart ached at the thought of my daughter not having both parents in her life. The picture-perfect, white-picket-fenced family that she deserved. The most important role I'll ever have in life is being her mom, keeping her safe, protecting her from harm, and I failed her at conception simply because of who I conceived her with. I failed her by giving her a father who could walk away so easily, and it fucking kills. On top of being a failure, I had to mourn the life I thought I had designed for myself.

But then I look at the life we have, the life I created for us, and I realize that I never needed him. Maya never needed him. I've been blessed with an amazing support system—my family, my friends—they've been there for me through it all. Seb, my mom, and my dad were at every single appointment—even though I told them that was unnecessary. My mom was with me in the delivery room, squeezing my hand through every contraction, whispering encouragement, wiping the sweat from my face. Damn, I miss my parents. They're in Florida now, living their best snowbird life, escaping the cold while I brace for the first snowfall of the season. It'll be my first Christmas without them—my favorite time of the year—but they'll be back when the weather begins to warm up again.

I slide Maya's plate onto the table just as I hear her barreling down the stairs, excitement in every step. The day has barely begun, and I already feel like I've lived a thousand lives.

After Maya finishes her breakfast, we rush out the door, barely making it on time. Mornings always feel like a chaotic relay race: me flipping eggs while simultaneously packing her backpack, her getting distracted mid-bite to tell me an *extremely* important story about a butterfly she saw last week. Somehow, we pull it off.

It helps that I teach at Maya's school. One drop-off. One pick-up. One less logistical nightmare in my already chaotic life. Lately, though, I've been thinking about transferring to the middle school where Anna teaches. I always dreamed about teaching at the middle school. I'd love to focus on English, really dig into storytelling, help kids find their voices —but do I actually have the capacity for a career change right now? Probably not. My life is held together with coffee, Rizos curl refresh spray, and the occasional deep breath. And, honestly, it really is so much easier going to the same place as Maya every day.

Seb keeps telling me he can help more. Mateo, Seb's best friend, too. Hell, he practically begs me to let him spend more time with Maya. And I know they mean it. I know they love her. But I can't shake the guilt. They have their own lives. Their own responsibilities. The last thing I want to do is feel like a burden, like I'm taking advantage of the people who've already done so much for me.

I didn't get a chance to eat lunch today—shocker—so now I'm inhaling a questionable-looking sandwich at my desk while half-heartedly working on lesson plans. Seb and Mari offered to take Maya for a few hours, and instead of going home to an empty house, I figured I'd stay here and get ahead on work.

Mari told me I should use the time to do something fun. "Go out! Live a little! Maybe even—gasp—go on a date."

A date. The thought alone makes me laugh. I haven't been on a date in years. And sex? I mean. *Do I even remember how?* I think I do? Sometimes I miss it—not just the physical part, but the intimacy. The feeling of being so close to someone in a way that has nothing to do with parenting or lesson plans. But dating? Ugh. I would quite literally rather throw myself in front of oncoming traffic than endure the agony of a million first dates. The small talk. The awkward first impressions. The inevitable, *what's your favorite color?* questions.

I don't *want* small talk. I want *real* talk. Tell me about your wildest dream, the one you're scared to say out loud. Tell me the things that keep you up at night, the secrets you don't tell anyone else. That's what I want—not surface-level bullshit about sports teams and the latest trending TV show.

But even if I wanted to date, when exactly would I fit it in? Between working all day, making sure Maya has everything she needs, and collapsing into bed the second she falls asleep, I barely have time to *think*. The other day I came to work wearing two different shoes—I'm a mess.

So here I am. Sitting in my classroom, pressing play on my favorite true crime podcast, eating a sandwich that is at least one day past its prime, and tackling lesson plans while Seb and Mari spend time with the best kid I know.

And honestly? It's not so bad.

Chapter Two

MATEO

I'm halfway through my *second* breakfast—because one wasn't enough after the morning shift—when Andres flops into the chair across from me.

"I'm done, bro. I'm retiring from women," he announces, rubbing a hand down his face.

I snort. "Sure you are."

"Deadass. No more dating, no more flirting, no more—"

Seb passes by, slaps him on the back, and cuts in with, "No more getting left on read after sending 'you up?' texts?"

Andres flips him off, and I grin, chewing another bite of mangu and eggs. "What happened this time?"

"Same shit, different girl," he mutters. "Said she wanted to keep things casual, but now she's planning our future wedding in her group chat."

"Sounds like you need to start dating women who actually like you for you," I say, smirking.

"Like you're one to talk," Andres shoots back. "You're worse than me, *papi chulo*."

"First of all, thank you," I say, grinning. "Second, I make my intentions crystal clear. I'm an *honest* man."

Seb snorts. "Honest? The hell you are."

I hold a hand to my chest, offended. "I tell every woman I'm not looking for anything serious. No lies, no fake promises. Just fun. And they know that going in."

And it's true. I don't do commitment. Don't do feelings. Don't do complicated. Life is easier that way. Cleaner.

"Right, right. There's no locking Mateo down," Andres says, smirking.

I finish the last bite of my breakfast, set my plate in the sink, and clap a hand on his shoulder. "Now you're getting it."

After my shift, I'm dead on my feet—and starving. My gear bag hits the floor just inside the door, and I head straight to the fridge, already imagining a sandwich, maybe leftovers, something that doesn't involve standing for too long.

I pull open my fridge and am greeted with a case of beer and a bottle of ketchup—that's it. Coño. I stand there for a second, just staring, like something else might magically appear if I look long enough. Like maybe a rotisserie chicken will materialize behind the Modelo. Spoiler alert: it doesn't.

I scrub a hand over my face and sigh. I need to get my ass to the store. The couch is calling my name—hell, the floor would probably do—but I know if I sit down, it's over. I'll wake up at 2 a.m. with a stiff neck and a hunger headache.

So I grab my keeps from the table, still in my uniform, and head out the door before exhaustion talks me out of being a functioning adult.

Why is it that when you're exhausted, a ten-minute drive feels like forty?

Every red light feels personal. Every bend in the road feels longer than I remember it being. My back aches. My eyes sting. All I want to do is turn this car around and crawl into my bed.

I should've just starved. Or maybe gulped down the damn ketchup. It's made out of tomatoes, those are vegetables, right? Or are they fruit? Either way, it would've been better than this late-night mission to keep myself from wasting away.

Both the driver and passenger windows are rolled down, the cool October breeze knifing through the cab, doing its best to slap the sleep out of me. My left hand's locked on the wheel, stiff from gripping it too tight, while the right fumbles for the radio volume. I crank it up. Something upbeat, fast enough to drown out the temptation of silence.

My eyes flick to the road then to the streetlights blurring past, one by one.

I love the October air in Lake City. There's something clean about it—crisp and biting in a way that feels earned after the sweat of the summer.

Back when I left California, I didn't have a real plan. Just a destination that felt nothing like the place I was running from. I'd never lived somewhere with snow, or seasons, or this quiet. I didn't know if it'd stick. I didn't know if I would. But Lake City...it became home.

Not because of the weather or the quiet or the fact that I can walk down the street and actually breathe. It became home because I found people who let me show up with my baggage and didn't ask me to unpack it right away. People like Seb. Like Andres. Like Cap. People who made space for me, even when I didn't think I deserved it.

And that's the thing about starting over—you never expect to care again. To build something that could fall apart. To wake up one day and realize that you're not just surviving anymore. You're living.

These people—they've become mine. And that makes the idea of losing it terrifying.

I finally arrive at the supermarket and rush out of my truck, telling myself that it'll be a quick stop—twenty minutes max. If I can get out fast, I'll actually eat before eight and maybe even get my ass to bed at a decent hour.

But of course, that's wishful thinking. People say don't shop hungry, but the real mistake is grocery shopping in a small town. What I thought would be a quick trip turns into an obstacle course of conversations. With every aisle I cross, I bump into someone who *absolutely* needs to chat. At this point, I'm convinced there's a sign taped to my back that says, *Talk to me, I have nothing better to do.*

I take a hard turn into the produce section, and fuck, I see Letty. I spin the cart in the opposite direction, but I'm not fast enough. She spots me.

"Mateo? I knew that was you," she purrs, placing a hand on my arm, gently squeezing my bicep.

"Hey, Letty. Yup, it's me. How are you?"

"What? No, it's good to see you, Letty? You're not happy to see me, Mateo?" she teases, biting her lip.

"Uh, yeah, it's good to see you, Letty. I'm just in a bit of a rush—just got off a long shift, need to grab food and get home to bed before I pass out on my feet."

Her eyes flicker at the word bed. Shit.

She rubs her hand slowly down my arm. "Aw, poor baby. You must be so tired. You need a good woman to take care of you. You're a hardworking man, Mateo. You need a strong woman by your side. If you ever want a home-cooked meal, I'd be happy to come over...satisfy that appetite."

Nope.

"Uh...right. Well. I gotta finish up here. Thanks for the... chat."

"Okay, Mateo," she says with a wink, walking off with way too much hip sway.

I exhale the breath I didn't know I was holding and steer the cart down the next aisle. I start throwing things into it like I'm stocking up for a storm—pasta, rice, canned goods, frozen meals—anything that'll keep me from having to come here again for a week.

And then I see it. A can of Florecitas. Score.

I toss it into the cart without thinking. Maya loves these. I always keep some on hand at the firehouse for her, but we've been out for a while. I grab a second can and drop it in beside the first.

Maybe I'll leave one there and bring the other to her tonight—*after* I eat and take a quick nap.

Chapter Three

ANALYSE

I finally call it a night on lesson planning at 8 o'clock—Maya is going to spend the night at Seb and Mari's. The moment I got home, I rip off my clothes, unhook my bra, and throw on a big T-shirt. I honestly think anyone who willingly wears jeans while at home is insane and I absolutely cannot have that in my life—the second my feet land in my house and that door is closed, those babies *need* to come right off.

Now I'm lying on the floor of my living room, a glass of wine beside me, old school Daddy Yankee blasting from my speaker. What can I say? Sometimes a girl needs a little old school reggaeton to unwind. I'll never forget the day my mom walked into my room and heard me singing "El Telefono"—she was pissed, and I was punished for a month. In retrospect, an eleven-year-old singing a song about phone sex is completely inappropriate. Sorry, Mami, I was always a bit of a handful.

The weekend has been calling my name all week long, and since Maya won't be home, I can get all the chores on my list done. I miss her little face. Isn't it crazy how we want a break, but the moment we get one, we miss them immediately? She's my little best friend. I love hearing all about her day and all the stories she makes up—the girl has some imagination. She's so much fun to be around. Maybe I can call Seb to drop her off? It isn't too late. No, no. I should let her have fun with them. It's not her fault I don't have a life.

Three glasses of wine deep, I decide I should probably have something to eat so that I won't wake up tomorrow feeling like garbage. I'm too tired to cook, so I decide to toast some bread. While the bread is toasting, I close my eyes and tilt my head back. The alcohol is making me feel warm and fuzzy, and I let the beat of the music wrap around my body like a wave.

The bread springs out of the toaster, and I rush to grab it, burning the tips of my fingers. I take a bite, and it's definitely the wine, but this is the best piece of toast I've ever had in my life. Like, no one has ever made a better toast than this one right here in my hands. I wash it down with more wine and hear the sound of a car pulling up in the front of my house. That's weird, I'm not expecting anyone tonight—maybe Maya was homesick?

I peek through my blinds and see a red truck that I definitely don't recognize. I know literally everyone in this town—so, who the hell is that? My confusion lasts for a moment and quickly turns into shock and that quickly turns into rage. You have got to be fucking kidding me.

I throw on a pair of chanclas before I run out the door and yell, "What the hell are you doing here?"

Nico just stands there, staring at me, a stunned look on his stupid face. Why is he stunned? I'm the one who's stunned. He turns up here, unannounced, when I haven't heard a single word from him in nearly seven years. This has to be a hallucination. I got myself wine drunk and now for some reason my brain is hallucinating my daughter's dead-beat father. I'm contemplating taking my chancleta off to throw at him to see if he's real when he clears his throat.

Looking me up and down, he says, "Analyse—you look good."

Is he for real right now? "Don't 'you look good' me, Nico. What the hell are you doing here?"

"I wanted to see you."

"Great. You've seen me. Now get back into your truck and never see me again."

"Come on, don't be like that."

"I will be like that, Nico. I haven't heard a peep from you in seven years and you decide to show up—unannounced, I might add—and say you just wanted to see me? Be for real."

To myself, I mumble, "Este maldito estúpido."

"I was thinking about you, about our baby. I fucked up. I miss you," Nico says.

He says "our baby" because he has no idea that we have a daughter, because he never once called, checked in, or tried to glean any information. I can't believe the words coming out of his mouth right now.

"She's my daughter," I say flatly. "If you want to talk about this, come back in the morning. Maya isn't here, and I'm not doing this right now."

"I know, I know. I fucked up big time. But I want to make things right. I want to meet her. Be in her life. Be in your life. Be that family you always dreamed about."

My eyes roll so far back into my head I hear my mom's warning echoing, *They'll stay that way if you don't stop.* This fucking guy.

"Nico, you and I will never be a family. You lost that chance the moment you walked out on me all those years ago."

"Just give me a chance. Let me show you—"

Headlights sweep across the driveway, Nico's words die on his tongue. Ay dios mio. I run my hand down my face, landing at my neck. Why is everyone showing up to my house unannounced? Since when do I give off the vibe that I like visitors without notice? Do I have a sign on my front lawn that says *show up whenever the hell you feel like* or something? It's so dark I can hardly make out whose car that is, until he opens the driver's side door and steps out. Mateo.

And it's at that very moment that someone else completely takes over my body. because I say, "Mateo, mi amor, I'm so glad you're here—I missed you."

I walk over to Mateo, wrap my arms around his neck, pretend I'm giving him a kiss, and whisper, "Go. With. It."

Mateo quickly masks the shock on his face, pulls me in closer, and says, "Hola, querida. You know I couldn't stay away from you for too long." Looking between Nico and me, he asks, "Who's this?"

I quickly untangle myself from Mateo's arms. Wow those arms are strong; okay focus, Analyse. You can ruminate on those thoughts later. I glance up at Mateo. "Mateo, this is Nico...Maya's father."

His jaw ticks, and for a split second, I see the shock in his eyes before he schools his expression. He shifts closer, body angling ever so slightly between me and Nico.

Then I turn to face Nico and say, "Nico, this is Mateo— my boyfriend."

The shock is written all over Nico's face, and I can't help but feel a bit of satisfaction. I look up at Mateo and can only imagine what thoughts are running through Nico's head right now. Mateo is all man—6'5", brown skin, chiseled jaw, nearly black eyes, curly black hair, big strong biceps, and a thigh tattoo on strong legs that look like they can crush someone. Shit. Mateo is hot.

Nico looks between us. "Your boyfriend?"

Before I can say anything, Mateo cuts in, holding out his

hand to Nico's and says, "Yeah, man. I'm her boyfriend. Is there something you need or are you on your way out?"

Nico doesn't move to grab Mateo's hand—asshole. Instead, his gaze stays on me. "Analyse, just think about what I said, okay? I was serious. I'm going to be around for a while."

And with that, he turns around, gets into his car, and drives away, leaving me to face Mateo—and the mess I've created.

Chapter Four

MATEO

This wasn't how I expected my night to go. When I pulled up and saw the red truck parked outside Analyse's place, my stomach dropped. For a second, I thought I was interrupting a date, and the rush of relief that hit me when I realized I wasn't is something I'll have to unpack later.

But the last person I expected to see was him. I've heard about Maya's dad over the years—his name always coming up in hushed voices, half-whispered stories that Analyse never wanted to linger on. Nico. I'd imagined him a hundred different ways, but never as the guy standing on her porch, making her look so tense and pissed that her whole face was pulled tight. And then he had the nerve to tell her to "think about what he said." What the hell does that even mean? Has he been in touch with her? What did he say?

Every muscle in me screamed to lay him out right then, to put him in his place the second I knew who he was. But for Maya's sake, I had to keep my cool. That's her dad. No matter how much it twists me up inside, I can't be the guy who takes a swing at him in front of her.

My gaze drifts back to Analyse, because in the middle of this shitstorm, she's impossible to ignore. She's standing there in an oversize T-shirt that skims her thighs, her curls wild around her face, her plump pink lips caught between her teeth. And God help me, she's breathtaking.

"So I'm your boyfriend, huh?"

Analyse pushes my shoulder. "Shut up, Mateo."

I laugh. "No, really, what was that about?"

She puts her hands over her face. "I'm sorry, Mateo. I just really needed him to go away and stop talking about 'our future.' I don't know why I said that, but I'll fix it as soon as I speak to him again."

I gently remove her hands from her face and hold them. "Hey, talk to me, start from the beginning, like for starters, where's Maya? Did she see him?"

She takes a deep breath. "No, she didn't see him. She's spending the night with Seb and Mari."

"Okay, that's good. So tell me what happened between him coming to your house and you telling him that I was your boyfriend."

"I didn't even know he was coming. He showed up and started spewing some shit about wanting to be a family— AFTER SEVEN DAMN YEARS—and I hated the idea of him thinking I was alone. Thinking that I spent all this time pining after him, waiting for him to come to his senses. Then you showed up, and I don't know what took over my body, but it just came out, and I'm sorry. I'll tell him I lied. I doubt he'll actually come back, but if he does, I'll make it clear."

I shake my head. "Seven years..." I let out a low whistle. "Analyse, that's not something you have to face alone. If he does come back, let me be here. Tonight, tomorrow morning, whenever. I'll stay over, or I'll come back first thing."

She gives a short, sharp laugh. "I doubt he'll actually show up again. Disappearing is his thing, Mateo. I don't think he has it in him to stick around."

I study her, the set of her shoulders telling me she wants to believe that. But underneath, I see the way her hands tremble when she crosses her arms.

The silence stretches for a beat, then she says softly, "Why were you here, anyway?"

"Oh, right." I jog back to my truck, grab the little paper bag off the seat, and hand it to her. "Florecitas. I know they're Maya's favorite."

Her face softens, surprise flickering before a real smile breaks through. "That's really sweet, Mateo. She'll be so happy."

"Good." I shove my hands in my pockets, fighting the urge to stay. "I'll see you tomorrow, Lyse."

She hugs the bag to her chest, still watching me like she isn't sure what to make of me anymore.

When I slide behind the wheel and pull away, one thought keeps circling my head. *What the hell did we just step into?*

Chapter Five

The sun streams through my window, my left eye peeking open. I'm sprawled across my bed, my bonnet halfway off my head. One arm dangles off the mattress, and my pillow is somewhere near my knees.

I blink slowly, trying to decide if I'm ready to get out of bed or if I should just roll over and fall back asleep. My mouth is dry—I could really use about a gallon of water right now. What a night. After Mateo left last night, I began to panic about the situation I've gotten us both into and popped open another bottle of wine—a decision I'm currently regretting.

A sharp knock rattles the front door. My stomach drops. Please don't let that be who I think it is.

Another knock, louder this time. "Analyse, it's me. We need to talk."

Shit. Nico.

I stumble out of bed, tug a hoodie over my oversize sleep shirt, and yank open the door. Nico is standing there, looking infuriatingly casual, like he didn't abandon me seven years ago.

"You didn't give me a chance to explain last night," he

21

says, his voice almost pleading. "I just want to talk. Please. About us. About our daughter."

The words hit like a stone in my gut. "She's my daughter," I snap before I can stop myself. "And there is no us, Nico. Not anymore."

His jaw tightens, but he steps closer. "I know I screwed up. But I'm here now, and I'm not going anywhere. We can fix this, Analyse. We can be a family. That's all I've ever wanted."

Anger flares hot in my chest. "Seven years too late," I shoot back. My throat tightens. God, I hate that part of me still wants answers. "And for the record, about last night—Mateo —" I swallow hard. "Mateo isn't—"

"Isn't what?" a deep voice cuts in.

I whip my head up, heart leaping into my throat. Mateo is striding up the walkway, a coffee carrier in one hand, as calm as ever. His gaze flicks between me and Nico, sharp and unreadable. He steps right into the space beside me like it's the most natural thing in the world.

"Isn't what, Lyse?" Mateo repeats, his tone smooth. He shifts the drinks into one hand and slips the other casually around my waist. "Because I could've sworn I heard my name."

Nico's face hardens, but his eyes never leave me. "So this is real, then? You and him?"

My pulse hammers. Words clog my throat, but Mateo doesn't hesitate. He squeezes my side and answers for me. "Yeah. It's real. Analyse and I are together."

The lie burns hot against my tongue, but I can't bring myself to correct him. Not with Nico watching me like a hawk, waiting for me to fold.

Nico exhales, shaking his head like he can't believe it. "Fine," he mutters. "If that's how it is, I'll respect it. But I'm still not going anywhere. I'm going to be in Maya's life whether you like it or not."

He turns on his heel and stalks back to his truck, slamming the door shut and peeling off down the street.

The second he's gone, I step out of Mateo's hold and press my shaking hands to my face. "Oh my god."

Mateo sets the coffee carrier on the porch railing, his eyes locked on me. "You almost told him, didn't you?"

I nod miserably. "I couldn't keep the lie straight. I was about to tell him you weren't—"

"Good thing I showed up, then." His voice low. "Because that lie? It's the only thing keeping him from thinking he still has a chance."

I open my mouth to argue, but no words come out. Because he's right. Nico's face, that little flash of hope when I almost told him the truth—it scared me more than I want to admit.

By the time Mateo leaves, the weight of what just happened presses down on me until I can barely breathe. I stumble back inside, shut the door, and collapse onto my couch. My head is pounding, and when I finally check my phone, I nearly drop it. Twenty notifications. All from Anna.

I open the first text.

ANNA

Call me.

Then proceed to scroll down and see that all the texts are different variations of her telling me to call her as soon as possible. That's weird. She left a voicemail. I press play and put the speaker on to listen. *"Lyse, it's Anna, obviously, I don't know why you haven't answered your phone, but Libby said she was taking a walk last night and saw you with Mateo and that you two were having sex against your car? What the hell? Call me back."*

I stare at my phone in disbelief. What is Libby talking

about? Having sex against my car? My anxiety rises, and I quickly dial Anna's number.

"Fucking finally!"

"Anna. What's with that message you left me? What are you talking about?" I say, panicked.

"Okay, so...Libby told Hilda and Hilda told me that she saw you last night with Mateo and you were canoodling."

"Canoodling?"

"Yup."

"You said that she said we were having sex."

"Right, I needed you to call me back right away and you weren't answering. I figured that would get those fingers dialing."

"For fuck's sake, Anna! I was damn near hyperventilating!"

"Why? It's obviously not true. You wouldn't be caught dead doing anything with Mateo."

The silence is deafening. Shit. I'm really going to have to do this, aren't I? I'm really telling people that I'm dating Mateo?

"Lyse? Right?"

"Well..."

"Holy fuck balls. You're fucking Mateo!"

"No! I mean! Yes! No! Oh my god, Anna!"

"Well, which is it? Are you or aren't you?"

"We're not fucking—we're dating."

The other end of the call is so silent that for a moment I think Anna hung up. I'm about to speak when she says, "Dating? You? And Mateo? Together? You and Mateo are dating? Each other?"

"Yes, we're dating each other. That's usually what that means."

"Wow. I'm shocked. Didn't you say he was a walking red flag? And I didn't think he *did* relationships."

"Yeah. I did think he was a walking red flag, but you know, we spend a lot of time together because of Maya—they love each other so much—and I got to learn about who he really is as a person."

"And who is that?"

"A nice guy, Anna."

Anna sighs. "Shit. I can't believe this is actually happening. Seb is going to be pissed. You know he gets all macho big brother and tells everyone to stay away from you."

"He'll get over it. He just needs to hear it from me first."

Anna laughs. "Well, you better talk to him soon, because Libby is running her mouth. You're the best piece of chisme we've had in months."

I roll my eyes. Shit. Living in a small town can be really hard when you're trying to keep a secret. I need to get to Seb before he hears it from someone else and blows a gasket.

"Ugh. Thanks for the heads up, banana. I need to get ready so I can go tell him."

"Okay, yeah...and Lyse...just be careful."

"With Seb??"

"With Mateo. I don't want you to get hurt."

"I'll be okay, An. But thank you for looking out for me."

"Always."

By the time I hang up with Anna, my anxiety is through the roof. The whole damn town already thinks Mateo and I were going at it in my front yard, and Nico now believes we're a couple. This is spiraling so far out of my control, and I can barely keep up.

Later that day, I'm pacing outside of the bakery when Mateo pulls up. The second he gets out of his truck, I throw my hands in the air.

"We are screwed," I blurt. "Completely, utterly screwed."

He raises a brow. "Nice to see you, too, querida."

"Don't." I point a finger at him. "The entire town thinks we had sex against my car last night."

Mateo barks out a laugh. "Against your car? That's creative."

"This isn't funny!" I snap. "Nico already believes we're together, and now everyone else does, too. I can't tell him it was a lie without looking insane, and I can't tell the town it was a lie without making things worse. Oh my god, what do we do?"

He tilts his head, considering me. "We keep the lie."

"Excuse me?"

"Think about it. Nico sticks around, he believes you moved on. Everyone else thinks we're together, so they stop talking about him and start talking about us instead. Problem solved." He shrugs.

"Mateo, this isn't some simple problem! This is my life! This is Maya's life!" I rake a hand through my hair. "We can't just fake date. We'd have to sell it to Seb, to Mari, to literally everyone. Seb is going to lose his mind."

"Seb can deal with it," Mateo says firmly. His eyes lock on mine. "What matters is that you don't have to face this alone. We pretend until Nico leaves. Until the gossip dies down. Whatever comes first."

I open my mouth to argue, but the truth is—I don't have a better plan. Slowly, reluctantly, I nod. "Fine. But we need ground rules."

He smirks. "Ground rules, huh?"

"Yes, Mateo! Ground rules. No kissing, no touching, no breathing on me."

He leans in closer, wrapping one of my curls around his finger. "Lyse, I don't think anyone is going to believe that we're together if we don't touch. They know me—and if you're my girl, there's no way I'm going to go a second without touching you, being near you, kissing you."

Heat creeps up my neck and face, and I clear my throat. "Right. Okay. So there will be touching...but we don't have to kiss."

"Okay. No kissing. Unless you ask for it."

I roll my eyes. "Well, we don't have to worry about that."

He barks out a laugh. "Whatever you say, Lyse. Anything else we should go over?"

"I kinda already told Anna and Mari. But everyone else is going to want to know how this started."

"So you already told them but you weren't sure if we were actually going to do this?"

"I panicked, okay? Everyone else is going to wonder how this started."

"Easy. We say it's new. We spent a lot of time together and things just naturally progressed. The rest is nobody's business."

"So we're really doing this, huh?"

"Yes, Lyse, we're really doing this. But if you don't want to, just say the word."

I'm quite for a few beats, and for a second, I think about backing out. Finally, I shake my head. "No, I want to do it."

A smile spreads across his face. "Great." He leans down and presses a kiss to my forehead. "Now you're my girl.

Chapter Six

ANALYSE

I need to get to Seb before Libby's big ol' mouth makes its way to him—so much for checking things off my to-do list today.

I turn the key in the ignition, and the sound of the next episode of my favorite podcast fills the car.

"The thing about small towns is that secrets don't stay buried—unless, of course, someone makes sure they do."

I take a deep breath, pulling out of the driveway, gravel crunching beneath my tires. The host's voice is smooth, calming my nerves as I prepare myself for this conversation I'm about to have. I chew on my bottom lip, practicing what I'm going to say, preparing myself for what he might say in return.

As I'm hyping myself up, I can't help but to feel frustrated. Why do I feel like a sixteen-year-old on my way to tell my dad that I crashed our car? Seb can't tell me shit. I may be his baby sister, but I haven't been a baby in a long time, and who I date—or pretend to date—is none of his business.

~

I pull up in front of Seb's house and freeze when I see a familiar car idling in the driveway. Mateo. *What the hell is he doing here?*

I glance at my reflection in the rearview mirror, trying to wipe the hangover off my face with a quick swipe of my sleeve. Then I step out of the car, walk over, and tap on Mateo's window. He's looking down at his phone and jumps at the sound. Dramatic.

He steps out of his car and says, "You scared the shit out of me."

I cross my arms. "You scare easily."

"Only when it's you, baby." He winks.

I roll my eyes, but the corner of my mouth twitches before I can stop it. "Cut it out, Mateo. What are you doing here?"

"What?" He grins, leaning against his car. "Can't a guy stop by to see his girlfriend?"

"This isn't even my house. What are you doing at Seb's— and why are you just sitting here in your car?"

"Anna called me." He rubs the back of his neck.

"Fantastic." I fold my arms tighter and glance toward the house, my stomach churning. I can't tell if it's the lingering hangover or the looming conversation, but either way, I feel sick.

"She said Libby's been running her mouth, and that you were coming to talk to Seb." Mateo shifts his weight, his eyes scanning mine.

"So she told you to come save me?" I raise a brow.

"You never need saving, preciosa—and she didn't tell me to do anything." He steps closer, voice low but steady. "I came because I wanted to." He pauses then adds, "And even if you don't need saving, we both know how Seb gets, I wasn't going to let you do this alone." He shrugs, but there's nothing casual about the way he's looking at me. "We're in this together."

I stare at him for a moment, unsure what to say. Finally, I settle for a mumbled, "Okay," and walk toward Seb's door.

Before I can knock, the door bursts open and Maya comes flying out, running straight toward me. But at the last second, she skids to a stop—her eyes lighting up when she spots Mateo.

"Mateo!" she squeals, launching herself at him.

He laughs, bending down to catch her easily. "Hi, princesa. Did you miss me?"

"Yes!" She wraps her little arms tight around his neck. "We played dress-up, did puzzles, baked cookies, and watched movies!"

"I'm glad you had fun." He gives her one last squeeze before setting her down gently. "But I think someone else is waiting for a hug." He tips his chin toward me.

That's all it takes. She pivots and runs the last few steps into my arms. "Mami!"

I scoop her into my arms with a laugh. "Hola, mamita! Te extrañé muchísimo, bebesita"

She snuggles in closer, her curls brushing against my cheek. "I missed you, too!"

I press a kiss to her head, warmth spreading in my chest. "I have to go in and talk to Tio, is he inside?"

"Yup," she says with a pop of her lips.

I get inside and glance around—and I see so much of Mari here. It's beautiful. For so many years, Sebastian was alone. Heartbroken. Just...getting by. And then Mari came back. She put the light back into his world, and I'm grateful every damn day for it. What's better than having one of my best friends as my sister-in-law?

I know I talked all that shit on the way over, but I can't help but feel nervous. Seb always has a way of making me feel like a kid again. I spot Mari first and exhale loudly.

Mari laughs. "Girl. Good thing you're here, because I've been trying to distract him from looking at his phone."

"So you know, too?"

"Of course, I do. Libby told Hilda and Hilda called me right away. Now, why you didn't tell me is the real question."

I begin twirling a curl around my finger. "I wasn't sure there was even something to tell. I was feeling it out."

"I get that. Go talk to Seb, he's in the back building a bookshelf for my library—but I want all the juicy details later." She reaches for Maya's hand and says, "Come on, Maya, let's go eat cupcakes!"

"Yessss!" she excitedly screams.

I stand there for a moment, not quite ready to make a move, when I hear someone clearing their throat and jump. I turn to see Mateo waiting for me. Shit. I forgot he was here.

"Do you need more time?"

"Let's just get this over with."

I see Seb hammering away and wonder if maybe I should've waited until he didn't have a weapon in his hands. Would he really hit Mateo? No. Maybe not? I don't know.

Seb looks up and smiles. "Hey Lyse. I wasn't expecting you this early." Then he looks at Mateo, and confusion dawns on his face. "Mateo? What's up, man? I wasn't expecting you at all." He chuckles.

"Seb, I need to tell you something," I say nervously.

He immediately stands straight. "What's going on? Are you okay?"

"I'm okay!" I say quickly. "It's nothing like that. I just need to tell you about..."

"About...?"

"Me and Mateo," I mumble.

"Come again? I have no idea what you said."

"MateoandIaredating," I say quickly.

"Lyse, I really need you to speak up here."

Mateo jumps in and says, "She said that she and I are dating."

Seb whips his head to Mateo. "What the fuck did you just say?"

"I said—"

Seb interrupts. "I fucking heard what you said. Is this your idea of a joke?"

I sigh. "He isn't joking, Seb. Mateo and I are really dating."

Seb looks really pissed. He's just standing there, staring at us, looking as if he's seconds away from exploding. He looks over at me, and I know he's going to go off.

"Analyse, what the hell are you thinking? You're my little sister. He's my best friend. This is a bad fucking idea."

"Seb, please. I'm a big girl, I can make my own decisions. I know what I'm doing."

"You know what you're doing." He laughs. "She knows what she's doing." He's pacing back and forth now. I can barely make out what he's saying, but I can feel his anger rolling off him.

"Coño, Sebastian! Ya, me estás dando un maldito pique," Mateo snaps.

"Yo te estoy dando pique? Yo?! Mira, cabrón—"

"The both of you shut the hell up!" I yell. "Mateo, I don't need a savior, and, Seb, I don't need you acting like you're my goddamn father. You're pissing me off!"

"But, Lyse—"

"I don't want to hear it," I say, cutting Seb off. "Listen to me closely, because I'm only saying this once—I can date whoever I want. I can do whatever I want."

Seb opens his mouth to speak, but I lift a finger and say, "I know that you love me, Seb. I know that you care about me and only want what's best for me. But you have to let me make my own decisions. Even if you think it's a mistake, you have to let me make my own mistakes. I love you, and I appreciate everything you've ever done for me and Maya. But let's get one thing straight—you don't get a say in this. And if you make me remind you of that one very specific summer secret and tell Mom about it, I absolutely will. Don't test me. You know she taught me how to pinch your ear in a way that makes you cry, and I won't hesitate to do it right here in front of everyone. So maybe just be a good brother and give us your support, okay?"

Seb's face softens. "Okay, fine. I get it. I'm sorry. I just worry, you know? But I'll support you. Of course, I'll support you. You're my baby sister," he says, pulling me in for a hug.

He looks at Mateo now, and says, "I'll support you guys, but I swear, Mateo, if you hurt my sister, you're dead."

Then he leaves the room to go play with Maya before I leave with her. That conversation actually went a lot better than I expected. I feel guilty about lying to him, but we're already all in on this, no turning back now.

I'm lying on the couch, Maya cuddled up on top of me, fast asleep, her curls a wild mess. These are the moments I look forward to. Being a single mom isn't easy, even with all the support in the world. Things can get really hectic, not leaving me with a lot of downtime. So when we have these quiet moments, just her and I—I relish it. I look down at her little face, eyelids fluttering, lips pouting, soft even breaths. She looks so peaceful.

It's been two weeks since Mateo and I told Sebastian that we're dating. I haven't seen either of them since. Mateo and I have been texting each other here and there, but I've been so busy helping the town plan the Fall Festival that I haven't had time to do much else.

Unsurprisingly, Nico hasn't turned up either. So much for

wanting to be back in our lives. I don't know if I'm irritated or relieved. I know he's still in town, because the people of this town can't keep a secret if their lives depended on it and they've been muttering about him all around town. Maybe all of this worry, all of this waiting, was for nothing.

This weekend is finally the Fall Festival—Maya is so damn excited, and admittedly, so am I. She's excited for the pie eating contest where she's certain she'll beat Alejandro, and I can't wait to get an apple cider donut in my hand—or maybe two donuts.

This weekend also marks the official debut of my relationship with Mateo. He'll be with Maya and I at the festival, pretending to be in love with me. Sure, everyone in town has been whispering about us. Libby really knows how to spread some bochinche. But, as of right now, that's all it's been because no one has actually seen us together.

Now that I think of it, we should probably set some ground rules. Especially with Maya being there. I don't want her getting mixed into this mess. With that thought, I pull out my phone and shoot a quick text to Mateo.

ANALYSE

We need rules.

MATEO

What happened to hello? How are you? How's your week been?

ANALYSE

Hello. I spoke to you yesterday. You're fine.

MATEO

What if I wasn't fine today? What if I had a horrible day?

I read the text and roll my eyes—and they call me dramatic.

ANALYSE

Fine. How are you, Mateo? Was your day a horrible one?

MATEO

Why thank you for asking, Analyse. My day has been terrific, actually. No complaints here.

ANALYSE

Oh my god. All that for nothing.

MATEO

Just teaching you manners, babygirl. So what's this about rules? What do we need rules for?

ANALYSE

You know what…I'll let that slide, for now. We need to set ground rules for this "relationship." I don't want Maya catching wind of this. I don't want to confuse her.

MATEO

That—we can agree on. We'll just act like friends in front of her, think you can manage that?

ANALYSE

Hmm. It'll be hard. Very hard. But I'll manage.

MATEO

Good girl. And we can let everyone else know that we're taking it slow and don't want her to know yet.

ANALYSE

Yup. Okay final rule…

MATEO

More rules? What now?

ANALYSE

You can't fall in love with me.

MATEO

What?? Wow Analyse, you're so damn humble. Really, you gotta get more confidence.

ANALYSE

I'm serious! Don't fall in love with me. I'm fantastic, but this is strictly business.

MATEO

Uhuh. Fine, I won't fall in love with you.

ANALYSE

Promise??

MATEO

Yeah, yeah. I promise.

I place my phone on the end table next to my couch and lay my head back, hugging Maya tight. Now that we have a plan in place, I feel like I can breathe a bit better. I really hope this doesn't all blow up in my face.

I fold the same dish towel for the third time and set it down, only to pick it up again. Across the kitchen, Maya is curled up on the couch with a coloring book in her lap and her socked feet tucked beneath her. She hums to herself—completely content, a pink marker streaking over the outline of a dinosaur in a tutu. She has no idea how much my heart is breaking right now.

I lean against the counter, arms crossed tight over my

chest, and take a deep breath. I've rehearsed this conversation a dozen different ways. Practiced it while driving, while brushing my teeth, while standing in line at the grocery store. Nothing makes it easier.

How do you tell your daughter that the man you've only ever called "your father" in vague, faraway terms is suddenly interested in being part of her life? That the man who never showed up before wants to now?

That you agreed—after years of silence, of anger, of carefully chosen explanations—to let her meet him?

I run a hand over my face. She deserves to know the truth. She always has. But there's a difference between protecting your child and preparing her for disappointment. And I'm still not sure where that line is.

"Mami?"

I look up.

Maya's head is tilted to the side, marker still in hand. "Are you okay? You're looking at the wall weird again."

I force a smile. "Yeah, baby. Just thinking."

"About dinner?"

"About something important."

She narrows her eyes in that very serious, very Maya way. "Is it bad?"

I shake my head and push off the counter, walking over to sit on the arm of the couch beside her. I smooth a hand over her hair, fingers catching in one of her curls. "No. Not bad. Just...big."

She puts her marker down and turns toward me fully, hands folded in her lap like she knows something is coming.

I pause then speak softly. "I want to talk to you about your dad."

Her expression shifts—slightly. Not fear. Not excitement. Just...alert. Like she's listening more carefully now.

"You know how we've talked about him before?" I start. "How I told you he wasn't around when you were born?"

She nods. "You said he had to leave."

That's one way I said it. When she was four and asking why everyone else's daddies were around but hers wasn't. And then later, I said he couldn't be what we needed. That sometimes, people don't know how to love the right way.

And she accepted that—because kids trust their moms. Especially when their moms hold their world together like glue. When they're there for their children every single day, with unconditional love.

"Well..." I breathe in slowly. "He's reached out recently. He wants to meet you."

Maya's eyes widen. "Meet me?"

I nod. "You've never met in person. But he asked for the chance."

She's quiet. I let the silence stretch, let her process it in whatever way her six-year-old brain can.

Finally, she asks, "Why now?"

The million dollar question.

"I don't know," I answer honestly. "But I think...he wants a chance to know you. Even if it's just once."

She chews on her bottom lip, eyes flicking back to the half-finished dinosaur on the page, then back to me. "Does he know what I look like?"

"No," I say softly. "Not yet."

She nods again. Then, after another beat, asks, "Did he not want me before?"

God. My baby. I close my eyes, just for a second. "It wasn't about you, baby. It was never about you."

Her voice is small. "But it feels like it was."

I slide off the arm of the couch and onto the cushions beside her, pulling her into my side. She comes easily, curling into me. "He didn't know how to be what we need," I say into her hair. "That's not your fault. You're so easy to love, Maya. The easiest. He just wasn't ready to be the kind of person you deserve."

"Are you sure I want to meet him?"

"I don't know," I admit. "And you don't have to. But he asked for a chance to meet you, and I wanted to ask you how you felt before I said yes."

She's quiet again. Her fingers fidget with the sleeve of my shirt. "Will you come too?"

I smile, though it doesn't quite reach my chest. "Of course. I'm not going anywhere."

She exhales, a little sigh of relief, and rests her head on my arm. For a long moment, we just sit there in the soft quiet of the living room. The TV hums faintly in the background, a cartoon menu looping with cheerful music no one's paying any attention to.

Maya traces her finger along the seam of a throw pillow. "What if I don't like him?"

I run a hand down her back in slow, even strokes. "Then that's okay."

She tilts her head to look up at me. "But he's my dad."

I smooth her hair back. "He's your dad by blood, yes. But being a dad is about showing up—and he hasn't done that. You don't owe him anything. Meeting him doesn't mean you have to feel anything. You just have to be honest with yourself."

She nods slowly, but I can see her chewing on it, the way she does with big thoughts.

"Will it be weird?" she asks.

I laugh softly. "Probably."

That earns me a tiny smile, and I hold on to it like oxygen.

"We're going to meet somewhere public," I continue. "Somewhere that feels safe. I told him I didn't want it to be in a house or anything too private. I wanted you to feel comfortable."

She's quiet again. "Do I have to hug him?"

"Absolutely not," I say, firm and immediate. "You don't have to do anything you don't want to. Not now. Not ever."

Her shoulders relax a little. "Will he look like me?"

That one catches me off guard. I picture Nico—sharp jawline, confident smile.

"A little," I say. "Your eyes are like his. But the rest of you? That's all me. My little twin."

She hums, filing that away. "I have questions," she says. "If I meet him."

"That's good. Ask whatever you want."

She looks at me seriously. "Even hard ones?"

I nod. "Especially hard ones."

She leans her head back on my arm again. "Okay."

And just like that, the decision is made. Not because she's excited. Not because she wants it. But because she's brave enough to face it, even if it scares her.

I press a kiss to the top of her head and close my eyes for a second. I don't trust Nico. I never will. But Maya deserves to decide who she lets into her life...even if I want to shield her from anything that could possibly hurt her.

Even if it kills me a little to open that door.

The first thing I feel is the wind.

It's a chilly Saturday morning, one of those crisp fall days where the air smells like damp leaves and distant barbecue smoke. Maya walks a few steps ahead of me, her curls bouncing with every stride, her little fists stuffed deep into the pockets of her jacket.

She hasn't said much since we left the house. I haven't either.

A few days have passed since I told Maya about Nico, and now we're meeting at the park near the library—the one with the big stone fountain and wide walking path. It's public, open, neutral. Somewhere safe.

He was already here when we pulled into the parking lot. I saw him from the car. Sitting on the bench near the fountain, tapping his foot. He stood when we got out, and for a second, he looked exactly the way he used to. Tall. Put together. Clean-shaven.

Maya slows down and turns back to me. I nod once, just enough to say *you've got this*, even though every part of me wants to scoop her back into the car and drive away to the safety of our home.

She steps closer to my side. I rest my hand gently on her back as we walk the last few feet together. Nico straightens. He looks at Maya, really looks at her, and for a second, he doesn't say anything. Just stares.

Finally, he clears his throat. "Hi," he says, voice quiet. "You must be Maya."

She nods once.

"I'm—" He glances at me then back to her. "I'm..."

"Nico," I cut in, my tone calm but firm.

His eyes flick to mine, startled.

"This is Nico, Maya." I smooth a hand down her back. "He wanted to meet you."

For a beat, no one speaks. The title he clearly wanted to claim—dad—hangs in the air, unsaid. Maya tilts her head, studying him.

"It's really good to meet you," Nico says quickly, adjusting. "You...you look just like your mom."

Maya glances up at me then back at him. "I don't know what you look like."

41

I feel his discomfort like static in the air. But he nods. "That's fair. I haven't been around."

"Why not?" she asks plainly.

He shifts his weight. "That's a good question."

"She's allowed to ask," I say, my voice soft but firm.

"I know." He swallows. "I wasn't ready. I was scared. And I made mistakes."

Maya studies him for a long time. "You missed my first day of school. And my birthdays."

"I know," he says, quieter now. "I'm really sorry."

Maya turns to me. "Can we sit?"

I nod and guide her to the bench across from Nico's. She hops up and swings her legs. Nico sits, too—tentatively, like any wrong move will make Maya bolt.

He tries to make small talk. Asks her about school, favorite subjects, cartoons. She answers in short sentences, polite but distant. She doesn't smile.

He tells a joke that probably worked in his head. She blinks at him. I want to step in. Smooth it over. But I don't. I let the silence stretch. Because she's handling this. And I promised myself I'd follow her lead. And because it isn't my job to make things more comfortable for him.

Nico leans forward, forearms on his knees. "You know, when I was a kid, I wanted to be a doctor."

Maya shrugs. "I want to be a ninja."

He nods, unsure what to say next. Maya picks at a loose thread on her sleeve, quiet, staring at him.

"I used to play baseball," he tries again. "Maybe I could take you to a game sometime?"

That's when she finally looks at me again. And I know that look. I invented that look. It's her help me look.

I clear my throat. "I think we're okay for today."

Nico blinks. "Oh. Yeah. Of course."

He looks like he wants to say more. Like there's a speech in his head that he's been practicing and he's just now realizing that this isn't the time to get it out.

Maya hops down from the bench, brushing her hands on her jeans. "It was nice to meet you," she says.

Nico stands, too. "Yeah. You too, Maya. Really."

She walks to me, slips her hands into mine without a word, and we start to leave.

"Analyse," Nico calls softly behind us.

I pause, turn slightly.

"I meant it," he says. "Thank you. For bringing her. For... for giving me this chance. I know I can win you back if you'll just let me."

I let out a slow breath, tired down to my bones. "Just don't make it harder than it has to be."

We walk away—hand in hand, her grip tight in mine, the breeze catching the edge of her jacket, lifting it. Once we're settled in the car, I start the engine and let it idle for a moment before pulling out of the lot.

"Was that okay?" she asks.

I glance over at her. "You were perfect."

She leans her head against the window. "I don't know how I'm supposed to feel, Mami."

"That's okay," I say gently. "You don't have to figure it all out right now. And I'll be here with you, helping you, every step of the way."

She's quiet for a while then says, "I love you so much, Mami."

"I love you, too, mija. More than you could ever imagine."

As we pull into the lot, I notice something waiting on front porch—a small white paper bag, folded neatly at the top. My chest tightens as I step out and peek inside. Florecitas for Maya. Pan sobao for me.

A note in Mateo's messy scrawl sits on top:

For my girls. Thought you might need these today.

I glance around, but he's not here. He didn't stay. Didn't hover. Just...knew.

Maya peeks into the bag and grins, wide and genuine, for the first time all day. "He remembered."

"Yeah, baby," I whisper, brushing a curl off her forehead. "He did."

Chapter Seven

ANALYSE

Maya comes racing into my room and jumps onto my bed. "Mama! Mama! Wake up!"

I begin to slowly open my eyes and see a wide-eyed Maya smiling at me, excitement rolling off her in waves. I let out yawn and look around the room. It's still dark out. "Maya? What are you doing up this early, bebecita?"

"Mama! We have to get up! Today is the big day and we need a big breakfast!"

I let out a laugh. "Ahh yes, you need the breakfast of champions for the pie-eating contest later. But...did we really need to wake up now? The sun isn't even out yet."

"We *had* to, mama. I have to eat super early so that I won't be too full for the pies later!"

My clever girl. She's clearly been thinking about this a lot.

"You're absolutely right! How's huevos revueltos sound?"

"Mmm con jamón, cebolla, y tomate?" she says excitedly.

A girl after my own heart—she's such a foodie, like me.

"You got it, mamita. Let me get up and ready, and I'll make breakfast for us."

~

The rest of the morning goes off without a hitch. I get ready and make breakfast for Maya and I, which she wolfs down. Now she's watching cartoons while I clean up the mess I left in the kitchen. Mateo texted me while we were eating, letting me know he would pick us up by nine—he said it would make more sense if we showed up together, in one car.

Anna and Mari have been blowing up the group chat all day; they still can't believe that Mateo and I are dating. Neither can I, if I'm being honest. They're going to be at the festival, and I just know that they're going to be watching Mateo and I like hawks.

Mari is a hopeless romantic, so to her, this is perfect. She loves the idea of me dating someone they're all already friends with—no having to worry if they're going to hate the guy, or if he's an asshole. Anna, on the other hand, is skeptical. She isn't sure that my dating Mateo is a good idea; he doesn't exactly have a reputation for getting into serious relationships.

I hear the crunching of gravel outside my kitchen window and look up to see Mateo pulling into my driveway. He steps out of his car, and I call to Maya to let her know to grab her jacket because it's time to leave.

Maya runs out of the house and straight into Mateo's arms. He lifts her into the air, and I can hear her little squeals of excitement. I begin to make my way over to my car for Maya's booster seat when Mateo stops me, placing a hand on my arm.

"I already have a booster setup in my truck."

Mateo must see the confusion etched on my face, because he repeats, "I have a booster seat setup in my car already, for Maya, so no need to grab yours."

"You have a booster seat?"

"Yes, Lyse. That is what I said. Man, we have to work on those listening skills, huh?"

"But why?"

"Well, babygirl, listening to others is important for—"

I cut him off. "No, not that part. Why do you have a booster seat?"

"For Maya," he says, as if it's the most obvious thing in the world.

"Where did you get a booster seat?"

Exasperated, he runs a hand through his hair. "The store. I'm pretty sure that's where everyone gets these."

I look at him blankly, and he continues. "Look, Maya is coming in my car, she needs a booster, so I got her one. I actually feel a bit like an asshole that I didn't think of getting one sooner. Why should I make you have to drag the seat back and forth between cars when I could just have one already in my truck for her? She's in my car frequently. It makes the most sense."

My stomach flips at his words. I can't believe he bought a seat for Maya. To just keep in his car. It shouldn't make me feel warm inside, but it does.

"That's really thoughtful. Thank you, Mateo."

He rubs the back of his neck, a little sheepish. "I, uh... might've peeked in Seb's car to check the model. Just wanted to get the same one Maya's used to."

That knocks the breath out of me. He didn't just think about convenience—he thought about *her* comfort.

He winks at me then, trying to play it cool. "You're welcome, chula."

A blush creeps up my neck. Shit. This is going to be a long day.

⁓

We arrive at the Fall Festival, and Maya immediately gets swooped away by Hilda—owner of the local bookstore—to get their faces painted. The pie-eating contest doesn't start for another hour, so there's time to kill.

I inhale deeply. I love the fall. I especially love the fall in Lake City. The temperatures are cooler, the air is crisp. The changing leaves fall from the trees, surrounding us in all their beauty of reds, yellows, and oranges. The scent of pumpkin spice, nutmeg, and cinnamon bring a sense of nostalgia—to a life where my biggest worry was how to get Seb to let me tag along with him and his friends. To the moments where my mom, dad, Seb and I would huddle together on the couch, watching scary movies with a batch of my mom's cookies. Seb would always get scared while watching, although he would deny it now. But not me. I lived for the nights of watching and rewatching *Scream*, *Halloween*, and *I Know What You Did Last Summer*. I guess that explains why I'm obsessed with true crime podcasts, and all things spooky season.

Mateo wraps an arm around my shoulder and leans in toward my ear, whispering, "You're ready to put on a show?" then plants a kiss on the side of my hair.

I look up at him, quirking an eyebrow. "I was born ready, baby."

He barks out a laugh. "That's what I'm talking about, chula."

Mariana, Anna, Seb, and Andres begin walking toward us, and suddenly, I'm filled with nerves.

"Look at the happy couple!" Mariana croons.

Seb nods a hello at Mateo and wraps me in a tight hug. "Good to see you, little sis. Where's Maya?" he asks, looking around for her.

"Now you *know* the moment we got here Hilda stole her away. Those two love to spend time together."

Andres claps Mateo on the shoulder. "My man! Look at you with a girlfriend. Our boy is all grown up."

Mateo looks over at me. "What can I say? I'm smart enough to lock down a good thing," he says sweetly.

At that, Mariana looks as if she has hearts in her eyes, Anna pretends to gag, and Seb just stares at us intently. The tension rolling off him is thick. I stare right back at him. Daring him to say a word that will set me off.

He's still unhappy about Mateo and I, and I sort of get it. Mateo's known for breaking hearts, and Seb's worried that I'll be broken in the way that I was after Nico. But he has to trust me and my judgment. I know what I'm doing...at least, I think so.

Sensing my frustration and Seb's trepidation at the situation, Mariana clears her throat and says, "Let's go do the sack race!"

A chorus of groans leaves us all.

"Ugh, you guys! We have to! What's the matter? Scared that I'm going to kick all your asses?" she says, placing her hands at her hips.

Seb brings Mari in close to him, whispers something in her ear that thankfully I can't hear, and kisses her hair. I feel a tug in my chest. Seb and Mari are so disgustingly in love with each other, but it wasn't always easy.

Seb and Mari met when they were kids and dated in high school. Their journey to get to where they are right now was a long one, and it makes me happy to see them both finally where they're meant to be—with each other. But there's this other part of me, this part that can't help but to feel this twinge in my chest at the sight of their love. Not jealousy. Or maybe it is. Not at them, exactly...but at what they have. Will I ever have someone look at me the way they look at each other? Will there ever be someone who loves me so deeply that they would do anything to make sure I'm happy? Someone who loves Maya and me, and will give us both the world.

I could never regret Maya. Not ever. She's my whole world, the best thing to ever happen to me. But Nico abandoning us without a second thought changed me. It scared me from even considering dating.

Mateo wraps his hand around mine, large and warm. It's almost as if he knows that I need someone at this moment. That I needed the warmth you get from another person's touch. His eyes stay locked on mine as he says, "We're in. But, Mari, I think my girl might give you a run for your money."

Laughter breaks out around us, but I can't look away from him. There's a warmth spreading through me. One that I don't want to think too hard about.

"Damn, chula. I thought for sure you'd let me win," Mateo says, grinning at me.

"Let you win? Me? Never, babe. I have to keep you humble," I say sweetly.

I kicked all of their asses. No question. Mari—I adore her —but she's too sweet for this kind of thing. Me? Please. I wasn't about to let a sack slow me down.

Seb went first. One well-timed shift and he lost balance— technically, I didn't push him. He just...stumbled near me. Mateo tripped, but that's on him for getting too close to me. Mari turned around when I told her someone was calling her. My sweet trusting, Mari. It bought me at least two hops.

And Anna—my girl—I may have squeezed her hand too tight when we were hopping, and we both nearly ate it. She laughed so hard she couldn't breathe, and I couldn't stop laughing either. We recovered, barely, but it was worth it.

I kept going. Sack to ankles, chaos in my wake, grinning

like a maniac. I grew up with an older brother. I had to learn early on how to win with grit. I'll play dirty if I have to. Elbows out, eyes on the prize. I guess I know where Maya gets her competitiveness from.

Speaking of which, it's finally time for the pie-eating contest, and I am ready to watch my baby girl take all those kids down.

We make our way over to the pie-eating contest—me, Mateo, Seb, Mari, Andres, and Anna—walking across the grass. The sun's lower now, golden and soft, casting long shadows as families crowd around the long table lined with aluminum pie tins.

Maya's already there, bouncing on her toes, her hands clasped behind her back like she's trying to play it cool. But I know she's filled with nervous energy.

"Ready for this?" I ask, smirking as we walk up.

She grins, wide and mischievous. "I was born ready to kick Alejandro's butt."

We all crack up.

Andres lets out a low whistle. "Just like her mom," he says, shaking his head with a smile.

Mateo crouches down in front of her, brushing a stray curl out of her face. "Remember, bebe—small bites, big heart. And if all else fails, distract them with your dimples."

Maya giggles, throwing her arms around him in a tight hug. He lifts her off the ground for a second before setting her back down.

"You got this," he says, pressing a kiss to her forehead.

She beams and walks over to the table with that same fire in her eyes I'd seen in the sack race mirror—determined, a little reckless, and completely her own. She takes her seat like the champion she knows she is.

The announcer calls it, and the contest begins.

A bell rings, and the kids dive in like wild animals. Faces

51

plant into whipped cream and crust, arms pinned behind their backs, laughter and cheering echoing around the field. Maya goes full beast mode—her curls bouncing with each determined bite. Her face is already a mess, and I've never been prouder. I'm mid-laugh when I feel someone step up beside me. I glance to my left—and freeze.

Fuck. It's Nico.

He's standing there like he belongs, hands in his pockets, smug as ever. Before I can even get a word out, Seb's already moving. His body cuts through the group like a storm.

"What the hell are you doing here?" Seb growls, grabbing the front of Nico's shirt and shoving him back a step.

Nico raises his eyebrows. "What? I can't watch my daughter compete in a pie-eating contest?"

Seb's lip curls. "*Your* daughter? You haven't been around for a day of her life and now you want to show up like you've been father of the year? Are you fucking kidding me?"

His voice is low but sharp, slicing through the noise like a blade.

Nico's smirk doesn't budge. "Touchy," he says.

Mateo's suddenly between them, arm outstretched to push Seb back. Calm, but tight with restraint. Protective. Controlled in that way that always makes me nervous—like he's the last step before a detonation.

Nico shifts his gaze, now settling on Mateo. "Oh, what's this? The little boyfriend's got something to say now?"

Mateo steps in closer, smiles cold and steady. "Yeah, this little boyfriend will lay you the fuck out."

Nico snorts. "Chill, man—"

"No." Mateo cuts him off. "You wanna watch Maya? Fine. Stand back and keep your damn mouth shut. But you say one more word to any of us, and I swear to God, I'll make sure you'll be eating your next meal through a straw."

Nico blinks, and the smugness flickers for just a second.

Mateo doesn't flinch. Doesn't blink. Seb's fists are still clenched, but he steps back, jaw locked.

I exhale slowly, heart pounding in my ears. Around us, the cheering continues—clueless, chaotic, joyful—like none of this is happening.

Maya's laughter carries through the crowd, loud and proud, and I turn my eyes back to her. She's got whipped cream on her nose and pie crust in her hair. She's winning. She's perfect. And I'll be damned if Nico ruins this day.

~

After the pie-eating contest, which Maya won, Nico promptly left, giving Maya a quick congratulations and an awkward hug.

But before I can stop myself, I storm after him, heat rushing through me. "You don't get to swoop in and confuse her life whenever it suits you."

He spins, hands raised like he's the victim here. "I just wanted to be part of it. That's all."

"Part of it?" I snap. "You've missed all of it. Every birthday. Every milestone. Now you want to walk in and play dad? Not happening."

I feel a warm, steady grip on my arm—Mateo. "That's enough for today, Nico. Time to go." The way he says it leaves no room for argument. Nico mutters something under his breath, but he turns and stalks off without another word.

My whole body is vibrating with leftover adrenaline when I turn back toward Mateo.

He smirks, shaking his head. "Remind me to never piss you off, chula. Seeing you go crazy like that? Hot as hell."

I let out a disbelieving laugh, shoving lightly at his chest. "You're insane."

"Probably," he says easily, eyes glinting. "But still true."

I suck in a breath, watching Nico's figure disappear into the crowd before finally turning back toward the festival. Maya knows that Nico is her father. She's always known of him. She doesn't know much of why he hasn't been around; I've kept it vague. I don't know if it's been for her sake or for his. Maybe a little bit of both. She's still so young, and I didn't think she was ready to learn that her dad simply made the choice to not be around. That he wasn't man enough to be the father she needed.

Seb was furious that Nico was there. He's also upset with me because I didn't tell him that Nico showed up in town. But, fuck. *I'm* still trying to wrap my head around it. I'm trying to come to terms with my own feelings about it all, and as much as I love Seb, I can't manage his feelings too. It's too damn much, and I have Maya to consider.

I have to admit...Mateo looked sexy as hell getting in Nico's face. Other than Seb, and my girls, no one has ever gotten so protective of Maya and me. It was nice. I think I could get used to it.

For the rest of the day, we walked around the festival eating copious bowls of chili, apple cider donuts, and pies. So many more pies.

Chapter Eight

ANALYSE

I'm exhausted. I hardly slept a wink last night, tossing and turning, stressing about this situation with Nico. I'm so damn mad, and the more I think about it, the more pissed off I get. He can't just show up unannounced like that. We need to set some ground rules.

I'm gulping my coffee when my phone pings with a text, I reach for it and see that I have several messages from The Council of Chaos.

ANNA

Are we still pretending like nothing happened yesterday or can we ask questions now?

MARI

Anna, we're giving her time. Remember?

ANNA

I actually don't remember that. What was I doing when you told me this?

MARI

Literally sitting in my car. It was last night.
On our way home from the festival.

ANNA

Ahh, see, that's where you went wrong. You
had Aventura playing in the background,
and you know I can't focus on anything else
when my baby Romeo is singing to me.

MARI

Omg, Anna. You weren't listening to
anything that I said?

ANNA

I'm sorry, Mari. But we have to get back to
the point.

MARI

Which is?

ANNA

Mariana Camila Vargas! Now you're not
listening! Nico, obvs! Lyse, where are you
girl?

I laugh to myself as I scroll through the messages. These girls are absolutely unhinged, but they're *my* unhinged girls. Sisters, not by blood but by choice. I truly can't imagine life without them driving me insane, drowning in wine nights, and offering advice I never asked for but always need.

Of course, Mari's playing it cool, giving me space when it comes to the whole Nico mess, while Anna's basically two seconds away from demanding a full breakdown with time-stamps. God, I love them.

ANALYSE

I'm here. But, reading your messages,
maybe I should hide?

MARI

Take whatever time you need!

ANNA

Don't you dare hide! I have questions.

ANALYSE

Okay, okay. Ask your questions.

ANNA

When did Nico show up?

ANALYSE

Two weeks.

MARI

Same time that you told Seb that you and
Mateo were dating. Crazy timing.

ANALYSE

Right...it was crazy timing, alright.

ANNA

Okay, I think this conversation will be better
over wine. Girls night?

MARI

You know I'm in.

ANALYSE

And you know I'll bring the good wine.

ANNA

Tonight?

MARI

You can drop Maya off with Seba! He'd love
that.

ANALYSE

Perfect. See you guys tonight!

I put my phone down on the kitchen table, and Maya runs into the room, happily calling for me, "Mami! Mami!"

"Yes, mi amor?"

She wraps her arms around my legs. "Is it pancake time?!"

I crouch down and kiss the top of her head. "You bet. And you know I need my best little helper!"

She gasps. "Yes! I'll help, Mami!"

Before I can begin grabbing any of the ingredients, the doorbell rings. Weird. I wasn't expecting anyone today. Please don't let it be Nico. I walk over to my front door and swing it open, mentally crossing all my fingers that he hasn't decided to pop up again uninvited. When I open it, it's not Nico standing there...it's Mateo.

"Mateo? What are you doing here?"

"Hello to you, too, Chula," he says, grinning.

"Right. Right. Hi, Mateo. What are you doing here?"

"Taking my girls to breakfast."

"I have no idea what you're talking about. Did we have plans?"

"Does your man need formal plans to take you out?"

"First of all, you're not my man—"

He opens his mouth to speak, but I lift a finger to stop him. "And second of all, yes. You should absolutely let me know in advance about our plans. What would you have done if I wasn't home?"

He lifts an eyebrow. "Where you would be, Analyse? You're always home or at the school. If you weren't here, then I would've driven to the school."

I roll my eyes. "Not true. I'm out all the time. Doing tons of fun things. I'm the life of the party, remember?"

He barks out a laugh. "This is coming from the girl that wants to be in bed at eight so she can binge episodes of *Law & Order: SVU* she's already seen."

My mouth drops open in offense. Before I can fire back,

Maya comes running in, and launches herself straight into Mateo's arms. "Mateo! Yay! Mami, Mateo's here!"

He lifts her up into the air. "Hi, baby girl. What do you think about us going for breakfast?"

At the exact same time I say, "We actually were about to make some pancakes."

And Maya goes, "Yes! Let's go to the diner! They have the bestest pancakes."

Little traitor. Looks like we're going to breakfast with Mateo.

The bell above the door jingles as we walk into the diner, that familiar scent of bacon, syrup, and fresh coffee wrapping around us like a hug. Maya practically skips ahead, her little sneakers squeaking against the tile floors.

"Booth or table?" Mateo asks, glancing at me.

"Booth," I say without hesitation. "Less chance of Maya falling off a chair trying to reach the syrup."

"Rude," Maya says, climbing into the booth. "I'm a big girl now."

Mateo grins as he slides in next to her, and I take the opposite side, setting my purse down. He grabs a couple of menus from the edge of the table and hands one to me.

"Let me guess," he says, leaning back with that annoyingly smug look of his, "you're going to order the same thing you always get—two eggs, bacon, toast, and exactly one bite of Maya's pancakes."

I lift an eyebrow. "That's bold of you to assume I'm that predictable."

He shrugs, grinning. "I pay attention."

Before I can respond, Maya pipes up, "And she drinks her

coffee with two sugars and just a little bit of milk, but not too much or she says it tastes like sadness."

Mateo bursts out laughing, and I bury my face behind the menu, trying not to smile.

"She's not wrong," I mumble.

A few minutes later, a waitress walks over, pen tucked behind her ear and a grin already playing on her lips.

"Well, if it isn't my favorite fireman," Letty says, all sing-songy and syrup-sweet, like the damn pancakes. "Didn't know you were in this morning."

Mateo gives a polite smile. "Hey, Letty."

Then her eyes flick to me, taking in the scene. Me across from him, Maya beside him, the easy vibe between us. Her smile falters for a blink—barely there—but she recovers fast.

"Didn't realize you had company," she says, sweet but sharp. "Just catching up with an old friend?"

Mateo doesn't even blink. He reaches across the table and threads his fingers through mine. "Not exactly," he says. "This is my girl."

My stomach flips. Letty has only lived here for about a year, so I don't know her very well. But from the looks of it, she's got a thing for Mateo.

Letty's smile tightens. "Right...well. What can I get you guys?"

Maya rattles off her order first, no hesitation: chocolate chip pancakes with extra whipped cream. Mateo goes next, but I barely hear what he says over the pounding in my chest. When it's my turn, I answer automatically, eyes locked on Mateo's thumb brushing slow circles against my skin.

Letty scribbles our order down, gives a final, lingering glance at Mateo, then walks away with her pride just a little bruised.

I raise an eyebrow. "Your girl?"

He smirks. "What? I'm committed to this relationship."

I glance down at our hands—still joined across the table. "Well," I say, schooling my expression, "you're doing a really convincing job."

He leans back slightly, that maddening smirk still playing on his lips. "You think so?"

I shrug. "Honestly? You're a little too good at this. Makes me wonder how many women you've fake dated before."

He lets out a low laugh. "You're my one and only, chula. But I've seen enough rom-coms to know the key is confidence. And you know me, baby, I drip confidence." He raises our joined hands and presses a light kiss against my skin.

I shake my head, trying not to laugh. "You're ridiculous."

He winks. "Ridiculously committed."

The moment lingers just long enough to feel like maybe we're playing the part a little too well.

Maya—completely zoned in on her coloring sheet—suddenly holds up her paper and announces proudly, "This is a dog, but I gave her a crown, because she's a princess now."

Mateo releases my hand and leans over to look. "That's one royal pup."

I nod, grateful she's too focused on her crayons to notice the moment that just happened across the table.

"Queen of Pancake Kingdom," I say, and Maya beams.

The next two hours, we eat our breakfast, Mateo hanging on Maya's every word, laughing at her stories like she's the funniest person he's ever met. She is. She tells him all about her favorite princesses, how she's going to be a ninja-clown when she grows up, but also how she wants to be a vet to help the animals, and how her teacher always saves her red jelly-beans. He listens to her so intently, giving her his complete attention.

I sip my coffee, chiming in here and there, but mostly just watching them. The two of them together are loud, chaotic, and weirdly perfect. He really matches Maya's energy,

By the time the plates are cleared and Maya's halfway through her third crayon masterpiece, I realize I've smiled more this morning than I have in weeks. It's just pretend, I remind myself as I gather my things, slide out of the booth, and thank the universe that Maya didn't ask too many questions.

∼

By the time I get back from dropping Maya off with Seb, the house is quiet. Blessedly, perfectly quiet. I take a deep breath, soaking in the silence, before grabbing wine glasses and setting them on the coffee table. Two bottles of red sit beside them, already breathing.

Mariana arrives first, holding a pink pastry box in one hand and a bottle of sparkling water in the other.

"I brought the goods," she says, waltzing in like a bakery fairy godmother. "Coconut shortbread, guava turnovers, and some new dulce de leche bars I'm testing. I need honest feedback and zero judgment on sugar intake."

"You had me at guava," I say, taking the box from her and placing it on the table.

"You okay?" she asks softly, slipping off her shoes.

I nod. "Getting there."

She doesn't push. She just smiles and says, "Then we eat," and starts arranging the pastries on a dish.

Anna bursts in ten minutes later, wearing hoop earrings and holding a Tupperware container above her head. "Arepas con queso, bebés! Fresh. From. My. Mom. We need to enjoy all the arepas we can get from her before she moves back to Colombia," she declares. "And I have questions. So many questions."

She hands me the container, kicks off her sneakers, and immediately pours herself a very full glass of Cab.

"You look good," she says, eyeing me up and down. "Suspiciously good."

"She does," Mariana agrees, smiling. "The *I'm getting laid* glow."

Anna waggles her eyebrows. "We'll get to him in a second. But I want to talk about the cursed man first—what the hell? When did he come back? And what does he want?"

I pour my own glass of wine, settling onto the couch with a guava turnover in one hand. "He showed up two weeks ago," I say.

"I can't believe you didn't tell us when he showed up. I would've egged his car!" Anna says, mouth full of arepa.

"He said he wants to be in Maya's life. That he wants to have his family back."

"His family? I don't like it," Anna says immediately, eyes narrowing. "I never liked him."

"You and I both," Mariana adds gently, picking at a piece of shortbread.

"And now he thinks he can just show up with that sorry little smirk and act like the last several years didn't happen?" Anna goes on, hands flying. "Absolutely not. I'm telling you, just give me his license plate and a ten-minute head start."

I take a sip of wine, letting the warmth spread through my chest. "It's been...complicated. He showed up here, and she didn't recognize him. Because she's never freaking met him. And he looked so shocked, like it hadn't occurred to him that disappearing before she was even born would actually mean something. What did he think I was doing? Showing her pictures of her long-lost shithead father?"

Anna groans. "Ugh, the male audacity."

"Textbook," Mariana says with a small nod.

"And then he has the nerve to show up at the festival. It's bullshit, and I'm sick of it."

"You need to set boundaries. He absolutely cannot show

up whenever he feels like it. This isn't good for you or Maya," Mariana says, her voice calm but firm.

"I know," I sigh. "It just pisses me off. He shows up acting like everything he missed out on—the pregnancy, the diapers, the sleepless nights, the first words, all of it—can just be erased because he suddenly wants to play dad."

"Too little, way too damn late," Anna mutters, biting into an arepa. "He doesn't get to call himself a father just because he remembered he has a kid."

"Exactly," I say. "Maya doesn't even know who he is. I'm not letting him confuse her just to soothe his ego."

"And what did he expect?" Mariana adds. "That you'd just open the door and roll out the welcome mat? He's delusional."

"I would've accidentally spilled hot coffee on him," Anna mutters.

"Tempting," I say, swirling the wine in my glass. "But I have a kid to protect. And he doesn't get to drop in and make things harder for her."

"Good," Mariana says. "Because he will if you let him."

"That's the thing," I say. "I'm not. He doesn't get access just because he showed up."

Anna exhales. "You're handling it better than I would. I'd be in jail. Smiling in the mugshot." Then she adds, brushing crumbs off her lap, "At least you've clearly upgraded."

I blink. "What?"

She shoots me a look like I'm being dense. "Mateo."

Mariana smiles into her wine. "He's...surprising."

I snort. "That's one word for him."

"No, but really," Anna says, tipping her glass toward me. "You two just strolled into the festival like it was no big deal. Holding hands. Looking all cozy. The entire town practically short-circuited."

"It wasn't that dramatic," I say.

Mariana tilts her head. "It kind of was."

I try to act casual, reaching for another guava turnover. "We were just walking around."

"Walking around holding hands," Anna corrects. "And he brought you lemonade."

"He offered. It was hot."

"So was he," she shoots back, grinning.

Mariana hides a smile behind her glass. "We just didn't see it coming. That's all. You've known each other for years, and suddenly...there's something there."

"There's nothing sudden about it," I say, maybe a little too quickly. "We're just...figuring things out."

Anna leans back with a satisfied nod. "Well, I support it. Tentatively. With questions."

"I'd expect nothing less," I say.

"I just want you to be happy," Mariana says, soft as ever. "No pressure. No expectations."

Anna grins. "But if he's the real deal, I call maid of honor."

I laugh, tossing a pillow at her. "Relax. It's not that deep."

"Not yet," she teases.

I shake my head and reach for my wine again, grateful the attention shifts back to food, music, and Maya's latest obsession with wearing her rain boots indoors.

By the time the pastries are picked over and the wine is nearly gone, I'm full in a way that has nothing to do with food. This was exactly what I needed.

Chapter Nine

MATEO

The slam of my boots against the ground echoes through the bay as I finish another sled push and stand up straight, breath sharp in my throat. My shirt's already clinging to my back, and I haven't even hit the rope yet.

I grab the chalk and start working it between my palms, trying not to let my brain go where it keeps going. Analyse.

The way she looked the other day at breakfast—head thrown back, hair falling over her face, laughing so hard she snorted. Her and Maya's relationship tugs at my heart. Watching the two of them together is really something special.

She gives Maya her complete, undivided attention, love, and devotion. Analyse is a damn good mother, and I find it so fucking sexy.

I shouldn't be thinking that. I know better. She's so much more than her beauty. Although, shit, she is drop dead gorgeous. It's the way she parents with her whole heart. The way she listens to Maya like nothing else exists in that moment. How she always knows when to be soft, when to be firm, when to just be there.

I feel a pang of pain in my chest. It catches me off guard. The ache I feel in my chest when I was the two of them together. A reminder of everything I once had. Everything I once lost.

I shake my head free of those thoughts, not allowing myself to go to a place that I've kept locked away for so long. A dark place that I can't show to anyone.

"Yo, lover boy," Andres calls out, cutting into the quiet. He's standing by the engine, dripping with sweat. "You looking a little slow over there. You praying that Cap's gonna come end you of your misery?"

I shoot him a look, grabbing my bottle and dumping water over my head. "Yeah, right, asshole. You know I'll smoke you in a sled push any day of the week."

Andres grins, cocky as hell. "Talk is cheap, Rodriguez. Let's see it."

Seb whistles low from behind me. "Careful, man. You don't wanna embarrass yourself in front of the guy Maya says could lift a car with one arm."

Andres barks out a laugh. I shake my head, biting back a smile. I should've known better than to tell those jerks what she said.

"What can I say," I toss back with a half-smirk, "kid knows what she's talking about." I start walking toward the sled, glancing over my shoulder. "Too bad her uncles are trash."

Andres lets out a dramatic gasp. "The disrespect! Alright, lover boy—put your legs where your mouth is."

I roll my shoulders back, smirking. "That's a weird way to ask me to beat your ass, but okay. You want this, too, Seb?"

Seb chuckles behind me. "I'm just here for the show."

"Okay, grandpa, enjoy the entertainment." I plant my feet at the edge of the sled and glance over at Andres. "You want a head start? Preserve your ego?"

He flips me off and drops into position on the sled next to mine. "Just don't cry when I leave you in the dust."

Captain Nathan walks in just as I tighten my grip on the bars. His eyes flick between us, unimpressed. "Am I gonna regret letting this happen?"

"Probably," Seb mutters.

For the next hour and a half, we push our sleds across the bay. There's no quit in either of us. Not with our dignity on the line.

We should've tapped out ten rounds ago, but neither one of us is willing to be the first to fold. Every time I stop to catch my breath, I see Andres resetting the weight, and I get my ass right back in line.

By the time Cap comes back, we're both half-dead, chests heaving, shirts drenched, legs shot.

"I hate you so much," Andres wheezes, leaning over the sled.

I drop to the floor beside him, gulping air. "Hate you more."

"Impossible. No one has ever felt the hatred that I feel for you right now. You smell like actual regret."

Seb strolls by, taking a sip from his bottle of Gatorade. "You idiots done, or should I call for backup?"

I flip him off without looking up. Andres mutters something that sounds like "funeral arrangements."

Cap pauses next to us, eyeing the two of us collapsed on the ground. "Glad to see all my training methods are in use."

"Yup," I manage to breathe out. "Peak conditioning."

He snorts and walks away.

Tonight is our weekly family dinner at the firehouse, and

Analyse and my first time attending together as a couple. The first time in front of Cap.

Cap—Nathan—isn't the kind of guy to pry, but he can call bullshit from a mile away. Always has. I hope Analyse and I can pull this off, because if Cap suspects something is off, this whole thing will unravel.

Analyse and Maya step through the bay doors, a tray of pastelón in Analyse's hands. Her hair pinned up, curls fighting for freedom, and she's wearing that soft hoodie I accidentally left at her place last week. I haven't asked for it back. It looks better on her.

Seb and Mariana are in the kitchen. Seb is prepping the chicken for the oven while Mariana starts on a pot of rice. Andres has music blasting from a Bluetooth speaker. He's chopping tomatoes, cucumbers, and romaine for a salad. And Anna is layering her postre de milo.

Maya beelines toward the kitchen, shouting, "Titi Mariana! Mami made pastelón and I got to mash the plátanos!"

Mariana beams at Maya, inhaling deeply. "Mmm, huele riquísimo!"

Maya grins, chest puffed out. "Right? I helped Mami with everything! I even got to taste the meat. But only a little bit. Mami said we had to save it for dinner."

"She's right," Andres chimes in. "We're going to be desperate for her pastelón once we get a load of Seb's dry chicken."

"I'll have you know that this is going to be the world's juiciest chicken. Right, mi tesoro?" he says, glancing over at Mariana.

"Uhhh...of course, Seba. It'll be the best chicken ever," she says, voice dripping with sarcasm, and then shoots the rest of us a look.

Andres immediately snorts. I press my lips together to

keep from laughing, and Analyse is hiding her face behind a dishtowel.

"Wow," Seb says, holding a hand to his heart. "The betrayal in this kitchen is unreal."

~

The food's finally ready, and we all crowd around the long table. Everyone's loud. Talking over each other. Plates being passed in every direction.

I pile food onto my plate, trying to stop myself from devouring the entire tray of the pastelón, when Analyse spots me.

"Your favorite," she says softly.

She settles in next to me, thigh brushing mine, her knee bumping against mine under the table. I feel every single point of contact like it's fire. Maya's across from us, scarfing down the food as if she hasn't had a single meal in days.

"Slow down," Seb says, passing her a napkin. "You're gonna choke."

"I'm going to have seconds," she replies between bites. "Maybe thirds."

Andres looks over at Analyse. "You starving our girl, or what?" he asks with a grin.

Analyse scoffs. "Yeah, right. The kid can eat. She's got a great appetite."

Cap chuckles from the far end of the table. "Gotta respect that she knows good food."

Mariana raises her fork in agreement. "And an appetite that would have made my mom proud."

Seb wraps his arms around Mariana's shoulders, and Anna gently squeezes her hand. Mariana's mom, Lucia, died a few months ago, and it was really hard on Mariana for a while there. It still is.

Lucia was a loss for the whole town. She was a pillar of the community. Someone who remembered birthdays, showed up with a hearty meal when you were having a bad day, and always, always, *always* made you feel seen and heard whenever she was near. Everyone who knew her loved her. Hell, the moment I stepped a foot into this town, she was one of the first faces I saw.

I blew into town with a heavy heart, battling demons no one here knew about, but she *saw* me. I packed up my life in California hoping a change of scenery would somehow make everything hurt less. I didn't have a job. I didn't have a place to stay. Just pain in my heart, and no idea what came next.

She took one look at me, and said, "You look like someone who could use a good meal."

I was completely caught off guard by the moment, but somehow, I found myself following this woman to her house for a home-cooked meal. And damn...that meal was incredible. She asked me a few questions, and by the end of that meal, she'd made a few calls and lined up a place for me to stay, and handed me Seb's number and told me I should think about joining the firehouse. Said I had the look of someone who was built for helping others. She barely knew me, and yet, she changed my life in a way that she would never understand. And now, sitting here at this table—laughing, eating, watching the family I have now—I realize how many of us she saved just by being who she was.

I'm quiet for a moment too long, caught in it—everything she gave me, everything she left behind. Then I feel her. Analyse slides her hand into mine and gives it a gentle squeeze. She leans in and presses a quick kiss to my cheek. Casual. Easy. Just a girlfriend being sweet to her boyfriend in a room full of people who already believe it.

I give her a grateful smile and squeeze her hand back.

~

After we've all eaten too much food, Cap and I clear the table while Andres and Seb argue over who's actually washing the dishes and who's just "supervising."

Seb's got a sponge on his hand but hasn't touched a plate in five minutes, and Andres is talking so much trash I'm not sure anything's actually clean. The girls are packing up the leftovers, leaving Cap and me to collect the used plates, empty trays, and crumpled napkins.

"A relationship looks good on you," Cay says.

I pause, a plate in my hand.

He doesn't look at me, just keeps moving. "You've always carried things quiet, but this is the first time I've seen you... light."

"She's easy to be around," I manage.

He nods. "I've known Analyse for a long time. She's a good woman that's dealt with a lot. I'm glad you both found something in one another."

I don't know what to say to that. Because I know he means every word. And I can't help the guilt that gnaws at me from this lie we've built. Cap's looking at me like I deserve her. Like I've finally found something good, and solid, and lasting. But he doesn't know that this is all a lie that started as a favor. And I hope this won't blow up in my face one he finds out.

Before I can say anything, she walks in with a stack of plates and that teasing smile of hers. "Talking about me?" she asks, smiling sweetly.

"Always," I shoot back.

"Hopefully all good things."

"I could never say a bad thing about you, chula," I say, giving her a wink.

She rolls her eyes, but I catch the corner of her mouth twitching like she's trying not to smile.

Cap watches us for a beat then steps closer, claps a hand on my shoulders, and says, "Good man," before heading out of the room.

The ride home is quiet. Maya's passed out in the back seat, head tilted at an impossible angle, clutching a Tupperware of Anna's dessert. One of her curls is stuck to her forehead.

"She's going to crash so hard when we get home," Analyse whispers from the passenger seat.

I chuckle. "She already did."

We both glance back at the same time then look at each other and share a quiet laugh. It feels easy with Analyse. Comfortable.

I pull into the driveway and kill the engine. The porch light is still on, casting a warm golden halo over the front steps.

Maya stirs in the backseat, and I step out of my car, walk over to her side, and unbuckle her. I lift her into my arms, her head immediately dropping to my shoulder with a sleepy sigh.

"I told you I get the shower first," she mumbles against my neck.

I smile. "I think you've earned it."

Analyse is already at the door by the time I reach the porch. She opens it quietly, steps inside to flick on the hallway light, and then turns back, watching me with something soft in her eyes.

I carry Maya through the door and gently lay her on the couch, pulling a throw blanket over her. She doesn't even stir. Just turns on her side and hugs the nearest pillow.

"She'll probably be out until the morning," Analyse whispers.

"Probably."

Analyse turns to me. "Tonight was a great night. Really."

I glance at her. "It was."

She leans against the doorframe, arms folded loosely in front of her. "You want water or something before you go?"

I shake my head. "Nah. I should let you get some sleep."

She nods but doesn't move. Neither do I. A curl slips free from the clip in her hair, falling into her face. Without thinking, I reach out and gently brush it back, tucking it behind her ear. My knuckles graze her skin, and she stills beneath my touch. Her eyes flick up to mine.

She doesn't smile. She doesn't say anything. But she doesn't move either. I let my hand drop.

"It was nice seeing you in your element," she says quietly.

I glance over at her. "You see me at the firehouse all the time."

"Yeah...but not like this."

I tilt my head. "Like what?"

She hesitates and then shrugs. "I don't know. Tonight just felt...different."

Another curl falls. I leave it this time.

"Goodnight, chula," I say, stepping back.

"Goodnight, Mateo."

She opens the door slowly, pausing in the frame like she's about to say something else—but she doesn't. And then she's gone.

I walk back to my car, but my chest's still tight, and my hand still remembers the feel of her skin.

Chapter Ten

ANALYSE

The next few days pass in a whirl.

We're a few weeks away from Thanksgiving break and then Christmas following soon after, and my students are feral. I'm pulling out all the tricks to try and keep them engaged—mini whiteboards, very dramatic and theatrical read-alouds, bribery via snacks. None of it sticks. These kids are bloodhounds, and they smell that the holidays are right around the corner.

"Miss Garcia," one of them groans mid-math lesson, "can't we just watch a movie?"

"Sure," I say sweetly, "as soon as you can multiply three-digit numbers without crying."

The class groans in unison. Internally, I'm groaning as well. Truthfully, I don't want to be doing this any more than they do. My head's not in it today, my patience is hanging by a thread, and I've already refilled my coffee three times just to survive the morning.

I love these kids—I do—but today, I'm struggling, and it's not even their fault. Damn Nico for getting into my head while I'm at a job that I actually love.

He's been calling more. Texting, too. Little check-ins disguised as the doting father. But I know what he's doing. He doesn't miss me. He misses having access to me. It must eat at him to think I'm in a happy relationship. That I had the audacity to move on from him. To be happy without him. He thought he would leave me on my own—with our baby—and I'd be here waiting for him when he was ready. That I'd be waiting, always, for him to come back.

I realize now that that's the kind of man Nico is. The kind that walks away and still expects the world to revolve around him. But I didn't wait. I built a life without him. And now, the idea that I might actually be happy—without him, because of someone else—it's crawling under his skin. Good.

"Miss Garcia, Umberto is trying to turn his desk into a spaceship again!"

Dios mio. I blink, refocus, and look up just in time to see Umberto on his knees beside his desk, arms flapping, making rocket noises while taping two rulers to the sides of his chair.

You've gotta be kidding me.

"Umberto," I say as evenly as possible. "What did we say about aviation projects during math?"

He freezes mid-launch. "Not to do it?"

"That's right. And yet, here we are."

He stares at me for a beat, then he sighs, peels the rulers off one at a time, and mutters, "Nobody respects visionaries."

I raise a brow but say nothing, and he takes his seat with exaggerated drama. I turn back to the board and try to remember where I left off. Something about fractions. Or maybe it was subtraction. Shit, I need to check my notes.

But at least I'm not thinking about Nico and his bullshit anymore.

~

That afternoon, I'm in the teacher's lounge eating a less than desirable salad that I regretted making the moment I took the first bite. I'm debating whether I'm desperate enough to eat the sad tomato that's trying to roll off my fork when my phone pings with a text.

I glance down, expecting a text from the girls, but it's from Mateo.

MATEO

What's for lunch?

ANALYSE

Sad salad. Tomatoes are mushy. 0/10 don't recommend.

MATEO

Damn. Tragic.

ANALYSE

Tell me about it.

MATEO

Hang tight.

ANALYSE

??

MATEO

Just don't move.

I frown at my phone, certain he's just messing with me. I poke half-heartedly at the salad again, already dreading another bite, when my phone pings once more.

MATEO

Come outside.

I blink. I look around the empty lounge. Confused. I type back quickly.

Why?

Three dots appear, disappear. Reappear.

MATEO

Because if you don't then this pollo guisado
is going to get cold.

I stare at my screen. He did not. He wouldn't actually—
Pollo guisado. My stomach rumbles at the thought.

I chew the inside of my cheek and glance toward the door.
I shouldn't go. I have a million things to do that he'll be a total
distraction from. But damn it, I'm starving.

I grab my badge and toss the salad into the trash. Fine. Just
a few minutes. For the food. Can't let the food go cold. That
would be a travesty.

I push the door open and step into the late afternoon sun,
already spotting him across the lot—leaning against his truck.
He's got a brown paper bag in one hand, and two cold drinks
balanced on the hood.

As soon as he sees me, he grins. My stomach flips. I tell
myself it's the hunger.

"Hey, chula," he says with a cocky grin.

I roll my eyes. I hate that stupid grin. Not really. But really.

"Weren't you ever taught to call before showing up places
growing up?" I say, crossing my arms as I stop in front of him.

His grin widens, he steps impossibly closer to me, voice
dipping just enough to make my pulse stutter. "Weren't you
ever taught to say thank you when someone brings you hot
food?"

I tilt my chin up, refusing to lean back even though he's
well within the too close zone now. The smell of the pollo
guisado is doing things to me. So is the smell of him—soap

and something warm and musky that shouldn't be allowed near me when I'm starving and vulnerable.

"I was also taught not to talk to strange men hovering in parking lots."

"Strange?" he echoes, mock offended.

"Uninvited."

He shrugs, completely unbothered. "Pretty sure bringing lunch gets me a pass."

I open my mouth to say something, but before I can, he lifts the spoon and places a bite of the pollo guisado right into my mouth.

Oh, fuck. That's good.

My head tips back, eyes rolling slightly, and I groan at the heavenly taste.

I hear him laugh—low, pleased, way too damn satisfied.

"Didn't think that's what I had to do to get you to make that sound," he says, voice dipped in smugness.

My eyes snap open. I chew slowly. Then I glare at him. "You're lucky that was incredible. You're also lucky I don't stab you with this fork."

"For you," he says, that damn grin returning, "I'd risk it."

I huff, grabbing the container from his hands, and take a step back. "Did you want to sit here eating this meal with me?"

His brows lift, just slightly. "Do you want me to?" he asks, careful now.

I open my mouth. Close it. Because no would be a lie. But yes feels like he's winning.

Instead, I shrug. "It's a good meal. Would be rude to let you walk away without tasting how great it is."

He smirks, just a little. "So we agree—I'm great."

"I said the food was great."

"Right. And I made the food, which means I am great."

"Just eat before I change my mind."

He scoops a spoonful into his mouth, chews, and says, "You're right. This is good."

I roll my eyes, but don't argue. We lean against the truck, shoulder to shoulder, and for the next twenty minutes eat our lunch in a comfortable quiet. And it's nice.

Chapter Eleven

ANALYSE

One new text from The Council of Chaos.

ANNA

Lyse, get your ass up. We're picking pumpkins!

It's been a few days since I've seen the girls in person, and apparently, that's a few days too long. I'm not surprised. The Council of Chaos runs on group selfies, seasonal snacks, a shit-ton of wine, and wildly unsolicited check-ins.

I text back.

ANALYSE

Do I have a choice?

ANNA

Absolutely not.

MARIANA

We're bringing the flannel. Don't fight it.

> **ANALYSE**
>
> Are the guys coming along for this kidnapping?

MARIANA

Seba is. Andres said only if there's hot cider and zero photo obligations.

ANNA

Which means he's coming and we're forcing him into a leaf pile...and taking loads of pictures.

MARIANA

Tell your man to get his ass up and ready to go, too.

I smile despite myself. My man. If they only knew. But it's easier this way. Let them believe it's real. I toss my phone onto the bed, pull on a sweater, and grab a flannel for Maya.

Pumpkins await.

The pumpkin patch is about twenty minutes outside of town, tucked behind a farmstand that sells cinnamon donuts, fresh honey, and apple cider so good that you'll never want to buy the store-bought stuff ever again.

By the time we pull up, Anna's already texting where to meet her, and Mariana is sending selfies from between two hay bales. After I unhook her from her booster seat, Maya practically launches herself out of the car.

"Mami, can we get apple cider and donuts?" she asks, eyes wide, curls bouncing.

"Let's start with one," I say, grabbing our bag from the back seat. "Then we'll negotiate."

She grins, knowing she'll win in the end.

We spot the girls near a row of wagons lined up for hayrides. Anna's wearing her *it's fall y'all* sweatshirt, and Mariana's already clutching a latte.

"Oh thank God," Anna says when she sees us. "I was starting to think you were bailing and I was going to have to find a new best friend in the maze."

"Tempting," I say. "But I figured you'd haunt me until I gave in."

"Correct," Mariana adds. "Also, you look cute. Love the boots."

I glance down at the ones I only wear this time of the year. "Thanks. They're my 'pretend I'm not exhausted' boots."

Maya's already tugging at my hand. "Can we go pick pumpkins now?"

"Let's go!" Mariana says, looping her arm through Maya's. "We're finding you the biggest pumpkin here."

We make our way into the field, winding between rows of round, lopsided, dirt-covered pumpkins. Maya darts ahead, inspecting each one, wanting the perfect pumpkins for our front porch. She mentioned wanting to find white pumpkins as well. I hope she finds exactly what she wants.

Mariana trails beside her, nodding seriously every time Maya announces, "This one's almost perfect, but not quite."

Anna nudges me. "So...where is he?"

I blink. "Who?"

She gives me a look. "Your man, girl. Your tall, broody, makes all the ladies wanna drop their panties fireman."

"Drop their panties." I snort. "I don't know. I texted him where we'd be, and said he can come if he'd like."

"Not you trying to play it cool," Anna says. "He's already yours"

I roll my eyes. "Yeah...for now."

Anna's face softens. "Lyse. I know I said things when I found out you two were together—probably too much. But I think Mateo is making me eat my words." She nudges me lightly. "He shows up for you. Consistently. That's not nothing."

I don't say anything, so she keeps going.

"I think he loves you. And if this hesitation is about Nico…I get it. He's a monumental jerk. What he did to you was unforgivable. He left. And he let you carry everything alone. But I hope you won't let what he broke stop you from accepting something that's good. Something that's real.

"He's crazy about you," she adds. "Anyone with eyes can see that. Don't talk yourself out of something that feels right just because it's unfamiliar."

"Love," I scoff. "Let's not get ahead of ourselves. We're having fun."

"Where's my best girl?" A voice cuts in behind us.

His voice. I turn. Seb's leading the way, grinning and cracking a total dad joke. "What do you get when you drop a pumpkin? Squash."

Anna groans immediately. "Absolutely not."

"Yes," Seb says proudly. "I've been saving that one."

Behind him, Andres sips from a cider, unfazed. "He told it in the car. Didn't land there either."

And then I see him. Mateo. Trailing behind them, hands tucked into his jacket pockets, curls slightly mussed from the wind. His eyes find mine like they always seem to do.

My heart quickens, my stomach flips. Nope. Shut that down, Lyse.

Maya yells, "Mateoooooo!" and takes off running through the pumpkins toward him.

He crouches just in time to catch her, lifting her up effortlessly with a soft laugh that does things to my chest I'm not ready to think about.

"You came!" she says, wrapping her arms around his neck,

"Of course, I came," he says. "There's not a chance I'd miss pumpkin picking with my favorite girl."

Anna leans closer to me, smug as hell, and whispers, "I told you so."

Maya wastes no time. She tugs Mateo and says, "We're finding the biggest, most prettiest one. And maybe a white one, too."

She's a girl on a mission.

Mateo follows easily, letting her chatter fill the space. He glances back once, catching my eye, and I see a smirk that makes my stomach twist.

Mariana falls in step beside me, arms crossed over her chest. "Our girl's got taste."

"She also thinks a good pumpkin is defined by the vibes."

Seb veers into a row and immediately picks up the first pumpkin he sees. "This one. No notes."

"It's shaped like a deflated basketball," Anna says, wrinkling her nose.

"Exactly. It has character!"

Andres leans over. "I swear you pick the worst pumpkins on purpose."

"Hey!" Seb says, offended. "The pumpkins I pick tell a story. A story of the journey they had to go on to get to this patch. We want those stories!"

Andres barks out a laugh. "Riiiight. You keep telling yourself that. You're definitely not just a bad picker."

Farther down the row, Maya points at a massive pumpkin halfway buried under vines. "That's it! That's the one!"

Mateo crouches beside it, inspecting it. "That's a good one, princesa. You've got a good eye."

"I want it. Can I pleeeease have it, Mateo?"

"Of course," he says, lifting it easily.

Maya gasps, hands over her mouth. "See! I told you, Mami! He's so strong! He can lift a car with one arm, I know it!"

Mateo chuckles, adjusting the pumpkin in his arms. "Don't let Andres here you say that."

Too late.

"I heard that!" Andres calls out from a few rows over. "And I can totally lift a car!"

I quirk an eyebrow at him.

"If the car is a toy. And plastic. And hollow." He continues.

Seb barks out a laugh and nearly drops the very sad-looking pumpkin he's carrying. Really. A truly unfortunate gourd that looks like it tells the story of constant emotional stress. Seriously. What did it have to go through to get here?

"She's just speaking facts," Mariana says, giving Maya a high five. "Mateo does have strong arms. Very visually verified."

I nearly choke on air. Mateo just grins.

Seb blinks at Mariana, hand to his chest. "Excuse me? Visually verified. Wow. Just wow. Should I just go home now, or...?"

Mariana pats his cheek. "You're strong, too, mi amor. The strongest."

He narrows his eyes. "That felt like a participation trophy."

Anna chuckles. "It was. But a sweet one."

Seb lets out a long, dramatic sigh and gently sets his tragic pumpkin into the wagon. "You hear that, buddy? We're nothing but a pity pair."

Maya leans over and gives the pumpkin a gentle pat. "It's okay. You can sit next to ours."

Mateo laughs, the sound soft and low beside me. "Our girl is too pure for this group."

Our girl. He says it so easily. Our girl. I try to retrace every conversation we've ever had since Maya was born. Has he always called her his girl, our girl? Maybe. I can't remember. But for some reason, right now, as he says it, the words settle differently. I can't help the butterflies it causes in my stomach.

I glance over at him, and he's still watching Maya, staring at her in awe. The awe I thought I only could have. As her mom. It tugs something deep in me.

Anna interrupts my thoughts, spinning around. "Alright, my fall queens and emotional support himbos—are we donut bound or what?"

"YES!" Maya yells. "Donuts! And the apple juice!"

"Cider," I correct automatically, but she's already grabbing Mateo's hand and tugging him toward the food stand.

And he lets her, of course. I have a little feeling he'd follow her anywhere she led.

We reach the stand, and the scent of cinnamon sugar and warm apples wraps around us like a cozy blanket. Maya's eyes go wide at the trays stacked with fresh donuts.

"Pick one," I tell her. "Just one."

"One for now," she says, already reaching.

The rest of the group fans out—Andres goes straight for the hot cider, Mariana's trying to convince Anna to split a caramel apple, and Seb is interrogating the teenager behind the counter about how many grams of sugar are there in a donut.

Mateo stands beside me, shoulder just barely brushing mine. "You want one?"

I glance at him. "Are you talking about the donuts or the cider?"

"Yes."

I huff a laugh. "Cider. But only if you're getting one, too."

He nods and signals to the vendor. "Two ciders, please. And one of whatever she's having," he adds, gesturing to Maya, who is already covered in powdered sugar.

We settle onto one of the benches just off to the side, where the group can still be heard arguing about donut rankings. Powdered over jelly. Bavarian cream over strawberry frosted.

Mateo passes me the warm cup, and for a moment, our fingers brush. I take the cider and sip. It's too sweet. So, of course, I love it.

I glance over at him and notice that he's watching me.

"You've got something," he says, gesturing to my face,

I blink. "What?"

He leans in, just slightly, and brushes his thumb gently against the corner of my mouth. Powdered sugar. The contact is brief. But it's enough to completely short-circuit my brain.

His hand drops back to his lap. "You good?" he asks, voice low.

I nod. Liar, liar. "Yeah," I say. "Just...sugar rush."

He smirks. "Sure."

I take a long gulp of my cider. "I'm serious," I say.

Mateo stretches one long leg out in front of him and bumps my foot lightly with his. "You've got your overthinking face on," he murmurs.

"I do not have an overthinking face."

He side-eyes me. "You absolutely do."

Before I can argue, Maya appears out of nowhere with powdered fingers and sticky cheeks. "Picture time!" she announces.

Anna is already waving everyone over toward the big photo wall set up by the cider stand—stacked hay bales, scarecrows, and pumpkins.

Mariana hands her phone over to one of the teens working

the stand. "Hi! Can you take a picture of all of us, please? Like, multiple? Don't be shy with the shutter."

Seb and Andres immediately start striking ridiculous poses —Seb throws his arm around the scarecrow, looking like he made a new lifelong pal, and Andres kicks a leaf pile into the air.

Mariana rolls her eyes and grabs Seb by the shirt, dragging him back in line. "You're taking one normal photo. Please. For the family album."

Maya plops herself in front of everyone, cheeks puffed, ready to burst with joy and excitement. "Mateo, come here!"

He steps in beside her, and without hesitation, lifts her into his arms. She squeals and wraps her arms around his neck, giggling.

Mariana looks at me, eyes sparkling, and says loud enough for everyone to hear, "Smile like you're in love!"

And that's the moment Mateo reaches for me. His arm slides around my waist like it's something he does every day, and then he pulls me flush against him, Maya still in his other arm.

My breath catches. I don't even have time to reach before the camera clicks. Once. Twice. Rapid fire.

I manage a smile, but my heart's racing.

He leans in, close to my ear, voice low and teasing, "You're smiling."

"I'm being held hostage."

"You feel pretty relaxed for a hostage."

"I hate it."

"You love it."

Maya giggles in his arms and kisses his cheek. "This is the best day ever."

❀

After a very good, but very long day, Maya is fast asleep in her bed.

She didn't even make it through her nightly bedtime story. One second, she was curled under her princess quilt, and the next, her eyes were fluttering closed mid-sentence. I finished the book anyway—out loud, like I always do—even if she wasn't awake to hear it. I'm not sure why. I guess I want to soak in every second of her, this small, as much as I can.

I kiss the top of her head before slipping out of her room, closing the door behind me with that soft, careful quiet only moms can master. Everyone knows that trying to keep your child asleep, and in their own bed, is like gently placing down a bomb so that it won't activate.

The house feels still. Peaceful.

I head into the kitchen, tug my hair into a loose bun, and lean against the counter with a glass of water, letting the silence stretch around me. The scent of fall still lingers faintly on my clothes—pumpkin, cinnamon, the worn cotton of flannel. A reminder of how good today was. Of how good it felt. Of how good it was to see Mateo with Maya. To see how good he is with me. The feel of his arm around my waist. Why did it feel like it belonged there? Why did I feel like he belonged next to me?

I shouldn't let myself sit in that feeling for too long. I shouldn't ponder a what-if that I know can never ever. Should never happen.

My phone buzzes on the counter. I blink down at the screen. Nico. Of course. Because he seems to have some sort of radar that goes off in his head whenever I'm happy. A radar telling him that he needs to disrupt my life, disrupt my peace.

I hesitate for a second before unlocking it.

NICO

I hope you're having a nice night.

ANALYSE

What do you want, Nico?

NICO

I just want to remind you of what I said
when I came back. I want you to know that
I meant it. I want to fix things. I miss you,
Lyse. I miss you so bad.

A second buzz. Another message.

NICO

I know I messed up. Shit. I fucked up big
time. But I want to be with you. I know that
now. I know I should have never left you.
Just give me a chance to prove I've
changed.

I stare at the messages, jaw tight.

He never asks about Maya. Never asks what she likes, how her day was, what her favorite color is this week. He doesn't know about her obsession with french fries with eggs or how she still sleeps with the same stuffed frog she's had since she was one. He doesn't know how hard she cried when she accidentally stepped on an ant in our backyard, singing sana sana colita de ran to it in hopes that the magical song of healing would resurrect it.

He doesn't know a damn thing. He spent one day with her since he's been back. He saw her for fifteen minutes after the Fall Festival's pie-eating contest. Then he went ghost. Again.

He isn't here for her. He's here for me. He wants me. He thinks I'm a prize for him to win, but he doesn't realize that she is everything. She's the goddamn prize. She's gold. She's sunshine. She's joy, happiness, and love.

But he doesn't care. It's a game to him. Win Analyse back.

He has no idea who I even am. He just wants the version of me that stood in the doorway crying when he left.

What he doesn't know is that woman? The one who begged? The one whose heart tore in two with each receding step of his... She doesn't live here anymore. She's dead and gone. Stronger and better than ever.

I lock my phone and set it down face-down on the counter, letting the silence reclaim the space. In the other room, the clock ticks softly. Upstairs, Maya sleeps without worry.

And me? I'm done begging.

Chapter Twelve

MATEO

I awake gasping for air, sweat dripping down the back of my neck. Nightmares.

I haven't had them in a while. I've been carefully evading them, hiding away from the pain. Avoiding triggers. Keeping my head down. Pretending that maybe, just fucking maybe, I had my shit figured out.

But I know better. Grief doesn't work like that. Grief doesn't just go away for good. It creeps in when you least expect it. It's tricky that way. One minute you're fine, sleeping in a bed you made yourself, in a life you've rebuilt piece by piece. And then within a blink of an eye, you're right back in the middle of it.

Grief.

It claws its way up your throat. Burns like smoke. Sticks to your ribs. Makes you forget how to breathe, even though you've done it since the day you were born.

Grief.

It doesn't ask permission to visit. It doesn't knock at your door. Doesn't send a carrier bird to notify you of its arrival. It just barges in unannounced, drags you under, holds you hostage, and dares you to act like it's not winning. As if it isn't killing you. As if you're not bleeding out in ways no one else can see.

I sit on the edge of the bed, elbows on my knees, heart still pounding. My fingers press into my temples, like I can squeeze the images out of my head. But I can't. I never will be able to. They're burned in too deep. Etched into every corner of who I am. They've become part of my very being. They are my mirror image.

The worst parts of me don't hide in the shadows anymore. They stare back at me in bathroom mirrors. In the silence between calls. In the faces of the people who were never supposed to become my family. And the worst part is that they will never know. Because I hide it.

I'm a master of hidden secrets. I lock it all away so deep, buried under the false pretense of normalcy and happiness. Hidden away by jokes and laughter.

I pretend the weight of the past, the weight of what happened, doesn't still sit on my chest every goddamn day. But it does. And the longer I pretend, the more I try to hide it, the more it tightens. Like a rope around my neck. I can't breathe. Not really.

Every move I make, every word I speak, feels like it's happening through a filter. No one really sees me. Not the real me, anyway. It's as if I'm underwater, and everyone else is on land. They're all waving, laughing, living, but not me. I'm just here. Drowning with a smile plastered across my face. I can't breathe. But they can't tell.

Because I've gotten really fucking good at pretending.

I'm bone-tired. Tired of pretending. Tired of drowning in silence. Tired of carrying ghosts I never invited but can't seem to let go of.

Still, I get up. Because that's what I do.

I go through the motions. Get ready like I'm not unraveling at the seams. I put on my uniform—layer by layer, piece by piece—until I'm back in character.

Until I'm the guy everyone knows. The one who shows up. The one who always seems okay. And by the time I slide into the driver's seat and pull out onto the road, I almost believe it. I almost believe I'm that guy.

Almost.

The station's already buzzing when I pull in.

The bay doors are open, and the cold morning air creeps through the garage, brushing against the concrete floor and making the smell of smoke and engine oil just a little sharper than usual.

Seb's leaning against the engine with a protein bar in his hand. "You're late," he says around a mouthful.

"You're dramatic," I toss back.

He shrugs, biting off another chunk. "Both can be true."

Andres is squatting beside a pile of gear, tightening the straps on his bunker pants. "He's grumpy, because Cap made him redo his paperwork after he logged a ladder drill as 'spiritual growth.'"

I smirk. "Creative. I'll give him that."

"Creative my ass," Seb mutters. "It was a symbolic ladder. For the record."

Nathan steps out of his office just in time to hear that and lets out a sigh. "Drill starts in ten," he says. "Try not to be idiots until then."

With these guys, I don't think we can make that promise.

We suit up, the mood light on the surface—jokes flying, boots thudding, gear shifting—but underneath it, I feel that familiar tension crawling its way back up my spine.

The drill is standard. Hose pull, interior sweep, extraction with a child dummy. Nothing we haven't done a hundred times before. But I can't shake the feeling of the morning. No matter how hard I try. I feel off. I feel different.

Like I'm wearing my skin wrong. Like my gear weighs more today. Like the air's too thick, and I'm already halfway to drowning.

I force the images of my nightmares out of my mind. Focus, Mateo. This is your time to be the version of you everyone expects. Cool, calm, and collected.

I need to be the Mateo they all know they can trust to be there. The one they can count on. The one Maya calls strong.

This is time to put on my best show.

So I square my shoulders. I check my gloves. And I walk into the smoke like it's nothing. I'm not unraveling from the inside out. Definitely not.

I step inside the drill structure, and the second the smoke hits my face, my lungs tighten. It's not really smoke—we use nontoxic training fog—but it doesn't matter. My body reacts anyway. It's as if my brain knowing the difference doesn't matter.

I move forward, eyes scanning the dim hallway, dragging the hose behind me, steps practiced and sure. But nothing about me feels sure. Nothing about me feels right today. The hallway bends, and for a second, I can't see the training dummy at the end of the room.

My breath stutters. My heartbeat pounds in my ears. And that's when I see it. The shape. Slumped. Small. I force myself forward. I grab the dummy. My gloves shake.

It's just a dummy. It's just a dummy. I mumble to myself. I tell myself I'm here. In Lake City. I'm here with the rest of my crew. That this is now. That this is just a drill. So why doesn't it feel like a drill? Why do I feel frozen in the moment of my past?

My grip on the dummy tightens. Too tight. My hands ache, gloves creaking against plastic limbs that don't weigh nearly enough to feel real. But my body doesn't care one bit. My body doesn't care that this is fake. It reacts like it's real.

Fuck. My chest burns from the memory of a moment that changed my life forever. A moment that I shove down deep and won't let anyone in on. Not Cap. Not Seb. Definitely not Analyse.

My world is a broken hourglass, unable to move forward because of the shame I refuse to let go of. The failure that follows me like a second skin.

I stagger back a step, the hose still trailing behind me, and suck in a breath that doesn't quite reach the bottom of my lungs. My helmet feels too tight. My gear feels too heavy.

It's not real.

It's not real.

It's not—

"Rodriguez! You good?" Cap's voice crackles in my earpiece.

I force a breath in. Nod, even though he can't see me. "Yeah. Moving."

I haul the dummy over my shoulder, every muscle screaming. Push forward. Each step is harder than the last. Just finish. Just get through this.

The door opens ahead, daylight streaming in like a slap to the face. I break through it and lower the dummy to the pavement, my breaths ragged.

I did it. I passed. But deep down, I know I didn't really make it out. Not really. Not in the way I need to.

The sunlight doesn't feel warm. The air doesn't feel fresh. Everything feels too damn loud. Too damn sharp. Too damn bright. Seb claps a hand on my back as I step out of the way, cracking some joke I don't catch. I nod like I heard it, like I'm fine, and move toward the benches at the far end of the bay.

Helmet off. Gloves off. But I still feel a weight heavy upon me. I sit. Elbows on my knees. Palms over my face. I reach for my phone without thinking.

My thumbs hover over the screen. I don't know what to say. Don't know how to explain the knot in my chest or the way today cracked something open that I've been duct-taping shut for years. I type out a quick message and place my phone down beside me.

I may not know what to say, but I know what I need. Who I need.

Analyse.

~

By the time she knocks on my door, the sun's dipped low enough to stain the sky a bruised gold. I've changed into sweats and a clean T-shirt, but I still feel like I'm wearing the day. It's in my bones. My lungs. My silence.

I open the door, and there she is—Analyse, in a faded hoodie and leggings, her curly hair framing her face, holding two bags: one from the grocery store, one from Mariana's bakery, The Rolling Pin.

God, she's beautiful. I look at her and feel like I should be on my knees.

"Hey," she says softly.

"Hey." It's the only word I can manage right now, and it comes out a little rough.

She holds up the bags in her hands. "I didn't know what you'd be in the mood for, so I brought a few things. Comfort food. And snacks. Obviously."

"Obviously," I echo, stepping aside so she can come in.

She brushes past me, and suddenly, I feel like I can breathe. A gust of air creeping into my lungs.

She heads straight to the kitchen, and I quickly follow. She starts unpacking the bags—containers from The Rolling Pin, a small tray of arroz con gandules, pastelitos wrapped in foil, chocolate-covered almonds, sour gummies, and a bag of plantain chips.

"This is all very nutritionally sound," I say, leaning against the counter.

She glances over her shoulder with a small smile. "I'm told emotional damage can be reversed with carbs and salt. I'm just testing the science."

I huff a quiet laugh. "Thanks for this. For coming."

"You don't have to thank me," she says, softer now. "You needed someone. You called. I came."

She says it so simply. As if her being here for me at this moment, no questions asked, is completely normal. As if she'd show up for me whenever I need her. I watch her for a moment as she sets the last container down. And I think...I think maybe she would.

I grab two plates from the cabinet, and she begins piling them with food. We eat on the couch, shoulder to shoulder, plates balanced on our laps, and the TV on low. *Law & Order: SVU*, obviously. The moment I handed her the remote, she put it on like muscle memory.

"You're predictable," I murmur, nudging her lightly with my elbow.

She doesn't take her eyes off the screen as she replies, "It's called comfort TV. Some people meditate. Some people do yoga. I watch Stabler beat up bad guys."

I huff a quiet laugh and take another bite. "I didn't realize how hungry I was," I murmur.

"Well, I'm glad I'm here to remind you that you're human. Eat up," she says, nudging at my knee playfully.

I clear my throat. "This was really good. All of it."

"Next time you're spiraling," she says casually, "I'll bring flan and wine."

"You're already planning the next time?"

She gives me a look. "Uh yeah, Mateo. You're a man who bottles his emotions and thinks working out before the sun even rises will fix all your problems. There's going to be a next time."

I let out a soft snort. "Brutal."

"Honest," she says, eating another spoonful of rice.

The silence stretches between us. It's nice. Comfortable. After a while, she grabs the bag of plantain chips and holds it open toward me. I take a few, and she rests her hand between us, bag crinkling slightly.

"Look, I'm not going to ask what's wrong," she says softly. "I don't need to know. But I'm here. I'll always be here for you. And when you need me again—yes, I said when—I'll be here again. No questions asked."

My throat tightens. Analyse. She's exactly what I needed today. She doesn't even realize what she's done for me. I stare down at the chips in my hand, and then I let my eyes meet hers. There's no pity in them. There's just understanding.

I nod once. That's all I can manage. But I think she gets it. I think she knows. Because she smiles softly, turns her attention back to the TV, and pops another chip into her mouth.

We've been watching episodes of *Law & Order* for the last few hours. My eyes are growing heavy. I turn my head, and there she is—Analyse, curled up beside me, fast asleep. Her legs are tucked beneath her, one arm draped loosely over her stomach, the throw blanket rising and falling with each steady breath. A curl has slipped across her cheek, soft and untamed.

I shift slowly, careful not to wake her, and just sit there, watching her in the dim light of the TV flickering across her skin. I stare at her for a beat too long. She's devastatingly beautiful. Easy, Mateo. Remember that this is all a lie. This is all fake. A performance. We aren't really dating. She's here for me as a friend. Just that. Nothing more.

I tear my gaze away and sink back into the cushions, scrubbing a hand down my face. But the warmth of her beside me, the way her hand brushed mine earlier, the echo of her voice saying I'll always be here—it clings to me.

I sigh heavily, lean my head back against the couch, eyes on the ceiling, trying to will myself to sleep. It doesn't work.

My body's still, but my mind won't quiet. It's too loud up there—too many thoughts jostling for space.

What am I doing? Why did I ask her to come? Why did she say yes?

The answer is obvious. It's because she's Analyse. This is who she is. She shows up for the people she cares about. I just didn't realize I was one of those people. Sure, I've been in her orbit for years. I spend as much time as I can with Maya. That kid holds my heart, probably more than either of them know.

But somehow along the way, I missed it—how Analyse is also there. She's in my heart. In my world. Taking up space.

I quickly rid my head of those thoughts. We said we were pretending. That this was just a game. A way to keep Nico away from her. A harmless lie.

I glance at her again. She's curled in closer now, her arm brushing mine. A hundred different thoughts push up at once. I shoot each of them down.

I stay quiet. I lie here. Wide awake. And I let her sleep beside me like nothing in the world could possibly go wrong.

Chapter Thirteen

ANALYSE

I'm sitting in the teacher's lounge enjoying a much needed break—legs crossed, coffee in one hand, and half a donut in the other.

A couple of the other teachers walk in, chatting quietly between themselves. They settle at a table behind me, their voices low at first, the sound of crinkling wrappers and chair legs scraping tile filling the quiet.

I don't mean to listen. I swear, I really don't. But sometimes these bochinchera ears win the battle against the mature woman inside of me. I tear off another bite of donut, chewing slowly, pretending I'm not leaning back in my seat in their direction. I blame my mother for having me watch all those telenovelas with her—now look at me, living for the drama.

"Did you see him the other day?" one of the teachers says.

"No!" another scream-whispers. "He was here?"

"Yes! He was parked right out front. It looked like he brought her lunch."

Shit. My eye twitches. My coffee goes down the wrong pipe. I cough once, quietly...at least I hope I was quiet, and I take another bite of my donut to buy time while my brain short-circuits. Dammit. Please don't let them be talking about me. There has to be another nice guy who brought a teacher lunch in our school, right? Right??

"Wow," one of the teachers says, voice lowered. "I'm so confused. I thought he and Letty were a thing? That's what she said."

Another lets out a sharp breath. "I know. He's obviously going behind her back."

A third voice jumps in, tone dismissive. "It honestly doesn't surprise me. Mateo doesn't scream boyfriend material."

The second one snorts. "No, he screams get in my bed material."

Then the first one sighs. "Ugh. Poor Letty. She's going to be heartbroken when she finds out."

I put the rest of my donut down. I've officially lost my appetite. I'm equal parts furious and sick to my stomach. First of all, how dare they talk about Mateo like that?

They don't even know him. Not the real him. They only know what they think they see. The jawline, the arms, the sexy-as-hell thigh tattoo. Look, I get it. He's hot. Like...infuriatingly hot. But that's not him. That's now who he is as a person.

They haven't seen the way he crouches to talk to Maya like she's the most important person in the room. Or how he will dress up in any princess costume if that's what makes her happy, because her happiness means the world to him.

They haven't seen how he shows up for every single one of us. How he showed up for Seb during his heartbreak, or Mariana in her time of grief, or me. How he's shown up for me since the day Maya was born, helped me every chance he could, even agreed to be my fake boyfriend to get my ex off my back.

Mateo Rodriguez isn't just "get in my bed" material. He's

the whole damn home. And here I am, sitting in this lounge, listening to people who don't know a thing about him speculate on a story they made up out of scraps. The idea that Letty is a victim in this all? Laughable.

The anger inside me starts bubbling, rising fast and hot in my chest. It's a white-hot fury that makes you say things you can't take back. And I know myself, and my damn mouth. So before I say something that'll have me writing a resignation letter before noon, I stand, toss the rest of my donut and my half-full coffee in the trash, and walk out.

Fast. Head high. Heart racing.

The door swings shut behind me, muffling the gossip still spinning in that damn room.

~

The rest of the day goes by in a blur. I go through the motions of teaching my students. I smile when I'm supposed to. Laugh when I need to. But none of it really lands.

I'm too in my head. Too distracted. Too annoyed.

Every time I pause, even for a second, my brain goes right back to that lounge. Those voices. That gossip. The way they tossed Mateo's name around like it was nothing. Like he was nothing. And worse—like I was some side chick with no self-respect.

By the time the final bell rings, I'm emotionally tapped out. The kids race out of the classroom, and I'm left standing by the whiteboard, a dry-erase marker in one hand and a tension headache blooming behind my eyes.

Goddamn Letty. Who does she think she is? Why is she telling people that she and Mateo are together? Did they have a thing? Were they hooking up when Mateo agreed to fake date me?

I press the heels of my palms into my eyes, trying to will the thoughts away, but they're already in. Circling. Building.

The thoughts are gnawing at me so deep, it makes my skin itch. I close my eyes. Exhale. Try not to scream.

After a few deep breaths, I decide I know exactly what I need.

≈

I sit behind the wheel of my car, parked in the driveway with the engine off and the windows cracked, finishing the last few minutes of the podcast episode.

"...the killer had been in the attic the entire time," the host says in her calm, slightly breathy voice. "Watching. Waiting. Listening to her brush her teeth."

I suck in a breath and mutter to myself, "See, this is why I don't trust creaky floorboards. You're either going to be fighting off a chupacabra or a murderer. Either way, you lose."

The host moves on to the closing credits, thanking listeners and teasing next week's deep dive into a cult that lived in the middle of the country and worshipped a man named George.

I hit pause. There's nothing like a little bit of true crime to get your heart rate going, a reminder that I'm alive and well.

I glance in the rearview mirror. Maya's in the backseat, legs swinging, earbuds in, humming along to what I assume is that Halloween playlist she begged me to download. She catches me watching and flashes me a peace sign. I smile. I love my tiny weirdo.

I unbuckle, grab my water bottle, and open the door. The air is crisp enough to make me glad I grabbed a sweater.

"Come on, mamita," I call, stretching out the kink in my back as I round the car. "Let's make the most of the last daylight before it turns into murder hour."

Maya hops out, tiara crooked, hoodie sleeves pulled over her hands. "We should do the murder mystery game again!"

"Only if you promise not to yell 'this is where the body was found' loud enough to freak out the neighbors again."

She shrugs, unapologetic. "I make no promises."

I really am raising my mini-me.

She skips ahead of me into the backyard, already dragging the chalk bucket and our "Mystery Kit" across the patio. It's an old shoebox we decorated last year with Halloween stickers and filled with random clues, flashlights, and one incredibly dramatic feather pen.

"You're such a little weirdo, kid."

"I get it from you." She giggles.

"Alright, Detective Maya," I say, grabbing the clipboard she's scribbled all over in marker. "What's the case today?"

She pulls out a crumpled index card and clears her throat. "The case of the missing pumpkin cookie. Someone took it. We don't know who, but we have three suspects. Each left behind a clue."

"Was it the princess with sticky fingers, the titi with a sweet tooth, or the firefighter who says he doesn't like sugar but is totally lying?"

She gasps. "Mateo!"

I grin. "Let's gather the evidence and crack the case!"

We spend the next hour going through "clues" to crack that case. Muddy footprints made with water and chalk, a bite mark in a sugar cookie I definitely took a nibble out of earlier, and a suspicious glove we found under the patio table. Maya's convinced the thief is someone close to us. "It's always the ones you least suspect," she says, squinting through her magnifying glass.

We're mid-search when the back gate creaks open.

"Buenas noches," Hilda calls, her voice warm.

Maya gasps and bolts across the yard. "Hildaaaaaa!"

They meet in a hug that almost knocks Hilda backward. I walk over, smiling as Hilda steadies her tote bag full of snacks, pajamas, and definitely a storybook or two.

"You sure you're good with her tonight?" I ask, even though I already know the answer.

She pats my arm. "Please. I live for these sleepovers. We're doing movie night, popcorn, and a couple of Cam Jansen books."

"Cam Jansen!" Maya practically vibrates with excitement. "I want the haunted carnival one."

"Packed and ready," Hilda says with a wink.

I lean down to kiss Maya's forehead. "Okay, mija. Be good. No scaring Hilda with crime scenes."

"Only happy mysteries," Maya says solemnly.

I grin. "Good girl."

The second Hilda and Maya pull out of the driveway, my phone buzzes.

ANNA

We're two minutes away. I expect wine and popcorn to be ready.

MARIANA

Also…is your door unlocked or are we breaking in again?

ANALYSE

It's unlocked. But by all means, live out your little breaking and entering fantasy.

MARIANA

I'd need Seba for that.

ANNA

Yesss girl.

ANALYSE

Mari! TOO FAR!

Two minutes later, the front door swings open. Anna walks in first, arms full—one hand holding a bottle of red wine, the other clutching a jumbo-sized bag of popcorn. Mariana follows behind her with a tote bag that's definitely filled with snacks. We're all wearing our vintage scream sweatshirts—the faded black ones with Billy Loomis on the front, one finger raised to his lips and the other hand gripping a knife. That man was so damn hot. Psychotic? Absolutely. But hot. And I will not be taking questions at this time.

Anna drops everything on the coffee table and flops onto the couch with a sigh. "Why are we not married to murderers who look like Skeet Ulrich in 1996?"

Mariana snorts. "Well firstly, I think Seba might have a problem with that. And secondly, jail is apparently frowned upon."

I raise a brow. "And yet we all agree Billy was the moment."

"Unhinged," Anna says, pouring wine. "But in a sexy way."

"I stand by what I said," I add, grabbing my glass. "He could ghost me and stab me in the same breath and I'd say thank you."

Mariana throws her head back laughing. "Therapy. Immediately."

"Whatever," I say, curling into the corner of the couch. "It's movie night. Let me be delusional in peace."

～

We're about halfway through the movie, and the popcorn's long gone. Anna's stretched across the floor, dramatically clutching a throw pillow every time Ghostface shows up. Mariana's wrapped in my favorite fuzzy blanket, the one that technically belongs to Maya but we all pretend is communal.

Tatum is in the garage, tossing beers around and low-key flirting with Ghostface like she's not about to freaking die.

"She's literally flirting with him," Mariana says, horrified. "Girl, what are you doing?"

"She thinks it's Randy," I say. "To be fair, if I thought some dude was trying to prank me in a Ghostface mask, I'd flirt, too."

"Oh, we know you would," Anna says, reaching for more wine. "You'd be like, 'Nice knife. But are you emotionally available?'"

Anna snorts so hard she chokes on her drink. I hand her a napkin, and we dissolve into laughter. That big belly laughter that only happens with the people that you most care about, the people the truly get you—down to your twisted sense of humor and your lifelong fear of attic murders.

As the credits roll, we all slump into the couch, quiet for the first time in hours.

Anna yawns and stretches. "Okay, but real talk...Mateo."

I blink. "What about him?"

She sits up. "He's really into you."

Mariana hums in agreement. "Deeply. Like, 'I'll build a house with you in the woods' into you."

I roll my eyes, but my face warms anyway. "You guys are making stuff up again."

"No, we're not," Anna says. "We're observant. You're just scared."

I don't answer right away. I run my finger along the rim of my glass, watching the way the candle flickers on the coffee table.

"We're having a really good time together," I finally say. "There's so much more to him than meets the eye. He surprised me. He's...a good man."

Mariana's smile softens. "I love that. He is a good man. And that's exactly what you deserve."

Anna raises her glass. "To good sex, good men, and the hope that they're both with the same person!"

We laugh and clink our glasses one last time.

They head out a little after midnight, both of them swearing they're going to text me the second they get home, even though I know they'll forget. And this is why I make them share their locations with me...gotta make sure my girls are safe.

I lock the door behind them, turn off the lights, and sink back into the couch. It's quiet now. Still warm from their laughter and presence. My heart beats a little louder in the silence.

I check my phone. No new messages. I sigh and start to set it down—when it buzzes.

> MATEO
>
> I hope the ghost with the knife didn't get you.

Another buzz.

> MATEO
>
> Also...thank you again. For the snacks. For the quiet. I didn't say it that night, but I really needed you. I'm glad you showed up for me.

I stare at the screen for a long moment. My thumb hovers over the keyboard, unsure of what to say. Then I type:

ANALYSE

Always.

Chapter Fourteen

MATEO

I'm just trying to get through the damn day. That's it.

I'm running on four hours of sleep, I forgot my protein shake on the counter, and my shoulder's been acting up since yesterday's drill. But I figure if I don't move my body soon, I'm going to crawl out of my skin—so I hit the gym.

I'm halfway through my warm-up set—lat pulldown, shoulder twinging in that annoying way—when I feel it. That familiar weight, like someone's watching me. I glance up.

Shit. Letty.

She's posted up by the front mirror, tight black leggings, sports bra, hair tied up with two perfect curls hanging down her face. She catches my eye and smiles. Slow. Like she's been waiting for me to notice her. Fuck me.

I turn back to my set, keep going, pretend I didn't see her. But it's too late.

A second later, I hear her voice behind me. "Wow. Look who decided to finally show up."

I don't answer. I finish the set, keep my focus straight ahead.

"Mind if I work out with you?"

I wipe the sweat from my brow, still not looking at her. I'm not a total asshole. I don't want to be rude to her, but I wish she'd take a goddamn hint.

"I guess," I mutter. "Just...don't get in my way."

She grins like the cat that caught the canary. "Wouldn't dream of it."

I move to the free weights and start loading the bar for a shoulder press. Letty grabs a set of dumbbells and sets up beside me, just close enough that I can feel her eyes on me. I focus on my form, count my reps in my head, and try to ignore the perfume cloud creeping into my airspace. Two sets in, I feel her step closer.

"Damn," she murmurs, placing a hand on my bicep mid-rep. "You've been putting in work, huh?"

I shift away, rack the weight, and glance down at her hand. "Don't do that."

She pulls her hand back slowly, batting her lashes. "Relax, Mateo. It's not a crime to appreciate good arms."

I don't answer. I grab my towel and turn back to reset the weights. I keep working out, trying to stay in my lane, trying not to snap at Letty as she tosses out flirty remarks between sets. But then—

"Yo, Mateo!" a voice calls out.

I turn, towel in hand. And there he is. Nico. Strutting toward us, looking every bit the asshole that he is. What the hell is happening today? I just wanted to work out in peace.

He stops a few feet away, arms crossed, eyes flicking from me to Letty, then back. "Didn't mean to interrupt."

Letty smiles too big. "Hey, Nico."

I look between them. They know each other? Letty doesn't offer an explanation, just keeps that damn smile plastered across her face.

Nico's smirk sharpens. "What? Small town. Everyone knows everyone, right?"

Letty steps back, tucking her hair behind her ear. "I ran into Nico at the Fall Festival. We had some things in common."

The way she says it makes a knot in my gut pull tight.

"You're working out together now?" Nico asks. "That new? Or just...picking up where you two left off?"

I don't know what this guy is going on about. Picking up where we left off? Did I hit my head? Is it the lack of sleep? Either way, I'm confused and getting more annoyed by the second.

I exhale slowly through my nose, the towel clenched in my hand. "We're not working out together."

Nico chuckles. "Looked like it. Especially when she had her hand all over you."

Letty doesn't deny it. Doesn't say a word. Just crosses her arms and looks down at her sneakers.

I take a step forward. "What do you want, Nico?"

He shrugs. "Just saying hi. Seeing what my daughter's mom's boyfriend is up to. I mean, I'd hate to find out you've got side pieces."

My fists clench. "Watch your mouth."

Nico smirks. "Touchy, touchy. Didn't mean anything by it, man. Just looking out for Analyse. She deserves to know what kind of guy she's with."

The way he says it makes my blood simmer. "You done?" I ask, jaw tight.

He takes one last look at Letty, then me. "For now."

Letty adjusts the straps on her sports bra, still not looking at me. "Sorry. I didn't know he was gonna show up."

I stare at her. "Sure." And I walk away.

I grab my bag, slam my water bottle into the side pocket, and head for the exit, not bothering to look back.

~

Later that night, I decide I'm going to see my favorite girl. Maya. That kid can turn a bad day into a good one within minutes.

I knock twice, and the door opens before I even lower my hand.

"Hey," Analyse says, voice soft, already stepping aside to let me in.

She's barefoot in leggings and an oversize tee that says *Yo hago lo que me da la gana*. Yeah...that tracks. If there's a more Analyse shirt out there, I haven't seen it. Her curls are clipped up, a few stray pieces falling loose around her face. She looks tired, but still as beautiful as ever.

"I brought something," I say, lifting the brown paper bag in my hand.

Maya appears like a blur behind her, squealing, "Florecitas!"

I hand the bag over, and she snatches it excitedly. Analyse raises an eyebrow at me as she closes the door.

"She asked for them the other day." I shrug.

"You're ridiculous," she says, but her lips twitch like she's fighting a smile.

"Only a little."

We settle in the living room, Maya sprawled across the floor with her coloring books while we sit on the couch. The TV is on low in the background—some baking competition show. We sit down on the couch, and Analyse begins opening the can of Florecitas. I can't help but stare at her.

She's radiant. End of the day, hair a little messy, and she's still the most beautiful thing in the room. Hell, in every room.

"You okay?" I ask, my voice low.

She turns to me, eyes soft. "Yeah. Just a long day. The kids were wild. Full moon energy or something."

I chuckle. "Want me to bring them in for a drill? Fire-fighter bootcamp?"

Her eyes light up. "They'd love that. You might regret it, though."

"Nah," I say, nudging her shoulder with mine. "For you, I'd risk it."

She holds my gaze for a second longer than usual. There's something in her expression, something I can't name, but it makes my chest go tight in the best kind of way.

Maya eventually yawns, dragging her blanket toward the couch. "I'm tired, but I don't wanna go to bed yet."

Analyse scoops her into her arms. "Go brush your teeth, mamita. I'll come tuck you in."

"Okay," Maya says sleepily, with a full mouth of cookie crumbs.

While she's in the bathroom, Analyse gathers her blanket and wipes down the crumbs.

"You're good at this," I murmur. "The mom thing."

She shrugs. "Most days I feel like I'm winging it."

"You're doing better than most."

"You're just saying that," she says quietly.

I stand, close the space between us, and gently place both hands on either side of her face. "Lyse," I say, my voice low but firm. "I need you to listen to me carefully, okay? Are you listening?"

She nods, eyes wide, unsure.

"You're an amazing mother. Every single thing you do—every single move you make—is with Maya at the center of it. You love in a way most people forget how to. Completely. Unshakedly. So I want you to say it."

"Say what?"

"That you're amazing. Say it."

"Mateo..." she starts, shaking her head, "I don't think—"

"Nope. Not letting it go. Say it."

She lets out a breath, almost a laugh, but then— "Fine. I'm amazing."

"Louder."

"I'M AMAZING!!" she shouts, smiling now, despite herself.

I grin, brushing my thumbs across her cheeks. "Good girl. Now don't you ever forget it."

When she comes back from putting Maya down, I'm leaning back on the couch. She sinks into the cushion beside me and tucks her legs under her. She pulls a throw blanket over both our laps without asking.

I glance down at her. "This part of the fake dating package?"

She smirks, not looking at me. "Don't get used to it."

Too late. Way too damn late.

We sit in silence for a few minutes, watching some guy panic over burnt cupcakes. I don't know when it happens exactly, but her head ends up resting on my shoulder. It feels good. Like it belongs there. I don't move. I just let myself feel it. The warmth of her. The rise and fall of her breath. The quiet.

Then—her phone buzzes on the coffee table. She doesn't move right away. But then she straightens up a little, reaches for it, and unlocks the screen. I glance at her out of the corner of my eye. Her smile fades. Her whole body stills.

"Everything okay?" I ask.

She nods too quickly. "Yeah. Just...I forgot I have an early morning tomorrow."

"Oh." I sit up, pushing my blanket off my lap. "Right. I should go, then."

"Yeah. I'm sorry...I'm just really tired."

I stand. "It's fine. It's late. I should get going anyway. Thanks for letting me crash your night."

"Thanks for the snacks," she says, walking me to the door.

We stand there for a second, the porch light soft above us. She's got her arms crossed over her chest now.

"I'll text you tomorrow," I say, even though I'm already sure something shifted.

She nods. "Okay. Drive safe."

The door closes behind me. I stand on the porch for a beat, staring at the wood grain of her door. What the hell just happened?

Chapter Fifteen

ANALYSE

I close the door behind Mateo and press my back against it. The house is quiet now. Too quiet. I look down at my phone, the screen still lit up with the last message.

LETTY

Girl to girl...thought you should know what your man is up to when he's not with you.

Attached: 1 image.

I click it. And there it is. Mateo. At the gym. Letty's hand on his arm. His head turned. His face unreadable. But they're close. A little too close, if you ask me. My stomach twists.

I stare at it too long, taking in every detail. Telling myself that this isn't what it looks like. That it's nothing. But I can't shake the image. Because the longer I look, the more it starts to feel like exactly what it looks like.

And the fact that Letty sent it to me? Like she was doing me some kind of favor? Like she's worried about me? It makes my skin crawl.

A low, bitter laugh escapes me. We're not even really

together. Mateo and I...we're pretending. And yet, here I am —jealous. Hurt. Pissed the hell off.

Because even if we aren't really together, Letty doesn't know that. To the world, to her, what Mateo and I have is real. To her, he's my damn boyfriend. And now he's just...letting her put her hands on him?

I push off the door, start pacing the living room. It's not the photo. It's what it says. It's the whisper behind it. The implication. The way she's trying to make me feel small. Like I'm the one being played. Like I'm the fool.

I stop walking. Jaw tight.

And, what the fuck, Mateo? You couldn't keep it in your damn pants a little while longer? Not even until this thing is over? Not even long enough to make sure I don't look like an idiot in the middle of all this? You're out here playing pretend with me and playing whatever game this is with her?

I pace faster, my bare feet slapping against the floor, heart pounding like it's trying to punch its way out of my chest. How dare he. How fucking dare he.

Whatever. Get it together, Analyse.

He's not mine. He was never mine. This is all one big lie to help me save face. That's all it ever was. A favor. A temporary solution to a very specific, and very annoying, problem.

So what if he lets Letty fawn all over him? So what if he didn't push her hand away? So what if it hurt to see it?

That's on me. That's my mistake. I'm the one who started blurring the lines. Who let myself believe the touches meant something. That the look in his eyes was real. That any of it was. Stupid. So fucking stupid.

This whole thing was always going to end. I just forgot that somewhere along the way.

~

I'm sitting on the edge of my bed, phone in hand, legs bouncing like I've had three coffees too many. My thumb hovers over the keyboard, furious. Hurt. Stupidly unsure what the hell I'm even doing.

But I type anyway.

Enjoying your arm workout?

Delete.

You couldn't even wait until this whole thing was over before letting her throw herself all over you? Really?

Delete.

You know what? Go ahead. Be with Letty. At least she doesn't have to pretend.

I pause.

That one sits longer than the rest. It burns. So I delete it slower. Like dragging a knife out instead of pulling it clean. I toss my phone on the bed and stand, pacing. I'm not even sure what I want from him. An apology? An explanation? Do I even have a right to ask for that?

We're fake dating. That's literally the whole point. He never promised me exclusivity. He never swore off flirty gym interactions or Letty's stupid wandering hands.

But God, I didn't think he'd...entertain it. Not like that. Not with her. I sit back down and grab the phone again.

Letty sent me a photo.

No. Too direct.

Just a heads up...your side piece is doing PR damage.

Delete. Petty doesn't help. Petty just proves I care. Which I definitely don't. I shouldn't. I type something else.

Do me a favor and try not to make me look like an idiot in front of everyone, yeah?

Shit. Shit. Shit. Nope. Can't send that. Delete.

I exhale, tossing the phone onto the bed again. This is what rock bottom in a fake relationship looks like—sitting in your pajamas, staring at your phone, trying to decide if it's worth it to confront someone who technically doesn't even owe you a damn thing.

But he does owe me something, right? A little bit of care. A little bit of respect. I mean...the bar is low here. We're not talking flowers and sonnets. I'm not asking for the world. Just basic human decency. And the bare minimum of not making me look like a fool in front of a woman who clearly wants to tear me down.

I pick up the phone one last time. Open a new message. Start typing. But this time, the words don't come. I sigh, lock the screen, and set it down, face-down on the nightstand. The blue light fades, but my anger certainly does not.

I grab my earbuds, pop them in, and queue up the only woman who gets it. La India. Mi Mayor Venganza blares through my headphones, the opening drums punching in time with my pulse. I lie back on my bed, fists clenched, jaw tight.

Letty can send all the damn pictures she wants. Nico can keep running his mouth. Mateo can play clueless if he wants to. But I'm not going down quietly. And I sure as hell won't be the one crying when it's over.

I'm tossing and turning all night. It's impossible to sleep when my thoughts are going wild. It's like my brain is a computer with twenty different tabs open, and every time I close one, another one opens up.

Every time I close my eyes, I see that damn picture. Letty's hand on him. Her smile. The way he didn't pull back. I try to rationalize it—tell myself it was nothing. That she probably cornered him. I know Mateo. He's a good man. At least, I think I know him. None of this makes any sense.

Would Mateo actually do this? I can't believe that he

would make me look so stupid like this. I can't believe that he'd actually hook up with another girl while pretending to be my boyfriend. He knows that Seb would be furious. Mariana and Anna, too. He has to know that this would hurt me. So then, why do I have this picture?

I flip onto my back and stare at the ceiling. I check the time. 3:42 a.m. I don't think I'm going to get any sleep. I need to unwind. I need to clear my head.

I pull open the drawer of my nightstand and take out my vibrator. As I lift my shirt over my head, the cool air makes my nipples harden. Closing my eyes, I explore the contours of my breasts, relishing their fullness beneath my palms. Each gentle squeeze sends a ripple of warmth through me, and I gently roll my nipples between my fingers. Gradually, my hands move down my body, and I begin to rub my clit in small, firm circles.

My mind is filled with thoughts of Mateo. I can't help it. He's all I see. His strong arms. His sexy smirk. That tattoo on his thigh that runs down his leg. I imagine his hands replacing mine, his touch firm but gentle. The fantasy is so vivid I can almost feel his breath on my neck, his lips trailing down my collarbone. My breathing quickens as I switch on the vibrator, its soft hum filling the quiet room.

I slide it between my legs, gasping at the first contact against my sensitive skin. The pulsations send waves of pleasure through my body, and I arch my back, pressing deeper into the mattress. My free hand continues to caress my breast, pinching and teasing my nipple in rhythm with the vibrator's movements.

"Mateo," I whisper into an empty room, not caring how desperate I sound. In my mind, he's here, watching me with those dark eyes that seem to see right through me. I imagine him telling me how beautiful I look. How amazing I am. How badly he wants me. How badly he needs me.

The pressure builds inside me, and my hips begin to move of their own accord, seeking release. My breath catches as I press the vibrator harder against me, its insistent hum vibrating through every fiber of my being. The tension builds low in my belly, a familiar pressure that makes my thighs tremble. I'm close. So damn close.

The release crashes through me like a tidal wave, my back arching off the bed as I moan out his name. My body pulses with pleasure, each wave more intense than the last as I ride out my orgasm. The vibrator continues its relentless rhythm against my oversensitive skin until I can't take it anymore and pull it away, my chest heaving with each breath.

As the aftershocks ripple through me, I collapse back onto my pillows, skin flushed and damp with sweat. I switch off the vibrator and set it aside, my mind clear, my body satisfied.

This whole thing with Letty...it doesn't feel like him. Not the Mateo I know.

The next morning, the sun is too bright, and my tolerance for everything is low. I got maybe three hours of sleep, and I'm exhausted. But Maya has been begging for a new book all week, and I promised we could stop by Ink & Paper if we had time after her dentist appointment. And I can never let her down. So here we are.

Ink & Paper has the perfect smell—warm paper, wood polish, and the faintest hint of vanilla from the scones Hilda sometimes keeps behind the register.

The bell over the door jingles as we walk in, and Maya immediately inhales deep like she's taking it all in. "Mmm, it smells like all the books you're going to buy me, mama," she says dreamily.

"Hi, mis amores," Hilda calls from behind the counter,

her silver hair tucked into a scarf, glasses perched low on her nose. She waves us in with a warm smile, setting down a stack of cozy mystery paperbacks. "Dentist go okay?"

"No cavities," Maya says proudly, flashing a toothy grin.

Hilda walks around to give Maya a hug. "That means you earned something fun. Go see if anything on the new arrivals shelf calls your name."

Maya skips off without hesitation, already scanning the shelves, sure to find her treasure. I walk over to the register, offering Hilda a tired smile.

"You okay?" she asks, her voice low, kind.

I nod. "Just tired."

She gives me a look that says she doesn't buy it, but she doesn't push. That's one of the many things I love about Hilda, she knows when to ask and when to just be.

While Maya's deep in the middle grade section, I browse aimlessly. My eyes pass over titles I've already read, some I've been meaning to pick up. I touch a spine here, flip through a back cover there. But I can't concentrate. Now when last night is still circling in my chest like a storm cloud.

I check my phone. Still no message from Mateo. I lock it and slip it back into my pocket before the ache in my chest can settle in too deep.

Maya returns a few minutes later with a stack of books as tall as her torso. "I couldn't decide," she says sweetly.

I sigh, but I'm already reaching for my wallet. "You're lucky I'm tired."

We pay, and Hilda sneaks a small sticker pack into Maya's tote bag. "Because I love you," she whispers conspiratorially. Maya beams.

We step outside into the cold sunlight. Maya's still talking about one of the stories she just picked up—another fun mystery to solve—and I'm nodding along, distracted but trying to stay present.

The sidewalk is quiet. Calm. A morning that I'd normally be soaking in. It's the kind of morning that reminds me why I love this little town. But my chest is tight, my thoughts spinning in too many directions. I glance down at Maya—cheeks flushed, curls bouncing.

"Wanna get ice cream?" I ask.

Maya gasps dramatically. "For breakfast?!"

I shrug. "It's after a dentist appointment and before lunch. That's basically legal."

She squeals, already grabbing my hand. "You're the best, Mami!"

There's a tiny walk-up window two blocks from Ink & Paper. We order two scoops—one dulce de leche for her, one mint chocolate chip for me—and take our cones to a bench nearby. It's cold out and we're eating ice cream, but hey, loving sweets is a lifestyle.

Maya swings her legs beneath the bench, curls bouncing under the hood of her jacket as she hums to herself between the licks. "This is sooooooo good. I think this is what dragons would eat if they had tastebuds."

I snort. "Pretty sure dragons breathe fire, not ice cream."

She holds up her cone dramatically. "Exactamente! Opposites attract."

I lean back, trying to soak in the moment. The bite of mint chocolate hits the back of my throat, crisp and familiar. Maya's humming to herself, enjoying her ice cream, and I pull out my phone and fire off a quick text to The Council of Chaos.

ANALYSE

SOS.

Chapter Sixteen

MATEO

I walk into the station, dropping my bag with a bit more force than intended. I'm frustrated.

Cap glances up from the table where he's reading a report, brows rising slightly. "Morning, Rodriguez."

Seb's leaned back in one of the chairs, nursing a black coffee. "Damn. You look worse for wear. You good?"

I grunt. "Didn't sleep." I grab a bottle of water from the fridge and crack the top. "Weird night."

Cap sets down his paperwork. "What happened?"

I sit across from them and rub my hands over my face. "That's the thing. I'm not completely sure what happened. But it was really weird."

Seb makes a face. "What does that even mean?"

"It started with a trip to the gym."

"Oh, the horror," Seb cuts in.

I glare at him. Cap waves his hand at me to go on.

"Anyway. It started with a trip to the gym. I was already in rare form, bad sleep or whatever. Then Letty was there."

"Ahh. Not great," Cap says.

"Exactly. So, she spots me and decides she needs to work

127

out with me. And of course, has to put her hands all over me. Then Nico shows up."

Seb chokes on his coffee. "Nico? At the gym?"

"Yeah." I shake my head. "Just strolls up and starts running his damn mouth."

Cap leans forward, arms resting on the table. "What'd he say?"

I toss the bottle cap onto the table, the plastic skidding across the surface. "Some shit about Letty and I working out together. Said it looked like we were picking up where we left off."

Seb frowns. "What does that even mean?"

"Hell if I know." I lean back in the chair, scrubbing a hand over my jaw. "I've never had a thing with Letty. She's been... persistent since I moved her, but I've never given her anything to work with."

Cap watches me for a beat. "So, you two never hooked up?"

I meet his eyes. "No. Not once. I've never touched her."

Seb whistles under his breath. "Could've fooled her."

"Yeah," I mutter. "Tell me about it."

I run a hand through my hair and sigh. "The whole thing just felt...off. I don't know how to explain it. Not Nico showing up—him being annoying is par for the course—but the way they were both acting? It didn't feel random."

Cap narrows his eyes. "You think it was a setup?"

I shrug. "That's the thing. I don't know what it was. I don't even know what they'd be setting me up with. I'm confused as hell."

Seb leans forward, elbows on his knees. "Did Nico say anything else?"

I nod slowly. "Yeah. Something like, 'Hate to find out you've got side pieces.' Real smug, like he was waiting for me to react. I told him to watch his mouth, and then I walked."

Cap lets out a long breath and rubs his jaw. "Sounds like he was trying to get under your skin."

"Mission accomplished," I mutter.

Seb leans back in his chair again. "Yeah. You're dating my sister and he's pissed. That asshole thought he'd just leave her high and dry with a baby and she'd fall at his feet for him when he came back."

Cap grunts in agreement. "He underestimated her. And now he's trying to rattle the guy who's stepping up where he didn't."

I stare at the bottle in my hands, turning it slowly between my palms. "Yeah...that's true. The dope is jealous."

"Speaking of Lyse, how are things with you guys?" Cap asks.

"That's another thing!"

Seb's jaw tightens. "What do you mean? What did you do to my sister?"

I lift both hands in surrender. "Nothing! That's the problem. I didn't do anything."

Seb narrows his eyes. "Okay, walk me through it. Slowly. With all the context. Because if you're telling me you hurt her—"

"I didn't," I cut in. "I swear, man. But something shifted last night."

Cap sits back in his chair, arms crossed, watching me closely. "How so?"

"She was fine. We were fine. I brought Florecitas for Maya, hung out at the house, everything was normal. Then her phone buzzed, she looked at it, and everything changed."

Seb leans forward. "Changed how?"

"Her whole vibe. She pulled away, said she forgot she had an early morning, practically rushed me out the door. I could feel it in my gut...something was off."

"And she didn't say what was wrong?"

"Nope. She didn't say. Just...smiled tight and shut down."

Cap lets out a thoughtful hum. "You think it's connected to Letty and Nico?"

I pause. "I didn't before. But shit. Maybe?"

Seb exhales sharply, pinching the bridge of his nose. "God, Letty is so damn messy."

Cap's eyes meet mine. "You planning to talk to Analyse?"

"I want to. I just don't want to make it worse if I don't even know what I'm apologizing for."

Seb gives me a flat look. "You better fix it. Fast. I don't want my sister unhappy."

I nod, chest tight. "Yeah. I'm going to. I don't want her unhappy either, bro. I just need to figure out exactly what's going on."

The door swings open, and Andres walks in, clipboard in hand and a shit-eating grin on his face. "Cap, we got a call," he says. "It's Libby's cat. She ran up that damn tree again."

"You've gotta be kidding me," Cap mutters, rubbing his temple. "Seb, you're up."

Seb recoils. "Absolutely not. That devil cat hates me. Last time I tried to help her, she swiped at my face."

Andres barks out a laugh. "She's got taste."

"Shut up," Seb fires back, pointing a finger. "I still have a scar."

"Barely," I say, smirking.

Cap looks between us. "Someone go get that damn cat before Libby calls again and starts crying into the dispatcher's ear. I can't handle another voicemail about her cat's emotional distress."

I push to my feet. "Fine. I'll do it."

"You better bring her down gently," Seb says, grabbing a granola bar and tossing it at Andres. "Or Libby'll file a complaint with city hall again."

Andres catches it mid-air, scowling. "She can file that complaint under not my problem."

I glance at him, deadpan. "Oh, it's your problem now."

He blinks. "Wait—what?"

I jerk my thumb toward the door. "You're coming with me, asshole."

Andres groans, dragging his feet toward the gear room. "I knew taking that damn call was a mistake."

"You've gotta be kidding me," I mutter as Andres and I pull up to Libby's house.

"Third time this month," Andres says, cutting the siren just as we turn into her driveway. "I swear that cat's either suicidal or just really into high altitudes."

I glance up through the windshield. Sure enough, perched at the highest possible branch is the devil cat. Libby's demon in fur form. The spawn of Satan with whiskers. She's glaring down at us like we ruined her day.

Libby rushes out in slippers and a housecoat, her gray curls bouncing, cheeks either flushed from either panic or rage —or both. "She's been up there for an hour! What if she jumps? She's delicate!"

"She literally crawled through your drywall last week," I say under my breath.

Libby doesn't hear me, or she ignores it. "You have to get her down!"

Andres stretches, yawning. "Maybe she just needs some alone time. Cats are independent creatures."

"She's a princess!" Libby shrieks. "She'll get cold! Or bored! Or attacked by a squirrel!"

The cat lets out a meow so long and angry it echoes like a death wail.

Andres sighs. "Alright. You're going up."

I blink at him. "Why me?"

"Because she likes you."

"She does not like me."

Libby gasps. "She adores you. She let you pet her once!"

"She bit me immediately after."

"She was playing."

"Then your cat has some questionable ideas about foreplay."

We grab the ladder from the truck while Libby paces the yard, muttering into her bathrobe pocket.

"I swear if I die today because of a damn tabby," I grumble, planting the ladder under the tree.

"Don't say that," Andres warns. "She senses weakness."

I begin climbing, slowly, carefully. The cat narrows her eyes as I ascend, tail twitching.

"Nice kitty," I murmur. "Totally normal, not possessed kitty. Just gonna bring you down so your mom stops threatening to sue the department."

She hisses at me. Loudly.

I freeze mid-rung. "Andres."

"Yeah?"

"She's making the sound that comes right before she does something demonic."

"She's just vocal."

"She's hissing in another language, I swear to God."

I reach the branch she's on. She's glaring. I slowly reached out, trying to grab her scruff like we practiced in training. She lets me almost get there...then flings herself two branches higher.

"You've gotta be kidding me!"

Libby lets out a wail. "She's so brave!"

Andres snorts. "You mean insane?"

"Don't call my baby insane!"

I climb higher, practically hugging the tree at this point. "Come on, cat. Please. I am tired. I am hungry. I am slipping away from an early retirement."

The cat meows again. This time it sounds smug.

With one arm wrapped around the branch and the other slowly reaching out, I inch closer. "Come on. Be a good kitty. Just this once."

She leaps into my arms. I almost fall off the damn tree. "Got her!" I yell, hugging her to my chest.

She purrs. I blink. "Are you kidding me?"

"She does love you!" Libby cries, clapping her hands. "You're her favorite!"

The cat nuzzles my neck and immediately sinks her claws into my shoulder. "Favorite," I grunt, climbing down with one arm.

Andres helps me the last few feet, holding the ladder steady. "You good?"

"Yeah, aside from the minor blood loss."

We hand the cat over to Libby, who acts like we just rescued her child from a burning building.

"You're both angels!" she gushes, hugging the cat so tightly. "I'm going to bake you boys a pie!"

"No need, really—" I start.

"What kind do you want? Pumpkin? Cherry? Ooh, how about pear!"

Andres leans in. "Please say pumpkin. Her pear pie tastes like feet."

"Pumpkin," I say quickly.

Libby beams and disappears inside. Andres and I make it to the truck, blood on my shirt, tree sap in my hair.

He starts the engine. "Well...another heroic rescue."

I glance down at the fresh claw marks. "Next time, I'm faking an injury."

Andres grins. "That's fair. But deep down, you love her."

"Yeah, right."

We pull away just as the cat appears in the window, her glowing eyes watching me like she's already plotting her next tree stunt.

I shiver. "We're not getting hazard pay for this, are we?"

"Nope."

"Figures."

And off we go. Just another day in Lake City.

ANALYSE

Maya and I arrive at Mariana and Seb's house, and Seb quickly whisks Maya away for a tio date. If I know Seb, and I do, he's going to use this time to spoil her rotten and bring her back to me hyped up on sugar.

Anna arrives shortly after they leave. "Hola, amigas," she greets, dropping onto Mariana's couch.

Mariana hands her a mug of hot chocolate, and Anna raises it in a cheers motion. Mari and I sit on the couch beside Anna, Mari placing a throw blanket over us.

"I missed you both." Anna sighs dramatically, kicking her feet up on the ottoman. "It's been, like, a week. I was starting to shrivel."

"I saw you two days ago," I point out.

"Which is practically seven in chaos years," she fires back.

Mari laughs. "She's not wrong. This week has been long."

"Tell me about it," I murmur, reaching for one of the sugar cookies on the tray between us.

Anna eyes me over the rim of her mug. "Right. Let's get to it, Lyse. What's going on? What was the SOS sent for?"

I inhale deeply then exhale through my nose. "I got a text last night. From Letty."

That gets their full attention.

Mari straightens. "What did she say?"

I grab my phone from the coffee table and hand it over, the screen already pulled up to the message I've read at least forty times since last night. Anna takes it first. They both lean in, reading the screen in silence.

Anna's eyebrows shoot up as she scrolls to the photo. "Oh, hell no."

Mari lets out a groan as she peeks over her shoulder. "That's not even subtle."

"Girl to girl?" Anna's voice drips with venom. "Who does she think she's fooling with this fake sisterhood bullshit?"

"She wanted to get under your skin," Mari says, handing my phone back. "And it worked."

I nod, wrapping the throw blanket tighter around my waist. "I can't stop thinking about it. The picture. I've looked at it over and over."

Anna tilts her head. "Do you think something happened?"

I hesitate. "No. I mean...no. I don't think Mateo would. He's not like that. I don't think he is anyway."

Anna interrupts gently. "I hate to be the one to say this, because you know I love you, but...he is a known fuckboy."

I groan and sink deeper into the couch. "Don't remind me."

Mari shoots her a look. "Anna."

"I'm just saying," Anna continues, raising her hands. "That was his reputation. Until, like, five minutes ago."

"Yeah, well," I mutter, "maybe he's changed."

Anna shrugs. "Maybe he has. Maybe he hasn't. I really, really hope for your sake he has. But guys don't transform overnight."

Mari folds her legs under her. "But they do grow up. And I've seen the way Mateo is with Maya. With you."

Anna points at me with her mug. "And you've changed, too. Don't act like you haven't. All that talk about how you guys were just feeling things out, taking it slow. Blah, blah, blah. You caught feelings. Real ones. Big time."

I don't say anything. I just pull the blanket tighter, desperate to shield myself from the truth.

Anna reaches over and grabs my hand. "So, ask yourself this, Lyse. Is it worth throwing this all away over a text from a girl who wants what you have?"

I blink down at my phone in my lap. "I just don't want to be that girl," I whisper. "The one who defends a guy who's playing her."

Mari squeezes my knee. "You're not. You're the girl who's scared. And you have every right to be. But you also have the right to fight for something if it's real."

Anna exhales through her nose. "We're not saying trust him blindly. We're saying trust yourself. You know Mateo. Does that picture feel like him?"

I shake my head. "No. It doesn't."

"Then that's your gut talking," Mari says. "And your gut's usually spot-on."

There's a long pause. The only sound is the soft clink of Mari setting her mug back down.

And then Anna says, "Okay. But also...if he did cheat, we slash his tires. Obviously."

Mari nods solemnly. "And key his truck."

A laugh breaks through my chest. "God, I love you both."

"We're here for you." Anna grins. "Always, baby. Even when you're spiraling."

Mari smirks. "Especially when you're spiraling. Anyway, what does Mateo have to say about all of this?"

"I haven't spoken to him about it," I admit quietly.

"Analyse Josephine Garcia! Are you kidding me?" Mariana nearly shouts, her eyes wide with disbelief.

"I know, I know." I groan, covering my eyes with my hands.

"Lyse, how do you expect to get to the bottom of this when you haven't even spoken to him?" Anna asks, exasperated.

"I know I have to speak to him about it. But I'm scared."

"Sweetie, what are you scared of?" Mari asks gently, her voice softer now.

I stare down at my mug, watching the steam curl into the air. "I think..." I pause, trying to find the right words. "I think I'm scared that maybe I'm wrong about him. That I let myself fall for someone who isn't who I thought he was. And if that's true, then..." My throat tightens. "Then I have to admit that I let my guards down for someone that wasn't worth it."

Anna reaches over and places a warm hand on my knee. "That doesn't make you foolish, Lyse. That makes you human."

"But it still hurts," I whisper. "Even the idea of it hurts."

Mari sighs, leaning her head against mine. "Then let's find out the truth—so you're not sitting here letting fear make the story up for you."

I nod slowly, my heart pounding. "Yeah. I'll talk to him."

There's a pause. Not long, but long enough for the air to shift, for the heaviness of the topic to settle in. I can feel my brain starting to spiral again, and I don't want to go there. Not yet. Not tonight.

I inhale deeply. "Okay. Enough about me. Banana, how about you?"

Anna blinks. "What about me?"

I tilt my head at her. "First of all, how have you been feeling since your mom left?"

Mari nods, chiming in, "Yeah, you've been quiet about that. And you never shut up."

Anna lets out a short laugh, but it doesn't quite reach her eyes. "I'll be honest. It's been hard. I'm so used to having my parents here. I mean, they're only in Colombia, not gone forever. But it's so weird not being able to just walk over to their house, or do Monday night dinners. I didn't realize how much those little things grounded me until they were gone."

"Oh, Anna..." I reach for her hand and squeeze. "You have us. I know it's not the same as your parents. But we're here for you. Always. No matter what."

"I know, and I love you guys for that..." Her eyes glisten a little, but she doesn't let them fall. "But you both also have your person. Mari has Seb, you have Mateo. It just feels like I'm never going to have that."

Mari leans forward, her voice soft but firm. "Banana, you are the catch. Any guy would be lucky to have you."

Anna laughs through her nose. "That's cute, Mari. But the last guy I dated was planning our future, the five kids I would be a stay at home mom to, and the room where his mom would sleep in before our third date was even over."

Mari's eyes go wide. "Wait—what?"

I nearly choke on my hot chocolate. "He brought up five kids and a live-in mother before dessert?"

Anna lifts a brow, deadpan. "Before entrees."

"Oh no," I whisper. "That man had a blueprint."

"A blueprint, a family tree, and probably a Pinterest board," Anna mutters, taking a dramatic sip of her drink. "And I'm just sitting there, trying to eat my damn mozzarella sticks in peace."

Mari clutches her chest. "That's unhinged behavior."

"I panicked and told him I was allergic to commitment and dairy."

I laugh so hard I nearly spill my mug. "And yet here you are, surviving both."

"Barely," Anna groans, sinking deeper into the couch. "Dating is a minefield. Every time I think I've met a normal guy, he ends up being a grown man who says 'nom nom' when he eats."

We all gag in unison.

"That's grounds for exile," Mari says. "From Earth."

"Right?" Anna says, shaking her head. "I just want someone who doesn't have mommy issues, weird eating sounds, or a criminal record. Someone who actually knows what it means to show up. I'm so tired of the guys who think commitment is a scary word."

Mari offers a warm smile. "You'll find him. Maybe he's already around."

Anna rolls her eyes. "Unless he's hiding in a firehouse or something, I doubt it."

I glance at her, but she doesn't notice. She's busy picking at the corner of the throw blanket, lost in thought.

"Maybe he is hiding in a firehouse," I say lightly, nudging her with my elbow.

Anna snorts. "Please. The only thing hiding in that firehouse is Nathan's stash of chili cheese Fritos."

Mariana chuckles. "You have to admit, though...there are worse places to stumble into love."

Anna raises a skeptical brow. "Please. Like someone like that actually exists—emotionally available, dependable, and hot? That's fantasy novel material."

Mariana laughs. "You do realize you're sitting on a couch with two women dating real-life firefighters, right?"

Anna points a finger. "Exactly. You two already snagged the good ones. The rest? Unavailable, uninterested, or unwilling to commit to someone." She exhales slowly, her gaze drifting toward the window.

Outside, the late afternoon light filters through the trees, casting soft shadows across the living room floor. The mood settles, the laughter fading into quiet. A long beat passes.

Anna clears her throat. "Can I say something kind of heavy?"

I nod immediately. "Always."

Mariana reaches for her hand, already sensing the shift in her tone.

"I want to be a mom," Anna says softly. "I know we laugh and make fun of all the bad dates, but it's not just about that. I'm in my thirties. I don't have anyone. And some days, it feels like that dream—the one where I have a family—is slipping further and further away."

She swallows, blinking rapidly. "And I know we're supposed to be all modern and empowered, and I am, but also...I want that life. I want a home, a kid, someone who chooses me back. And I don't want to be the only one still hoping for it while everyone else moves on."

"You won't be," Mariana says. "He's out there, Banana."

"If he is, he better hurry up," Anna mutters, half-laughing, half-heartbroken. "Unless he's been hiding in plain sight, I don't think I'm going to find him anytime soon."

I watch her carefully. Anna's the strong one, the sharp-tongued one, the friend who always has the comeback ready and the tissue box waiting if someone else starts crying. But now? She just looks...tired. A little worn around the edges. And I can't help but wonder how long she has been holding all this in.

"You know," I say, reaching for another sugar cookie even though I don't really want it, "there's nothing wrong with wanting it. All of it. Love, family, the works."

Anna snorts softly. "Tell that to the guy who ghosted me after I said I wasn't interested in a situationship."

"Was that the podcast bro?" Mari asks, grimacing.

"No. That one tried to pitch me his NFT startup. This was the guy who claimed he wanted something real and then disappeared the minute I mentioned wanting kids someday."

Mari raises her eyebrows. "They really just start running?"

"Like I pulled out a chainsaw," Anna says. "It's not like I said I wanted to elope tomorrow and start IVF next week. We'd been dating for a few months, and I just wanted to be honest about what I want in the future."

I nod, understanding more than I want to admit. "You deserve someone who doesn't see that as terrifying. Who sees it as a gift."

"Exactly." Anna pulls the blanket up to her chin and sighs. "I know it sounds dramatic, but some days I feel like I'm watching this little train—my dream, I guess—pull away from the station. And I'm still standing on the platform, trying to pretend I'm okay waving goodbye."

Silence falls between us.

Mariana shifts beside her. "Maybe he's not on the train at all. Maybe he's already at the destination, just waiting for you to get there."

"Wow," Anna murmurs, glancing sideways at her. "That was either very deep or totally nonsensical."

"Both," Mari says proudly. "You're welcome."

Anna laughs, a real one this time, but her eyes are still soft. Still holding that glint of sadness I know too well.

I reach for her hand. "You're not the only one who's ever felt like that. I've felt it. Mari's felt it. Everyone's just pretending they haven't. But you—" I squeeze her fingers. "You're going to get there. And when you do? It's going to be so worth it."

"I hope so," she whispers.

Mari tilts her head, studying her. "What if you already know him?"

Anna rolls her eyes. "If this turns into some cheesy Hallmark plot twist, I swear I'll throw this blanket."

"I'm serious," Mari says, grinning. "You've lived here most of your life. Maybe he's been here the whole time, and neither of you realized it."

Anna hums like she's about to dismiss the idea, but she doesn't. Instead, she glances toward the window and says, "Maybe."

Anna clears her throat and nudges me with her foot. "Alright, enough about my impending spinsterhood. What are you going to do next? About Mateo?"

I groan and flop backward onto the couch. "I was hoping you'd all forget."

"Not a chance," Mari says, sitting cross-legged. "We love you too much to let you spiral without at least sending you into the storm with snacks and a plan."

"Snacks, I have," I say, pointing at the now half-empty tray. "A plan, I do not."

Anna clicks her tongue. "Then let's make one. Step one: talk to him."

"Do I have to?"

They both shoot me a look.

"Okay, fine," I grumble. "But I'm not doing it today. Today is for hot chocolate and bad TV and pretending I'm not a total emotional mess."

"Then we support your delusion," Mari declares, grabbing the remote.

"I'll allow one episode," Anna says, lifting her mug. "Then we text him."

I grumble but don't argue. Deep down, I know they're right.

Chapter Eighteen

MATEO

I'm trying to relish my day off—emphasis on trying. I slept in. Made myself breakfast. I even managed to sit on the porch with my coffee and pretend things were fine for a full twelve minutes. But the silence? It's loud.

Analyse still hasn't texted or called. I've checked my phone so many times, and every single time I don't see that one new message notification, I have to suppress the urge to chuck my phone across the room.

Not a single word from her, and now I'm stuck in that weird space between should I give her room and should I just call her and get it over with. The worst part of all of this is that I'm still unclear on what is causing the sudden weirdness and silence. I don't even know what I did.

But I can't just sit on my hands either. Yesterday I dropped lunch off at the school office—real food, not the sad salads she pretends are meals—without signing my name. Just left it there because I knew she wouldn't take it otherwise. Last night I left daisies on her porch, no note. She's always loved them. They were gone by morning, but she never said a word.

This morning, I left a stack of new books for Maya on their porch with a note that said, *New mysteries for Maya*. Nothing back. Not a word. But at least she knows I'm thinking of her. At least she knows I'm trying.

Whatever it is, it's eating at me. I thought things were good. I thought we were good. But something's changed, something's shifted...and I hate not knowing what. I toss my empty coffee cup in the sink and head out. I'm in desperate need of a haircut.

~

I step inside Angie's shop, and I'm immediately wrapped in the warm scent of hairspray, coconut oil, and warm blow-dried hair. I should've turned around the second I walked in and felt the tension crackle through the air like static. But I didn't. Because I'm a damn fool.

"Rodriguez," Angie says without looking up from the head of curls she's working on. Her voice is flat—polite, but barely. "Didn't think I'd see you today."

I nod, a little caught off guard. "Hey, Ang. I'm just here for a quick cut," I say, trying to keep my voice light.

Angie hums, still not looking up. "You want the usual?"

"Yeah."

She finishes sectioning off the client's hair before finally glancing my way. "Take a seat. I'll be right with you."

I head to the second chair, keeping my eyes on the tile floor. The shop's quiet aside from the low hum of a dryer in the back. A few minutes later, she clips the cape around my neck with more force than necessary. Not painful, but definitely on purpose. What did I do to her? What's with the women in my life?

"You been keeping busy?" she asks, tone casual.

I glance at her in the mirror. "Yeah, I guess."

She raises a brow. "At the gym, maybe?"

And there it is. I shift in the chair. "You wanna ask something, Ang, just ask it."

Her eyes meet mine in the mirror, sharp and unblinking. "You and Letty. You two back on or something?"

I blink. "Back on? We've never been on before. There's no getting back with someone I've never been with."

"Hmm." She turns on the clippers and starts trimming the back of my neck, each stroke of the blades just shy of aggressive. "Could've fooled me."

I grit my teeth. "I'm not with Letty. I've never been with Letty. I don't know why this is even coming up."

"Funny," she says. "Because she's been acting like you are. Been in here twice this week, name-dropping you, saying how you always tell her that you and Analyse aren't serious."

My pulse jumps. "She what?"

Angie scoffs. "She told Dee and Jolene that you two are reconnecting. She said you've been working out together, grabbing coffee, and that Analyse is just a fling. And I have to say, Mateo, this really pisses me the hell off! You know what that girl has been through. I don't think I've seen her date since that idiot Nico left her, and now you're playing her? You've got some nerve."

I turned in the chair despite the cape. "That's a lie."

She levels me with a look. "You sure about that?"

"Yes!" I say, too loud. "She showed up at the gym. I didn't invite her. I didn't ask her to work out with me. And I sure as hell didn't say any of that."

Angie crosses her arms. "Well, she's saying it. And people are believing it."

I rub a hand down my face. "Jesus. Why would she even—"

"Because she wants you," Angie cuts in. "And she knows you're taken. Or...were."

I freeze. "What does that mean?"

Her voice softens a fraction. "I saw Analyse yesterday. She seemed off. Different. She looked...rough. She didn't say much, but I know heartbreak when I see it."

My stomach sinks. "She didn't respond to my last text," I mutter.

"Well," Angie says, spinning my chair toward the mirror, "now you know why."

I stare at my reflection. The cape is still snug around my neck, my jaw locked so tight it aches. My face looks the same, but inside, I'm unraveling.

"She won't even talk to me," I say again, softer this time.

Angie leans back against the counter behind her, arms still crossed. "Then maybe you need to do something more than talk."

I swallow hard. "I didn't know she was hurting. I didn't even know what was going on."

"That's the problem," she fires back. "You should've."

Silence stretches between us. The buzz of the clippers is gone, but the hum of tension remains.

"Fuck. I thought..." I shake my head. "I thought things were good. I thought she knew that I'd never do anything like that."

Angie snorts. "You thought she knew? No offense, Mateo, you know I love you, but you don't exactly have the best reputation. You've been with girls left and right. And Analyse doesn't have the luxury of taking chances, but she did take one, on you. You need to make her feel safe. Letty's out here writing fanfiction about you two."

I grit my teeth again. "Letty's lying. I never said any of that. And I haven't touched her."

"Then you better find a way to make that crystal clear. To everyone." She picks up a comb and towel, starts sweeping hair off my neck with more force than necessary.

"I didn't ask her to come to the gym," I mutter. "I didn't even want her there."

"Then why'd you let her stay?"

"I felt bad...I was trying to be a nice guy."

The door chimes as someone walks in. Angie lifts a hand to the new customer then gives me a pointed look and drops her voice. "I'm finishing your cut, but after that? You're on your own, lover boy."

I nod, guilt tightening like a vise in my chest. Minutes pass in silence. Snip, snip. Clip, comb. When she's done, she undoes the cape and shakes the hair onto the floor, not bothering to brush the stray pieces off my shoulders. I stand and slide the money on the counter. She doesn't reach for it.

"Fix it," she says. "Before there's nothing left to fix."

I nod again, unsure if my legs will even carry me out the door. The weight of everything Angie said sits heavy on my shoulders.

I push through the door, the bell overhead chiming behind me, and the later afternoon air slaps me in the face. I'm halfway to my truck when my phone buzzes in my pocket. I fumble to pull it out, my fingers suddenly clumsy.

One new message from Analyse. My heart jumps into my throat.

ANALYSE

Hey.

My thumbs hover for a beat too long. What do I even say? What tone do I take?

MATEO

Hi, chula.

148

Three dots appear. Vanish. Then come back again. My chest tightens with every passing second.

ANALYSE

Sorry I haven't texted you. It's been busy.

Busy. That could mean anything. Busy avoiding me. Busy untangling her heart from mine. Busy convincing herself I'm not worth the risk. I take a breath and remind myself this is her reaching out. She didn't have to.

MATEO

That's okay. I'm just happy to hear from you now. Are you okay?

Another pause. Longer this time. I start pacing the sidewalk in front of the barber shop, phone tight in my grip.

ANALYSE

Yeah…Can you come over? I think we should have a talk.

The bottom drops out of my stomach. A talk. That could mean anything. Sweat begins to creep down my neck.

MATEO

Of course. I was thinking the same thing.

I slip my phone back into my pocket, hop into my truck, and start it up. Every mile between me and her house suddenly feels like too many.

The drive to Analyse's place feels longer than it should. My thoughts keep cycling through everything Angie said. Letty's lies. Analyse's silence. Her face, looking "rough."

I park down the street from her house, heart hammering

against my ribs. The sun's just starting to dip, casting everything in dusky gold.

I step onto the porch and knock. Lightly at first, then again. Firmer. A full minute passes. No answer. I raise my hand to knock again, but before I can, the door creaks open. Analyse stands there in sweats, an oversize hoodie drowning her frame. Angie might have said she was looking rough, but that's not what I see. There are darker circles under her eyes than usual, and I swear I'll find out why, but even like this she's beautiful. She always is.

"Hey," I say, voice rough.

"Hi."

She opens the door, stepping aside to let me in. I step inside, and the door clicks shut behind me. Her scent lingers in the air—she smells like strawberries. I follow her into the living room.

"Where's Maya?"

"She's still with Seb. He said he hadn't had a proper tio date in too long."

"Ahh. Okay. How are you?"

"Fine."

"You're not fine."

"I am fine, Mateo."

"Yeah, so then why did you basically kick me out the other night?"

"I told you...I had an early morning."

"Bullshit."

"What?"

"I said bullshit. You've had many early mornings, Lyse, and not once have you ever run me out of your house the way you did that night. Talk to me. What's going on?"

She takes a deep breath and then sits beside me on her couch. "Letty texted me that night."

"And tell me, what did that she-devil say?"

"It wasn't so much what she said, but what she showed me."

"What did she show you?"

"It was a picture. Of you both. At the gym. Her hands were all over you. You both seemed cozy."

"A picture? Let me see it."

She pulls her phone out of her pocket, unlocking it, and shows me the picture. Oh, fuck. There it is. A picture of me and Letty at the gym, and her damn hands are on my bicep. This doesn't look good.

"That's not what it looks like. I swear."

"Look. It's fine. You and I aren't even together, not really. I just don't want to look stupid. It's embarrassing. You're supposed to be my man, and Letty's out there telling everyone that'll listen that you're with her. So whatever you're doing, couldn't it just have waited until you and I were done with this?"

I grab her hands between mine. "Slow down. You don't actually think that I'm sleeping with Letty behind your back? Do you?"

"I don't know what to think."

"Lyse. You know me. You know that I would never hurt you."

"Right...but I also know that we never talked about being exclusive, and you and I aren't actually dating."

"Chula, I need you to listen to me...I am not sleeping with Letty, or anyone else. I would never do that. I care about you, and I will never hurt you. As long as you and I are together, you are mine, and there's nothing that I will allow to get between us. I don't care if this isn't a real relationship—you are mine."

"I've been through a lot, Mateo," she says.

"I get it," I say, and I mean it. "I should've pushed her away," I admit. "I didn't invite her there. She just showed up.

And I thought ignoring her was the best move. I didn't want to give her more attention by making a scene. I didn't think she'd go this far."

"I hate that she made me doubt you. How did she even get this picture?"

"I think I know...Nico."

"Nico? What does he have to do with this?"

"He was there, too. At the gym. He came over while Letty and I were working out and started saying all this crap about me having a side-piece. I'd bet every dollar I have that he took that picture of us."

"Wow. But then how would Letty have gotten it?"

I think about this for a moment. And then it dawns on me...how they spoke to each other as if they knew one another. They seemed comfortable.

"They're working together."

"What do you mean they're working together?"

"He wants you back, right?" I say, and she nods. "And Letty wants me."

She grimaces.

"So they're going to be really damn motivated to break us up. You should've seen them there, talking to each other like they knew each other. I thought it was odd, but hell, I didn't realize how fucked up they really were."

"So you're telling me that Nico and Letty set this all up? They were both at the gym. Letty got her hands on you so that Nico can take this picture and have her send it to me?"

"Yes, that's exactly what I'm saying."

I can see Analyse's anger begin to boil over. Shit. She's pissed.

"Those assholes!" she yells. "I can't believe that they'd stoop so damn low. How fucking dare they? I'm going to call Nico right now!"

She begins to go to his contact in her phone, but I stop her.

"No, don't call him. Not now. Not while you're this angry. Take a beat. I know you, chula. You don't want to blow everything up. Deep down, you want him to be in Maya's life. Not because you want him in yours, but because you think she needs her dad. I know that's something that always hurt you. Yeah, it might've hurt when he left you, but what hurt you the most is that he left her."

She sucks in a breath, and looks at me, eyes welling up. Her lips part like she wants to speak, but nothing comes out.

"You didn't have to tell me," I say gently. "I've paid attention. To every movement, every expression, every word since the day I met you."

She just stares at me, throat working like she's trying to swallow down the weight of it. The silence stretches, heavy and loud, until she finally whispers, almost disbelieving, "You see me."

Her voice is quiet. And yeah, I do. I always have.

She blinks quickly, like she's trying to push tears back in before they fall. "Sometimes, I don't think anyone really does. Thank you. And you're right. I just want Maya to have her dad. I hate that he left, but I sometimes wonder if this is their chance. Her chance to have everything I've always wanted for her. So what? I just say nothing?"

"Yeah. Let's just say nothing," I say, my voice low but firm. "Because they don't matter. We matter. And we're okay. That's all I care about. That you and I are good." I pause, swallowing the lump rising in my throat. "I couldn't bear it if you didn't believe me, if they succeeded in tearing us apart. My heart wouldn't make it, chula." I take a breath. "But I need you to promise me something, yeah?"

She nods, her eyes glassy. "Of course, anything," she says softly.

"Promise me that if they try again," I murmur, leaning in just a little, "that if they try to pull one of these stunts again, that you'll come to me. You won't shut me out again, please. I can't take it."

"I promise, Mateo. I swear it," she whispers, her voice shaking as she threads her fingers through mine.

She squeezes my hands once more then leans back against the couch, exhaustion finally catching up with her. I can see it in the slump of her shoulders, in the way her eyes flutter even as she tries to keep them on me.

"You should rest, chula," I say softly. "I'll get out of your hair."

She starts to protest, but I brush my thumb gently across her knuckles. "Mari mentioned she was holding some pastries for you. I'll swing by and grab them so you don't have to. Consider it handled."

Her lips part like she wants to argue, but she's too tired. Instead, she gives me the smallest nod. "Thank you," she whispers.

I press a kiss to her forehead. "Rest. I'll be back later."

The bell over Mari's bakery door jingles behind me as I step out, a paper bag of quesitos and pastelillos de guayaba in one hand, still warm. I barely make it two steps before a too-sweet voice cuts through the afternoon air.

"Mateo."

I turn. Letty's leaning against the brick wall, arms crossed. Her smile's wide, smug, practiced. "What, no Analyse today? Or is she finally letting you breathe?"

I exhale slowly. I should walk away. Ignore it. But after everything she's said, everything she's spread—no. Not this time.

I step closer, bag crinkling in my fist. "You done running your mouth yet, Letty? Or do I need to spell it out for you?"

Her smirk widens, but there's a flicker of nerves in her eyes. "Spell what out?"

"That you and I were never a thing. Not before. Not now. Not ever." My voice is low but sharp enough to carry to the people sipping cafecitos at the sidewalk tables. Heads are already turning. Good.

Her smile falters. "Come on, Mateo—"

"No." I cut her off. "You've been telling people Analyse is just a fling. That we're 'reconnecting.' That I've been saying we're not serious. Let me make this real clear: there was never a shot for you. Not then, not now, not ever. And dragging her name into your lies? That's the quickest way to make sure I don't even tolerate you in the same room."

I lean in, my voice dropping lower. "Understand this— disrespecting her is an automatic disqualifier. Analyse is mine, and anyone who can't respect her sure as hell isn't welcome anywhere near me."

The bakery door creaks behind me, and Mari's voice pipes up. "Everything good out here?" She's holding a rolling pin, flour dusting her apron. Her eyes dart from me to Letty.

"Fine, Mari," I say, not looking away from Letty. "Just clearing up a misunderstanding."

Letty shifts her weight, clearly uncomfortable now. I step in closer, lowering my voice. "You hear me, Letty? Even if Analyse and I weren't together." I shake my head. "You're an automatic no. Always was, always will be."

Her face goes pale. Mari raises a brow like she's ready to back me up if needed. Letty doesn't say another word. She just turns on her heel and stalks down the sidewalk.

I finally exhale, glancing back at Mari.

She lifts the rolling pin, smirking. "Guess I didn't need this after all."

"Appreciate the backup, though," I mutter, lips twitching.

She grins. "Anytime."

I adjust the bag of pastries under my arm and head to my truck, pulse still thudding but lighter. Analyse might not have been here to see it, but word will get back to her. It always does. And this time, I want her to know exactly where I stand.

Chapter Nineteen

ANALYSE

The last few weeks have been calm. Nico has been visiting Maya, and Letty hasn't said a word since that text she sent—hopefully she crawled back into the hole she came from. Now it's the day before Christmas Eve, which means prepping for our big Christmas dinner tomorrow. The meat is marinating, the pies are baking, and Mateo and I are making the coquito while Maya sits at the kitchen table decorating sugar cookies.

Mateo dips a spoon in the coquito mix and lifts it toward my mouth. "Tell me if it needs more cinnamon," he says, eyes gleaming.

I narrow my eyes but lean in, letting him feed me a small sip. "Mmm." I swirl it on my tongue, pretending to consider. "Maybe a pinch more nutmeg."

"Lies," he mutters with a smirk, already taking another sip for himself. "It's perfect. Admit it."

"You're awfully cocky for someone who didn't even know how to make coquito until a week ago."

He places a hand on his chest, feigning offense. "Wow.

First of all, the disrespect in this kitchen is real. Second, I'm a master of coquito, I'm basically Puerto Rican now."

I snort, turning back to stir the pot on the stove. "Okay, Mateito Rodriguez, slow your roll."

Behind me, I hear the chair legs scrape as Maya hops off the table and scampers into the living room with a tray of her half-decorated cookies, singing "Feliz Navidad."

Mateo steps up behind me, his hands sliding around my waist as he leans down to whisper in my ear. "Admit it," he murmurs. "You love how good I've gotten at blending into your chaos."

My pulse stutters, but I don't let it show. "Hmm. You do okay."

"Okay?" he repeats, pulling back just enough for me to catch his grin. "Mujer, I'm over here measuring the ingredients for the coquito like my life depends on it."

I fight the smile tugging at my lips. "You read the recipe off your phone, Mateo."

He leans in a little, his voice low and cocky. "Yeah, but I read with intention. You can't teach that."

I laugh, but my chest feels too tight.

"I'm just saying," he adds, resting his chin lightly on my shoulder, "I've basically earned honorary abuelito status. At this rate, your family's gonna ask me to host Nochebuena next year."

I roll my eyes and elbow him gently. "You're ridiculous."

"But you like it."

I don't answer. Because he's right. I do like it. Too damn much. For a second, I almost turn. Almost lean back into the warmth of his chest. Almost ask him what we're even doing— if he feels what I'm feeling, too. But I don't.

Instead, I turn back to the stove, focusing on the pot of rice. "You better focus," I say, voice light. "You still have to grate the coconut."

"Already on it," he says, stepping back, and I hate how much colder the room feels the second he does.

Mateo hums as he grates the coconut, shoulders moving with every stroke, completely in his element like this is just another Saturday morning. Except it's not. It's the day before Christmas Eve, and here he is, fitting into my life, my world, so seamlessly. He's here like he was always meant to be here. Like he has always been here. We move together in synchronicity as if we've done this our whole lives.

He glances up. "You're staring."

I blink. "No, I'm not."

He smiles knowingly. "It's okay, chula. You can admit you're impressed."

"I'm not impressed," I lie, turning back toward the stove. "You're just not as useless in the kitchen as I expected."

"That sounds like progress."

I laugh despite myself and shake my head. "You know what? I'll take it."

From the corner of my eye, I see him fake a bow. "Gracias, chef."

We fall into a rhythm after that—Mateo measuring and pouring while I work on the glaze for the ham. Every so often, Maya runs in from the living room to show off a cookie or ask if she can lick the spoon. And every time, Mateo lights up like she's the best part of his entire day. Maybe she is. Maybe we both are. I shouldn't think like that. We're not real.

This whole fake dating thing was supposed to be temporary. A Band-Aid to get Nico off my back and keep things simple for Maya. I'm stirring the glaze when I feel him behind me again, not touching, but close enough to feel the warmth of him.

"I forgot to ask," he says casually. "What's the dress code for tomorrow? Are we going Christmas sweaters or full glam?"

I smirk. "Mateo. Do you not know Latinas at all? This is our time to shine, baby. Full glam."

He chuckles. "How could I forget? You guys love getting dressed up to sit in the living room."

I spin around to face him, still holding the spoon. "If you want to survive tomorrow, you better iron a shirt. A real one. With buttons."

He makes a face. "Fine. But only because I like you."

My stomach flips. It's not the first time he's said it. Not the first time he's thrown a little line into a conversation like it's no big deal. But tonight, with the house smelling like coconuts and sugar, and Christmas music floating in from the living room, it lands different.

"You're going to make this complicated," I murmur, mostly to myself.

"What?" he asks, stepping closer. "What did you say?"

I shake my head, heart thudding. "Nothing"

But his eyes are sharp. "You said I'm going to make this complicated. Why?"

"It's nothing, Mateo. Please just forget I said anything."

"What if I don't want to forget?"

For a second, we just stare at each other. The air between us thickens, and I hate how much I want to close the space, to see how his lips would feel against mine. But I don't. I can't.

"Please, Mateo. Not today. Not right now."

Mateo's jaw ticks, and I see it—the flash of something behind his eyes. Frustration. Hurt. Maybe even disappointment. But he swallows it down like he always does, like he respects my boundaries even when they cut both of us open.

He nods once, slow and deliberate. "Okay," he says softly. "Not today."

The silence that follows is thick, but not angry. It's laced with everything we aren't saying. Everything we wish we could say. Everything I'm not ready to admit out loud. He steps back, just slightly. Just enough that I can breathe again.

Behind me, he clears his throat. "Do I at least get to know what color you're wearing tomorrow?"

I let out a breath. "Red. Obviously."

He lets out a low whistle. "You're gonna shut the whole dinner down."

"You better not wear green and make us look like a Christmas tree."

"No promises," he teases, voice lighter now.

A few hours have passed, and we've been working mostly in silence. Thankfully, we don't talk about the moment we almost had. Maya's in bed now, and the house is still.

I come out of her room, tiptoeing so I don't wake her, and find Mateo on the couch, one arm draped across the backrest.

"You stayed," I say, surprised.

He shrugs. "Didn't want to leave yet."

I should tell him to go. It's late. We've said what we needed to say. But I don't. I sit next to him, pulling a throw blanket over my legs. We sit in silence for a few minutes, the tree lights blinking in the corner, casting soft colors across the walls.

"I used to hate Christmas," I admit, eyes still on the tree. "After Maya was born, it just...hurt. Nico wasn't around. I felt like a failure. Everything felt heavy. But tonight, for the first time in a really long time, it feels like joy again."

Mateo turns toward me. "I'm glad."

"You did that."

He blinks. "Me?"

"You. Being here. Helping. Laughing with Maya. You gave us something we didn't know we were missing."

He doesn't speak right away. Then says, "You gave that to me, too."

I turn to face him.

"I haven't had a real Christmas in years. There are things in my past, things that have made me feel empty. But being here with you, with Maya, doing all the traditions—" He smiles, soft and reverent. "It's the first time I've wanted this again."

My throat tightens. "I'm scared," I whisper before I can stop myself.

He shifts closer, brows furrowed. "Of what?"

"Of giving in. Of getting used to this. To you. And then feeling the same hurt I felt all those years ago."

Mateo nods slowly. "That's fair. But can I tell you something?"

I nod.

"I'm scared, too," he says. "Because I've never wanted something to last so badly."

The words hang between us.

"I think I need to go to bed," I say, voice thin.

He nods again. "Yeah. Me too."

But neither of us moves. Not right away. Eventually, I force myself to stand. "Thank you. For today. For everything."

He looks up at me, something unreadable in his eyes. "Always."

And just before I turn to go, he reaches out and gently brushes a loose curl behind my ear. The touch is light. Barely there. But I feel it long after his hand moves away. I feel it deep in my core.

"Tomorrow," he says softly. "Let's just...enjoy tomorrow"

"Okay."

I walk away before I can do something stupid like kiss him.

Chapter Twenty

ANALYSE

The smell hits first—rich spices, roasted garlic, sweet cinnamon, citrus and slow-cooked pork. The house is full of music and warmth, and for the first time in a long time, it actually feels like Christmas.

Maya darts past me in a red dress covered in glitter, carrying a candy cane in one hand and a gingerbread cookie in the other. "Titi Mari brought the good treats!" she calls over her shoulder before disappearing into the living room.

I smile and shake my head, turning toward the kitchen where chaos has become a kind of love language. The dining table is overflowing. There's pernil on a carved wooden board, the skin perfectly crispy. A honey-glazed ham sits beside it, garnished with pineapples and cloves. Trays of arroz con gandules, ensalada de papa, buttery dinner rolls, and tower of pies take up every inch of space. Mari's bakery boxes are stacked near the end of the table, full of pastelitos and coconut macaroons dusted with edible gold. Anna's brought two trays of fresh Colombian empanadas that people are already sneaking from before dinner. Andres walks in behind her, both arms cradling bottles of wine like he's about to restock a bar.

"It's not too much, is it?" Andres says, placing the bottles on the counter.

"You brought nine bottles," I deadpan.

"We're a lively bunch," he replies with a wink.

Across the room, Mateo is wearing a white button-down —ironed, thank God—and red suspenders Maya picked out for him. His sleeves are rolled to his elbows, and he's crouched beside her, helping her hang an ornament on the bottom branch of the tree. He looks up at me mid-laugh, like he can feel me watching.

God, I'm in trouble.

By the time everyone arrives, the house is full. Seb's manning the music, bouncing between salsa, freestyle, and classic Christmas ballads. Anna and Mari are in the kitchen arguing over whether the empanadas need more aji. Maya is happily leading Nathan around the house on a tour, narrating every detail of our home.

Mateo slips behind me, placing a hand on my lower back as he leans in. "You okay?" he murmurs, just for me.

"Yeah," I breathe. "More than okay."

Nathan walks back into the room a few minutes later holding something in his hands—large, red petals, delicate and bold. He walks straight to Mari.

"These are for you," he says, holding out a bundle of flor de maga. "I know they were your mom's favorite."

Mari freezes. The room stills with her.

She blinks, swallows, then steps forward to take them, her voice barely above a whisper. "Thank you."

"I wanted her to be part of tonight, too," he says.

She presses the petals to her chest. "She would've loved that."

Someone turns the music down. A beat of silence settles over the group. Seb raises a glass. "To Lucia," he says.

"To Lucia," we all echo, glasses clinking.

Dinner is loud and messy in the best way. Everyone talks over each other, passing plates, laughing, dipping bread into sauce, licking sticky glaze off their fingers. Maya eats mostly dessert, and no one dares to stop her. Mateo takes two servings of arroz con gandules and moans dramatically at the table.

"This rice has no business being this good," he groans, eyes closed.

"That's because I made it," I tease, nudging him with my foot under the table.

"Marry me," he says without missing a beat, and the table erupts in laughter.

I glance around the room—at Nathan playfully throwing peas at Anna, at Mari leaning into Seb's shoulder while he quietly refills her drink, at Maya curled into Mateo's side— and my chest aches with something deep and certain.

This isn't pretend anymore.

Later, when bellies are full and wine glasses are half-empty, Seb insists on Christmas karaoke. Andres queues up "Feliz Navidad," and Mateo pulls Maya to the center of the living room, where they start dancing like no one's watching. Her laughter is loud and unfiltered, and he's twirling her in a circle while she squeals with joy.

"Alright, alright," Seb says, clapping. "Time for something slower. Let the romantics shine."

"Aw, Seb...my lover boy." Mari gushes.

He switches the song. It's "Have Yourself a Merry Little Christmas," slow and soft. Mateo glances at me. Offers a hand. I hesitate for half a second, then I take it. He pulls me in gently, one arm around my waist, the other holding my land like it's the most natural thing in the world.

"You're glowing," he whispers.

"It's the wine."

"It's not."

I look up at him, and his eyes are already on mine, steady and warm. We sway slowly in the middle of the room, the lights from the tree casting gold over his face. His handsome face. The hum of the room fades. And in this moment, everyone else has drifted away. It's just us.

"You look devastatingly beautiful tonight, chula," he says.

"You clean up pretty well yourself, coquito king."

He grins, but his eyes hold something deeper. "You feel this, too, right?"

I nod.

"Say it," he murmurs.

"I feel it, too."

"Good."

As the song ends, I pull back slightly. "I should check on—"

But then Maya shouts, "Mistletoe! They're under the mistletoe!"

Every head turns. I glance up, and sure enough, there it is —tied to the archway above us, slightly crooked.

Mateo's eyes stay on me. "Well?"

"It's okay, Mateo. We don't have to," I say, heart hammering.

"No," he says, stepping closer. "But I want to."

The music changes again—now it's "All I Want for Christmas Is You," soft and jazzy in the background.

"Lyse, I want to kiss you so badly I can barely hold myself

together," he says quietly, only for me. "But only if you want it too. Only if you need me as badly as I need you. Say the word."

My breath catches. "Yes," I breathe out. "I want it as badly as you do. Please kiss me, Mateo."

He threads his hands through my hair, fingers gentle, reverent, like he's memorizing the feel of me. Then he leans in and presses his lips against mine.

It's slow—achingly slow—tentative at first, like we're both afraid to take too much, like we're each holding a breath we've been waiting all year to release. His mouth moves against mine with a quiet desperation, and I feel just as desperate for him.

My hands slide up his chest, finding the curve of his jaw, and when I tilt my head, he exhales like he's home. The world around us fades. There's no music, no laughter, no mistletoe. Just this—just him, and me, and this kiss that feels like everything I've ever been missing. And I think he feels the same way too.

When we finally break apart, the room erupts in cheers. Mari whistles. Andres lifts his wine in the air. Anna wipes a dramatic fake tear from the corner of her eye. Maya grins so wide it looks like it might split her face.

Mateo presses his forehead to mine. "Merry Christmas, chula."

"Merry Christmas," I whisper back, my voice catching on something I don't have words for yet.

Chapter Twenty-One
ANALYSE

My phone buzzes while I'm in the middle of drying dishes, and I glance over to see a new group chat forming.

One new message from Let's Make Bad Decisions Tonight.

Immediately, I pause. Because nothing good starts with Anna and wanting to make bad decisions. I still remember the matching tattoos her and Mari got on Mari's twenty-first birthday because they were drinking too much.

> **ANNA**
>
> Let's go out tonight!

More messages follow in rapid succession.

> **ANNA**
>
> I'm talking dancing. Drinking. Reggaeton. Possibly karaoke.
>
> **MARI**
>
> You had me at dancing.

SEB

She had me at bad decisions.

ANDRES

If there's dancing, I'm gonna need a minimum of 3 drinks first.

NATHAN

I'll go, but I need to keep my bad decisions at a minimum. Anna, do I need to wear glitter again? I'll do it. But just know it'll be begrudgingly.

I laugh under my breath just as another message comes in.

ANNA

YES. ALL of you. Tonight. No excuses. We survived Christmas Eve, so this is our reward. We're going OUT.

MATEO

Out like…"out out"?

ANNA

YES, MATEO, put on your nice shoes.

I chime in finally.

ANALYSE

I'm in. I'll text Hilda to see if Maya can sleep over.

MARI

Yesssssssssss! We never go out anymore. This is the post-christmas detox we deserve.

SEB

No offense, but my detox includes rum.

ANDRES

God help us all.

I grin, already texting Hilda to confirm the sleepover. Within seconds, she responds.

HILDA

Of course, mi amor. Tell Maya to bring her pajamas with the little cats, I love those. I'll have hot chocolate waiting.

My heart softens at the message, and I type a quick thank you before dropping into the chat again.

ANALYSE

Maya's set. What time are we meeting?

ANNA

7:30 at my place. Drinks here first, then bar. LET'S GOOOOOOO.

MARI

I'm bringing lashes. Analyse, wear something HOT.

ANDRES

You're going to break Mateo.

ANALYSE

He'll be fine.

MATEO

Will I, though?

∽

Anna's room looks like a tornado of glitter, makeup brushes, and lashes passed through it...twice.

Mari is leaning into the mirror, applying a wing so sharp it could cut glass, while Anna blasts a Bad Bunny playlist and digs through a mountain of tiny purses. I'm sitting at her vanity, hair curled, makeup flawless, staring at the black dress draped across the chair. It's short. Like, short short. And tight. And maybe a little see-through in the right light.

"Okay," I say, fidgeting with the zipper. "I can't wear that."

"Yes. You can." Mari doesn't even look up.

"She absolutely can," Anna chimes in. "Mateo is not ready. And that's exactly why you should wear it."

"He's going to short-circuit," Mari adds, brushing highlighter across her cheekbones. "And it'll be so hot to witness."

I sigh, give the dress one last glance, then finally pull it on. It hugs every curve, the fabric soft and clingy, with a deep scoop in the back and a slit up the thigh. My heels add three inches to my height and make me feel so damn sexy. When I step out of the bathroom, Anna and Mari both go silent for a beat.

"Shit," Anne breathes. "You look dangerous."

"You look like you're about to ruin his whole life." Mari grins.

I glance at myself in the mirror. I mean...they're not wrong.

We're just finishing last-minute touch-ups—Anna reapplying her lipstick for the third time, Mari spraying perfume on all of us—when the knock comes at the door.

Anna practically squeals. "They're here!"

"Act casual," Mari says as she grabs her clutch. "Like we didn't just spend two hours contouring."

"Too late," I mutter, suddenly very aware of the pounding in my chest.

Anna opens the door, and the guys file in—Seb in a black button-down and jeans, Andres in a sleek navy blazer, Nathan in all black with a cheeky gold chain. And then...Mateo. Black jeans, a dark olive-green shirt that clings to his strong arms, sleeves rolled, and cocky smirk in place. Damn, that man is fine as hell.

His eyes land on me, and he stops moving. Completely. He just stares.

"Damn," Andres mutters under his breath, nudging Mateo. "You okay, bro?"

Mateo doesn't answer. He just keeps looking at me like I'm the only one in the room.

"Hi," I say, voice barely above a whisper.

He blinks, finally catching himself. "Hi."

Mari leans toward Anna, stage whispering, "He's broken."

Anna giggles. "Mission Accomplished."

Mateo steps closer, his voice husky and low. "You look..." He shakes his head slowly. "Chula, you look like trouble."

Heat rushes to my cheeks. "Maybe, I want to get in trouble with you," I say, leaning in whispering in his ear. "And you don't look so bad yourself."

Mateo's breath catches, and I swear his eyes darken just a little. His lips part like he wants to say something, but he doesn't. Instead, he leans in, his mouth brushing the shell of my ear.

"You better be careful, chula," he murmurs, voice low and full of promise. "Because if you keep talking like that, I won't make it through the night."

I pull back just enough to meet his eyes, heart pounding. "Then let's see how far you make it," I say, walking past him toward the door.

And I don't even have to look back to know he's watching every step I take.

The bar is alive with lights and bass and bodies moving in every direction. Our group takes over a booth near the back, drinks already flowing before we even sit down. Anna orders a round of tequila shots, Andres finds the wine list, and Seb somehow convinces the bartender to make him something called holiday jungle juice.

Mari slides into the booth beside Seb, her hand resting naturally on his thigh, and within minutes they're leaned in, heads pressed together, whispering and laughing like they're in their own little bubble. On the other end, Anna's chatting animatedly with Nathan and Andres, her arms flying, cheeks flushed from her second cocktail.

Mateo's next to me, his knee brushing mine. The heat between us has been building all night, like a spark waiting for the right breath of air to ignite it. I sip my drink and scan the crowd, pulse already syncing to the rhythm. The music thumps through the walls, but then—oh yes—then the beat changes. An old-school reggaeton track drops. The beat from "Prrrum" by Cosculluela begins to fill my ears. My eyes snap to Mateo's.

He doesn't even get the chance to ask. I grab his hand. "Come on."

He grins. "Let's go, chula."

We weave through the crowd, the music getting louder with every step. The moment we hit the dance floor, I turn, press my back to his chest, and start to move. His hands come down on my hips like they've always belonged there. Firm. Possessive.

We move together like we've done this a hundred times. The bass thrums through us, and I roll my hips, pressing into him, and I feel him. Every breath. Every shift. Every thought he's not saying.

His mouth is near my ear, my breath heavy. "You're going to kill me."

"Not yet," I murmur, grinding against him. "You're still standing."

His fingers dig in slightly, and the sound he makes? A low, guttural exhale that sends a shiver down my spine. I turn around, slowly, hands sliding up his chest. He watches me like he's starving and I'm going to be his next meal. The kind of look that turns my insides to molten heat. Then the music changes. A bachata track.

His hands find mine, and without a word, he draws me closer. His hand rests at the small of my back, the other clasping mine. Our steps fall into rhythm like they were made to. Dancing bachata is slow, sensual, intimate. Every move with him feels like foreplay.

Our bodies stay pressed, my thigh brushing between his legs with every step. His nose grazes my temple. Our mouths are so close. We're both breathing heavier now, and neither of us is pretending anymore.

"You're driving me insane," he says, his voice low and rough.

"Good," I whisper, my hand drifting to his chest. "I want to."

He stops moving. And I know it. I can feel it. The moment he makes a decision.

"Please," he rasps, like he can't take another second.

That one word undoes me, and I nod. He pulls me in and kisses me. Not soft. Not sweet. Hungry.

His lips crash into mine like he's been waiting his whole life for this moment. His hand slides up my spine, the other cupping my jaw as he deepens it. I melt into him, my hands threading through his curls, anchoring us together as the music fades beneath the sound of blood rushing in my ears. I've never had a kiss that drove me as crazy as this one is. The kind of kiss that makes me wonder how I ever went without it. How did I go this long without feeling the press of lips against mine, the minty taste of his tongue as it moves against mine? Now that I've had it, I don't think I'll ever be able to stop.

He pulls back slightly, his forehead resting on mine. "I need you. I can't wait anymore."

"Then don't," I breathe. "Let's go."

We weave back through the crowd, his hand tightly laced in mine. At the booth, Anna raises an eyebrow. Mari smirks knowingly.

"We'll see you all tomorrow," Mateo says, voice rough.

"Use protection!" Andres calls.

I roll my eyes. Mateo just laughs. And then we're out the door.

The second the door to my house closes, he's on me. His hands grip my waist, my back hits the wall, and our mouths crash together again, messier this time. Needier.

I gasp against his lips, my fingers tangling in his hair, pulling him even closer. My hands, trembling with adrenaline and something like need, knot themselves in his thick hair. I'm greedy for his mouth, the scrape of his teeth across my bottom lip. His hands are everywhere at once—fingers sinking deep into my waist, thumbs tracing the edge of my ribs, palms spanning the small of my back.

He lifts me in a single motion and pins me against the wall. My breath punches out of me as my legs wrap around his waist. His body presses into mine, heat radiating through fabric. Every muscle in him is taut, a coil drawn so tight.

He's kissing me like a man lost in the desert who just found a spring—hungry, reverent, wild. My hands skim his jaw, his neck, the slope of his shoulders, memorizing every inch with frantic devotion. He pauses only when we're both gasping, our foreheads pressed together, breath coming in hard, ragged waves. My heart hammers against his chest. He looks at me, eyes dark and dilated, trembling with the restraint it takes not to devour me whole.

His lips press into the hollow of my throat, hot puffs of breath branding the skin just below my ear. "You don't understand, chula," he says, voice rough. "I've wanted this. Wanted you. For so damn long." He pauses, the silence full of promise. "And now that I have you," he growls, dragging his mouth along my jaw, "I'm not going to rush. I'm going to savor every goddamn second. I'm going to take my time."

The words melt straight down my spine. Every cell in my body vibrates with anticipation. I clutch his shoulders, desperate to keep him anchored to me. His hands span the flare of my hip, his thumbs stroking slow, hypnotic circles that make my vision blur. His mouth finds the pulse beneath my ear and lingers for a breath.

His fingers curl around the thin straps of my dress and drag them slowly down my shoulders. The fabric slips away, exposing skin to the cool air. I shiver, not from cold, but from the intensity in his eyes.

"God, you're beautiful," he breathes, voice thick with want.

His palms cup the weight of my breasts, thumbs brushing over my hardened nipples in a way that makes my head fall back against the wall. I arch into his touch. The calluses on his hands create a delicious friction against my skin.

He lowers his head, replacing one hand with his mouth. The first touch of his tongue sends electricity shooting through me. I cry out, fingers tightening in his hair. He sucks gently, then harder, a low hum vibrating through his lips. My knees threaten to give out, but he has me caged in, his mouth relentless. Every flick of his tongue is a jolt straight through my core. I arch, clutching him harder. When he closes his lips around my nipple, a raw, involuntary cry escapes me.

"Mateo," I gasp.

He pulls back just enough to blow cool air across the dampened skin, then moves to the other breast, lavishing it with the same devastating attention. His teeth scrape lightly, a gentle bite, and my body bows in response. My head thuds against the wall. Every muscle in me is wound tight.

I can't catch my breath. I can't think. The only thing I can do is feel. And he's making me feel so damn good. He teases and tastes, alternating between soft and rough, gentle and greedy, until I'm trembling.

His hands slide down, tracing the curve of my spine. My dress is bunched around my hips. His fingers span the backs of my thighs, squeezing, kneading, dragging me closer to the hard line of his body. He rocks his hips forward, the ridge of him pressing against my pussy through our clothes. A strangled sound escapes me.

"Is this what you want?" he rasps, sliding a hand down to cup my ass, fingers digging in possessively. The sensation makes me arch, a moan slipping free.

"God, yes," I breathe, head falling back. "Please."

His mouth curves into a wicked smile against my collarbone. "Please what?" He rolls his hips again, more deliberately this time. The friction sends sparks through me.

"Don't stop," I pant, nails scraping down his back. "More, please." My legs tighten around his waist.

"Wasn't planning on it," he groans.

He squeezes my ass, using his grip to pull me tighter as he continues to rock against me. The delicious pressure builds. My thighs tremble. His hands slide between us, fingers dipping beneath the lace of my panties. The fabric is soaked.

"You're so wet for me," he whispers, voice rough. His

fingers explore, circling and teasing until my hips buck against his touch.

He withdraws slowly, eyes locked on mine as he brings his glistening finger to his lips. My breath catches as he slides it into his mouth. "You taste better than I could've imagined," he groans. "So sweet. So perfect."

I whimper as he presses against me again, the friction maddening. "Please, Mateo," I breathe, rolling my hips. "I need more."

"Tell me what you want, chula," he says, gripping my waist as he rocks against me harder. The pressure builds with each thrust.

"Fuck," I choke out. "I'm going to come," I gasp, body trembling. "Mateo, I'm—"

The world dissolves into a broken cry as pleasure crashes through me in violent waves. My body arches, every nerve igniting. My vision blurs as I shatter completely against him.

"That's it," he growls, tightening his grip. "Let go for me."

I'm helpless to do anything else. My body convulses, sensations rippling through me. When I finally come back to myself, I'm panting, still quivering.

Mateo eases back, eyes dark with hunger. He carefully sets me down. My legs wobble. "Dress and panties off. Heels stay on."

The commanding tone sends a fresh thrill through me.

"You like that, chula? Like when I tell you what to do?"

"Fuck, yes," I admit. "I love when you take control."

I unzip my dress and let it fall. My panties follow. The cool air hits my skin, but it's his gaze that makes me shiver.

"You're fucking perfect, Analyse. A goddamn goddess."

"Your turn. Everything off. Now."

His brows lift, but a slow smile spreads across his face. He strips quickly, and when I see him, all of him, I go still. Holy fuck. He's huge. Thick. Long. My thighs clench at the thought of him inside me.

"See something you like?" he rumbles.

I swallow. "More than like."

"Touch me."

My hand wraps around him. Velvet over steel, hot and pulsating in the palm of my hand. He groans as I squeeze.

"Just like that," he encourages, eyes hooded, dark with desire. "God, your hands are perfect."

I stroke him slowly, watching his face as pleasure washes over his features. His jaw tightens, a muscle ticking with restraint. It thrills me to see him fighting for control, to know that my touch affects him just as deeply as he affects me.

"I want to taste you," I whisper.

His eyes flash. "Are you sure?"

Instead of answering, I sink to my knees. The hardwood floor is unforgiving against my skin, but I barely notice the discomfort. All I can focus on is him. His scent, his heat. The way his breathing has turned ragged and shallow as he watches me with those dark, hungry eyes.

I take him in my hand again, feeling the weight of him, the silky smooth skin stretched taut over hardness. My lips part, and I flick my tongue out to taste the bead of moisture at his tip. The salty-sweet flavor makes me moan.

"Fuck," he hisses, one hand coming down to cup my face, thumb tracing my bottom lip. "You have no idea what you do to me."

I look up at him through my lashes, maintaining eye contact as I take him into my mouth. His fingers tangle in my hair, gripping tight, a raw desperate need in his touch. I take him deeper, hollowing my cheeks, savoring the way his breath catches when I swirl my tongue around him.

"Dios mio," he groans, his accent thick as he struggles to

maintain control. "Just like that, baby. Your mouth feels so fucking good."

I moan around him, the vibration making his hips jerk forward involuntarily. My hands grip his thighs, feeling the muscles bunch beneath my palms as I work him with my mouth. I pull back to lick along his length, then take him deep again, finding a rhythm that has him panting above me.

"Stop," he says suddenly, his voice strained. "I need to be inside you."

I release him with a soft pop, my lips swollen and slick. He helps me to my feet, his hands steady on my arms, and I find my balance on the heels.

"Bedroom," he says, but I shake my head.

"Here. I don't want to wait."

His eyes darken further. "Turn around. Hands on the wall."

I turn slowly, my pulse hammering as I place my palms flat against the cool surface. The anticipation is electric, making every nerve ending sing. I can feel him behind me, the heat of his body so close but not quite touching.

I hear the rustle of his pocket, the sound of foil crinkling between his fingers. I glance over my shoulder, watching as he prepares to tear open the condom.

"Wait," I whisper, my voice husky. "I want to feel you. All of you."

His movements pause, eyes meeting mine with a question burning in them.

"I have an IUD," I assure him, my breath catching as his hand slides up my spine.

His breath catches. "Are you sure?"

I nod, my eyes never leaving his. "I don't want anything between us. I want to feel every inch of you. Please."

A groan escapes him, primal and raw. The foil packet

disappears back into his pocket as he steps closer, his chest pressing against my back, lips grazing my ear.

"Spread your legs," he commands, his voice a rough whisper that sends shivers cascading down my spine.

I comply, widening my stance, the heels clicking against the hardwood. His hands skim down my sides before gripping my hips. I arch my back, pressing against him, desperate for contact.

"You're so beautiful like this," he murmurs, his lips brushing the shell of my ear. "So damn beautiful. Spread wide for me. So perfect for me."

I feel him position himself at my entrance, the blunt head of him pressing against my slick pussy. My breath catches as he slowly pushes inside, stretching me inch by delicious inch. The burn feels so good, a perfect blend of pleasure and pain that makes my knees buckle. His arm wraps around my waist, holding me steady as he continues his relentless advance.

"Fuck," he groans when he's fully seated, his forehead dropping to my shoulder. "Baby, you're so tight."

I've never felt so completely filled, so utterly possessed. He's everywhere—inside me, around me, his scent filling my lungs with each gasping breath. When he begins to move, slowly withdrawing before pushing back in, stars explode behind my eyelids.

"Mateo," I groan, my fingers curling against the wall. "Please..."

"Tell me what you need," he says against my neck, his teeth grazing the sensitive skin there. "I'll give you anything."

"Harder," I gasp, pushing back against him. "I need you to fuck me harder."

Something primal flashes in his eyes, sending liquid heat pooling between my thighs. His grip tightens, fingers digging into my hips hard enough to leave marks.

"Anything for you, mi vida," he growls, and then he's

moving with purpose, each thrust deeper and more forceful than the last.

The sound of skin slapping against skin fills the room, punctuated by my desperate moans and his guttural groans. I brace myself against the wall, my palms flat against the cool surface as he pounds into me from behind. Every thrust sends shockwaves of pleasure radiating through my body.

"You take me so well," he praises, voice strained with the efforts of his movements. "Like you were made for me. Only me."

His hand slides from my hip, tracing a path across my stomach before dipping lower. When his fingers find my clit, circling with perfect pressure, my entire body jerks. The dual sensation of his cock stretching me full and his fingers working magic has me careening toward the edge again.

"Oh god," I whimper, my body tensing as pleasure builds with frightening speed. "Mateo, I can't—"

"Yes, you can, chula," he murmurs, his breath hot against my ear. "Come for me again. I want to feel you squeeze around me when you fall apart."

His thrusts become more erratic, more desperate, as his fingers work faster. I can't stop trembling.

"Mateo," I cry out, my voice breaking on his name as the pleasure crests. "I'm—"

The orgasm tears through me like wildfire, my body convulsing as I scream his name. My vision whites out completely, every muscle seizing as wave after wave of pleasure crashes over me. I'm dimly aware of him cursing in Spanish behind him, his rhythm faltering as I clench around him.

"Fuck, Analyse," he growls, his movements becoming frantic. "I'm going to—"

His words cut off in a strangled moan as he buries himself deep, his body going rigid against mine. I feel him pulse inside me, hot and thick, marking me as his. The sensation draws out my own climax, making me shudder with aftershocks.

We stay like that for long moments, both of us breathing hard, sweat-slicked skin cooling in the air. When he finally pulls out, I whimper at the loss, my legs threatening to give out completely. He catches me before I can collapse, strong arms encircling my waist, turning me to face him.

"I've got you," he murmurs, pressing his forehead against mine.

He lifts me effortlessly, cradling me against his chest as he carries me toward the bedroom. My arms loop around his neck, face nestled in the crook of his shoulder. I breathe him in —sweat, sandalwood, and something so uniquely Mateo.

The sheets are cool against my heated skin as he lays me down. He follows me down onto the mattress, his body a welcome weight above mine. His thumb traces the curve of my cheek, eyes searching mine with an intensity that makes my heart stutter.

"You okay?" he asks, voice rough with concern. "I wasn't too rough, was I?"

I shake my head, still catching my breath. "No, you were perfect. It was perfect."

He presses a tender kiss to my forehead, then my nose, then my lips—soft, lingering touches that make my chest tighten with something deeper than desire. This gentleness is unexpected, a stark contrast to the raw hunger from moments before.

"Good," he whispers against my mouth. "Because I'm nowhere near done with you."

A shiver runs through me at his words. Despite the earth-shattering orgasms, I can already feel that familiar heat building again under his touch. His hands skim down my sides, reverent now, worshipping rather than claiming.

"Again?" I breathe, surprised by my body's eager response.

His smile is wicked. "I told you I was going to take my time with you," he reminds me, his voice a low rumble against my skin. "That was just the beginning."

His fingers trace lazy patterns across my stomach, each touch leaving goosebumps in their wake. I'm hypersensitive now, every nerve ending raw and exposed. When he dips his head to press his lips to my collarbone, I shudder beneath him.

"I want to memorize every inch of you," he murmurs, his breath warm against my skin. "Every birthmark, every scar, every place that makes you gasp when I touch it."

His mouth follows the path of his words, trailing down between my breasts, lingering at the small birthmark right below my breast. He takes his time, tasting and teasing, his tongue tracing patterns that make my breath hitch.

I arch beneath him as his hands slide down to my hips, fingers pressing into my flesh with just enough pressure to make me moan. Time seems to stretch and compress all at once. Each second feels eternal, yet I'm losing all sense of how long we've been tangled together in the sheets.

"Please," I whisper, not even sure I'm begging for.

He lifts his head, eyes dark with hunger as they meet mine. "We have all night," he promises. "And I plan to use every minute of it."

And for the next few hours, that's exactly what he does.

Chapter Twenty-Two

MATEO

The last few days with Analyse have been...something else. I keep thinking there aren't words for it, and then I look at her, really look at her, and I realize that maybe it's because I've never felt anything quite like this before. Maybe that's why there aren't the right words to describe how she's making me feel. Maybe it's why no words feel great enough.

It's New Year's Eve, and instead of going to a party or the club, Analyse and I decided that we wanted to stay home with Maya...ringing in the new year with our favorite little girl.

Outside, it's snowing like crazy. Thick, quiet flurries falling in sheets, frosting the windows and painting the world white. But in here, it's all warmth. Pillows piled high, fuzzy blankets everywhere, the scent of butter popcorn lingering in the air. And them—my girls—curled up on the couch beside me, laughter soft and easy. There's nowhere else I'd rather be. No one else I'd rather be with.

Maya is curled between us under a mountain of pillows, head on Analyse's lap, feet in my lap, holding the remote.

"Okay," she says, "one more movie and then we switch to the countdown."

"You've said one more movie three times already," I tease.

She gives me a look. "Princess rules!"

"Oh, you're right, milady." I hold up both hands. "I forgot that we are in the presence of royalty."

Analyse snorts, brushing a hand through Maya's hair. She looks over at me, eyes soft with affection, and for a second, it feels like time slows. This moment is one we'll carry into every new year from now on. And it hits me in the chest—how much I needed this. How long I've been longing for something like it. It reminds me of memories I haven't dared revisit in a long time. Moments I used to wish I could relive. And now, I think, I get my second chance.

The movie plays, something animated and with a lot of singing, but I'm not really watching. I'm too focused on the way Analyse smiles when Maya laughs, the way she absently traces circles along Maya's arm. The way she glances over at me sometimes. And every time she looks over at me, I swear my heart stops for a moment, in awe of her beauty, of the way she makes me feel.

When the clock finally hits 11:45, Maya jumps up. "We need hats! And noise things!"

Analyse laughs. "You mean noisemakers?"

"Yeah, Mami! That's what I said!"

She runs to the kitchen and comes back with a small stash of party supplies Analyse picked up from the party shop in town. Sparkly paper crowns, gold confetti poppers, and plastic horns. Maya hands me a silver crown and declares, "You're King Mateo for the night!"

I raise a brow. "Do I get a throne?"

"Nope. Just a crown and a horn. Blow it!"

Analyse doubles over laughing as I give the horn the saddest attempt of a celebratory honk. We switch the TV to the New Year's countdown, and by 11:59, Maya is bouncing in place, half from excitement, half from sugar. I sit with one arm around Analyse, the other resting on Maya's back, feeling like my whole heart is wrapped in this moment.

The countdown starts—ten, nine, eight...

Maya shrieks, jumping up and down on the couch.

Seven, six, five...

I look at Analyse. Her eyes meet mine.

Four, three, two...

She leans in, forehead against mine.

One.

Maya screams, "Happy New Year!" and starts blowing her horn like we just hit the jackpot. Confetti flies everywhere. One of the poppers explodes, glitter raining down on all three of us. But all I see is her.

I kiss her before I can think twice. It's soft and unhurried —full of promise. It's a kiss that feels like hope. The kind of hope that only comes when a new year begins, and you're lucky enough to start it with the person who already feels like home.

When we pull back, she whispers, "Happy New Year."

"Happy New Year, chula," I murmur.

And then Maya launches onto our laps, giggling, and we wrap her in our arms, holding her close. This is beginning to feel like forever.

After Maya finally comes down from her sugar and the New Year's high wares off, we tuck her into bed. She's out in minutes—curled up in a pile of blankets, arms flung wide, hair tangled around her pillow.

Analyse and I stand there for a moment, just watching her sleep. Both of us are tired, but it's a type of tired that also comes with joy. This past year...damn. It's the one I never saw coming. If you had told me in January that I'd be standing here, in this house, with a woman like Analyse and a kid like Maya—that I'd feel whole again, somehow—I would've laughed in your face. Hell, I would've told you you were out of your goddamn mind. And yet...here I am.

"You're staying, right?" Analyse asks softly as we walk back toward her room.

I glance over at her, heart thudding in my chest. "There's nowhere I'd rather be."

She smirks. "Good. Or else I'd have to handcuff you to my bed."

My lips twitch "Oh yeah? You threatening me with a good time, chula?"

"Always."

I reach for her hand and pull her gently toward me. She comes willingly, smiling up at me like she's already halfway in a dream. "Come on," I murmur, pressing a kiss to her temple. "Let's go to bed."

We slip into a quiet rhythm of getting ready for the night —side by side at the sink, brushing our teeth like it's something we've always done together. She goes through what has to be the most elaborate skincare routine I've ever seen, bottle after bottle, tapping her face with products I've never even heard of. I wash my face with a bar of soap and catch her shaking her head at me in the mirror, amused.

It's easy. Comfortable. Like muscle memory we never actually built—but somehow know. And that's when it hits me. How normal this feels. How right. Like we've been doing this for years instead of days. Like we've already built something incredible without even realizing it. And I pause.

Was I led here? To Lake City. To her. To Maya.

Was all the pain I've been dragging behind me...for this? Was it all part of some bigger plan? Something I couldn't see until now? God, Lyse. What are you doing to me? Why is it that every time I look at you, my heart whispers *home*?

We climb into bed, and she immediately curls into my chest like it's second nature. The thick comforter covers us, wrapping us in its warmth.

I tilt her chin up gently, just enough so I can see her face. "You're so beautiful."

She laughs softly. "Mateo, I'm in flannel pajamas, a silk bonnet, and I've got zero makeup on. I'm not exactly in beauty mode right now."

I shake my head. "You could be wearing a garbage bag and I'd still think you're the most stunning woman I've ever seen." I brush a knuckle along her jaw. "Lyse, you're so gorgeous that every time I look at you, I have to check my pulse—just to make sure I'm still alive."

She lets out a sound between a laugh and a breath then leans in and presses her lips to mine. I kiss her back, slow and tender, hands cradling her face like she's the most precious thing in the world...she is.

When we finally pull away, her eyes search mine. "Can I ask you something?"

"You can ask me anything."

Her voice is careful. "Why do you never talk about your family? Are they still in California?"

And just like that—walls I didn't even realize I'd rebuilt slam back into place. My chest tightens. Fuck. I knew we'd talk about this eventually. I just didn't think it'd be tonight. Not here. Not now, with her curled against me. But the look on her face—gentle, patient, loving—tells me she isn't asking to pry. She's asking to know me. All of me. And my heart starts racing.

I swallow hard, my throat suddenly dry. My fingers twitch, restless beneath the covers. "They're not in California, no."

"Oh...did they move?"

"Not exactly."

She tilts her head, confused but gentle. "What do you mean?"

I take a breath—long, shaky. My chest tightens. My hands clench into fists against the blanket. This is it. The moment I've been avoiding. The story I swore I'd never speak aloud again.

"I grew up in California," I begin, my voice rougher than I expect. "My parents met in the Dominican Republic, got married, and moved to the States for a better life. They picked California for the sunshine. They said no one could ever be sad in a place with that much light."

I pause, swallowing hard. Analyse doesn't say anything, just slides her hand over mine. Her thumb traces slow circles. It anchors me.

"I was born first. Then came my little sister, Maribel. She was smart—scary smart. And funny. Always singing, always dancing around the house. My parents were...incredible. Kind. Loving. My dad used to take us to the park every day. No matter how tired he was from a long day at work. He'd pitch baseballs to me then run around chasing Maribel."

A memory flashes. My father's laugh. My mother's voice calling us in for dinner. Maribel's curls bouncing as she ran.

"My mom..." My voice cracks. "She was love. Just...love in human form. Always helping someone. Always smiling. She made everything feel safe."

I feel my throat tighten, words sticking. But I force them out. "My plan was always to take care of them. I got a full ride to USC for baseball, and when I told them, they both cried. Even my dad. I'd never seen him cry before. They were proud."

A tear slips down my cheek, and I don't bother wiping it away. "I moved into the dorms, but we were still close. Every Sunday, I took them to lunch. I never missed a single one. And

Maribel? She was the team's little sister. Everyone loved her. And she loved telling them embarrassing stories about me."

I laugh, a short, broken sound.

"And then one night...I got a call. Two in the morning. Unknown number. I almost didn't answer."

Analyse's grip tightens around mine. I can feel her breath catch me, like she knows what's coming.

"It was a fire. At my parents' house. They think it started from an old outlet. The house was old. There wasn't a working smoke alarm. It should've had one. I should've checked. They were sleeping. My mom. My dad. Maribel. They were sleeping and they...they never woke up."

The words hang in the air like smoke. Heavy. Suffocating. I've said them a thousand times in my head, and somehow, they still knock the breath out of me.

"No," I whisper. "They couldn't be gone. I had just seen them. I got in my car and drove there anyway, still convinced it was a mistake. But when I pulled up..."

My voice tremblers. "The house was still burning. Flames everywhere. Firefighters were trying to control it. I got out of the car and tried to run inside, screaming that my family was in there."

I shake my head, the memory hitting me like a punch to the gut. "It took three grown men to hold me back. I fought them with everything I had. I begged. I *begged*. But they wouldn't let me in."

Tears pour down now, hot and relentless. I can't stop them. I don't try to. "I just stood there and watched. I watched as my family burned."

My whole body shakes. The pain crashes over me in waves. "I should've been there," I whisper. "I should've protected them. I could've saved them."

I say it again, louder. Desperate. "I could've saved them."

And again. "*I could've saved them.*"

The sob rips from my chest before I can stop it. I feel Analyse shift, and then she's wrapping her arms around me, pulling me tight against her. I collapse into her, shaking, sobbing into her shoulder like a child.

I bury my face in her neck, clinging to her like she's the only thing keeping me from falling apart completely. "I'm sorry," I choke out. "I'm so sorry."

"You have nothing to be sorry for," she whispers, her voice shaking. Her fingers run through my hair, slow and soothing. "You were a kid, Mateo. A kid. You didn't fail them."

I shake my head, but she holds me tighter.

"You loved them," she says. "And I know they knew that. I know they were proud of you. Are proud of you."

I don't say anything. I can't. The grief has taken over.

"I finished college because it's what they would've wanted," I eventually say, voice barely above a whisper. "And the day I graduated, I went back to that restaurant we always went to. I sat at our table. Waited for them to walk through the door.

"I couldn't bring myself to go to the cemetery after the funeral," I admit, eyes trained on the floor. "Not once. I know where they're buried. I know I should've gone. But I couldn't. I couldn't face the headstones. I couldn't face that they were really not here anymore.

"So I just kept...going back to the restaurant instead. Like maybe, if I just sat there long enough, they'd walk in. Mami in her Sunday dress. Maribel bouncing beside her. Papi with that same old baseball cap."

Silence.

"They never came."

Analyse presses a kiss to the side of my head. Her tears mix with mine.

"I left California the next day," I say. "The sun felt like it was mocking me. I needed cold. Pain. Something else. I packed everything and moved here. Picked Lake City off a damn map. I became a firefighter because I swore I'd never let anyone else lose their family the way I lost mine."

I pull back just enough to look at her, my hands still trembling. "I didn't think I'd find a family again. I didn't think I'd find you. But you...Lyse, you make me feel again. Like I'm alive. Like maybe it's okay to want something more. To have something more."

A small smile tugs at her lips through the tears.

"And Maya..." My voice breaks. "God, I love her. She reminds me so much of Maribel. The same light. The same stubborn streak."

I pause. Then say softly, "It's like the little pieces of you both...they're stitching my heart back together, one thread at a time. You two are saving me. Every day. Every second."

I cup her face, thumb brushing her cheek. "I'd do anything for you both. Anything. Day or night."

She leans her forehead against mine, our breaths mingling in the quiet of the room. "You already have," she whispers.

And in that moment, in her arms, I finally let myself breathe.

Chapter Twenty-Three

ANALYSE

We're still wrapped around each other, clutching like the world might come undone if we loosen our grip. Mateo's face is buried in the crook of my neck, his breathing uneven, his tears soaking into my skin. His hands are fisted in the back of my shirt like he's trying to keep himself from falling apart again. I hold him tighter.

There's nothing I can say that would touch the depth of what he just shared—of what he's carried. So I stay quiet, letting the silence speak for me. Letting my presence say: You're not alone anymore.

Eventually, the tremble in his body fades. His breathing begins to steady, still a little raw but no longer unraveling. When he finally lifts his head, the look in his eyes nearly undoes me. Red-rimmed. Shining. But soft. So soft it makes my heart ache.

"I don't know how to explain it," he murmurs, voice thick with leftover grief. "But being here with you...it's the first time I've felt like I might be okay again."

My heart swells and shatters at once. I press my forehead

to his, noses brushing, our breaths tangling in the quiet space between us. Then I kiss him.

It's gentle, tender, like we're both afraid of breaking the fragile thread tethering us together. But as his lips move against mine, I feel it shift. The kiss deepens, grows warmer. His hand cradles my cheek, the pad of his thumb brushing just beneath my eye. Like he's memorizing me by feel. Like he needs this, needs me, to stay grounded.

When my fingers drift under the hem of his shirt, I pause, giving him the chance to stop me. He doesn't. He lifts his arms, wordlessly letting me peel the fabric away.

Under the soft wash of moonlight, he looks unreal— broad shoulders, lean muscle. But it's not just his body. It's the look in his eyes, like I'm touching a part of him no one's been allowed near in years.

"I don't know if I deserve this," he whispers, eyes searching mine.

I shake my head, threading my fingers through his hair. "You deserve everything good in this world."

I pull him down to me again, and our mouths meet with more urgency. More need. It's no longer gentle...it's greedy, hungry. We kiss like we have lost time to make up for. Like we might never get another chance.

His hands move under my shirt, calloused palms sweeping over my bare skin, dragging a gasp from my lips. I arch into him, needing him closer, needing to feel all of him, all at once.

"Are you sure?" he rasps, voice shaking slightly.

"I've never been more sure of anything," I whisper.

Clothes fall away, slow and deliberate, piece by piece until nothing separates us. My body hums with anticipation, every nerve ending alive under his touch. His gaze drags over me like a caress.

"God," he breathes. "You're unreal."

His weight settles over me, warm steady. I spread my

thighs, and he nestles between them, his skin burning against mine. He groans softly at the contact, forehead pressing to mine.

"This okay?" he asks, breath ragged.

"More than okay," I whisper. "Please."

He reaches between us, lining himself up, and slides into me slowly. I gasp, my body arching as he fills me completely. He's thick, warm, and overwhelming, and I feel everything. He stays still, forehead still against mine, waiting for me to adjust.

"You feel like home," he whispers, and the words hit harder than anything else tonight.

I wrap my legs around his waist and roll my hips, urging him to move. "So do you."

He begins to thrust, deep and unhurried, his strokes deliberate, like he's trying to carve himself into my soul. I clutch at his back, fingers digging into his skin.

"Mateo," I moan. "Yes. Just like that."

He groans, his rhythm deepening, his mouth trailing down my throat to my collarbone, then lower. His tongue circles my nipple, sucking gently, and I cry out, hips lifting into his. Every part of me feels on fire. Needy and trembling and alive.

"You feel incredible," he pants. "You—God, Lyse—you're everything."

My nails scrape down his back, hips rising to meet every thrust, our bodies locked in rhythm. His hand fines the place where we're joined, thumb circling my clit in time with his movements. The pleasure builds, hot and unbearable.

"I'm gonna, oh God, Mateo, I'm gonna come."

"Come for me," he groans. "Let me feel you fall apart."

And I do. I shatter around him, my whole body locking up as waves of pleasure crash through me. I cry out his name, clutching him tighter, the orgasm ripping through me like a storm. I don't come down gently. I fall hard, breath stolen, vision blurred.

He follows seconds later, thrusts turning erratic, hips stuttering. His voice breaks as he groans into my neck, his release crashing into him. I feel him pulse inside me, his entire body trembling with the force of it.

We collapse into each other, chests heaving, sweat cooling between our skin. His head drops to my shoulder. My fingers trace his spine, lazy and tender, trying to memorize the moment. The weight of him, the warmth, the safety. Neither of us speaks for a while.

Then, softly, he murmurs, "I didn't think I could ever feel like this again."

I smile, brushing back the damp hair from his forehead. "You can. You do. With me."

He shifts onto his side, pulling me with him, keeping me tucked tightly against his chest. Our legs tangle. His hand rests on my waist, thumb rubbing slow, aimless circles.

"I never planned for any of this," he says, voice low. "But you...you're the best thing I never saw coming."

Tears sting my eyes again, this time for a different reason. "You've got me," I whisper, kissing the corner of his mouth. "Completely."

By the time the sun rises, the world outside looks like a snow globe. Thick flurries are still falling, blanketing the rooftops and trees in white. Everything is still and soft, the kind of morning that makes you want to stay in bed all day. But Maya has other plans.

"SNOW DAY!" she shrieks, bounding into our room with mismatched socks and a sparkly unicorn sweater that's three sizes too big.

Mateo groans beside me, lifting one arm dramatically over his face. "What time is it?"

"Time to play in the snow!" Maya answers cheerfully, tugging at the covers. "Come on! Come on!"

He peeks out from under his arms. "Don't you want pancakes first?"

Maya pauses. "Okay, but snow after."

I sit up, laughing. "Deal."

An hour later, pancakes have been devoured. Cocoa mugs are empty. Maya has dressed herself in no less than four layers of clothes, insisting it's her "snow armor." Mateo is pulling on his boots at the front door while I zip Maya's puffy pink coat.

"Do we have enough gloves?" I ask, checking the tote by the door.

Mateo lifts one of Maya's sparkly mittens. "One glove only."

"Sorry, Mami!" Maya says with a grin.

We finally manage to get out the door, bundled head to toe. The snow is deep, up to Maya's knees in some places, and still falling gently. The whole neighborhood is hushed beneath the weight of winter, but there's a buzz of life in the town square. Everyone in this town loves a good snowstorm.

"Where to first?" I ask,

"SLEDS!" Maya squeals.

Mateo slaps his glove against his palm. "To the hill it is."

Lake City's park has been transformed into a winter playground. Kids are running wild, their squeals echoing against the buildings. Someone's set up a temporary sledding hill using hay bales and packed snow. A small group is building an igloo near the gazebo, and there's even a hot cocoa stand staffed by the high school drama club.

Maya clutches her sled to her chest. "Come on, come one!" she says, already running ahead.

We take turns going down the hill with her. First me, then Mateo, then all three of us in a tangled, laughing heap. At one point, Mateo pretends to fall off and flops backward dramatically into a snowbank. Maya throws herself on top of him and announces she's conquered the Fire Knight of Snow Valley.

"I yield," Mateo says, eyes closed. "The Queen of Chaos has won."

Snowflakes dust his eyelashes. He looks up at me, grinning. My chest aches a little with how beautiful this moment is.

My phone buzzes in my pocket as we gather our sleds, the vibration sharp against the softness of the day. I slip off one glove just long enough to glance at the screen.

NICO

When can I see her? She deserves to know her dad. Don't drag this out.

My stomach twists. I lock the phone without answering, shove it deep into my coat, and paste on a smile. Not now. Not here.

Mateo grabs my sled in one hand, my mittened fingers in the other. Maya is already skipping ahead toward the square, cocoa on her mind, and I let myself follow.

Later that afternoon, we wander through the heart of the town, hand in hand, our boots crunching through the thick snow. The gazebo at the town square glows under a canopy of string lights, soft yellow bulbs twinkling against the pale sky like trapped stars. A local band plays classic holiday tunes with a jazzy twist—saxophones humming, a stand-up bass keeping time, and the gentle clink of tambourine bells keeping rhythm with the snowflakes that continue to drift lazily down.

Maya runs ahead, her tiny boots kicking up powder as she twirls beneath the lights like the snow itself is music. She's got a cup of cocoa in one mittened hand and the other thrown dramatically in the air as she spins in wild, clumsy circles.

Mateo slips an arm around my waist and pulls me close, pressing a kiss to the top of my head. His body is warm against mine, even through our thick coats.

"She's happy," he murmurs, eyes never leaving Maya.

I watch her, too, feeling the weight of it. The ease, the freedom, the laughter. It wraps around us like a blanket.

I nod, my own smile soft. "She's safe. She's loved."

The music swells as a new song begins, and Maya shouts, "This one's my favorite!" before launching into another round of chaotic twirling. She nearly slips on a patch of ice but catches herself with a laugh, then pretends to bow dramatically like a ballerina at the end of a show.

"Encore!" Mateo calls, clapping above his head.

She beams and launches into a shaky curtsy before taking a sip of her cocoa that results in whipped cream sticking to her nose.

"I can't handle how cute she is," I say with a laugh.

"She gets it from you," he replies, kissing my temple again.

After the music winds down and the band starts to pack up, Maya bounds over and grabs both our hands. "Can we make a snowman now? A big one? Like...huge. Gigantic. The biggest in the whole town!"

Mateo grins. "Only if we can give him a backstory."

Maya gasps. "Yes! Yes! He needs a name. A life. A job!"

CHAPTER TWENTY-THREE

"He's a CEO of sled technology," I chime in. "Very busy. Very important."

Maya's eyes go wide. "His name is...Mr. Sledsworth,"

"Sir Mr. Sledsworth," Mateo says solemnly. "Of the North Pole division."

With our mission set, we move to a wide patch of open snow and get to work. Maya directs us, pointing to where the base should go and demanding, "More snow, more snow!"

Mateo rolls the first ball until it's almost as tall as Maya herself, grunting dramatically like it weighs a thousand pounds. "I may not survive this snow boulder," he groans.

I help her roll the middle section while Mateo adds extra snow to the base for the "maximum snow stability." When the middle is stacked and secure, he lifts the smaller top piece on with exaggerated effort.

"Sir Mr. Sledsworth has arrived," Maya declares, standing with her hands on her hips.

We gather sticks for arms—long, crooked branches with little twigs on the ends that Mateo arranges in dramatic jazz hands.

"For flair," he says, stepping back to admire his work.

"He's fabulous," I say.

We use smooth black pebbles for eyes and a crooked little carrot for a nose. Maya takes off one of her scarves and wraps it around the snowman's neck.

Mateo brushes snow off Mr. Sledworth's "shoulders" then bows low. "Your Snowjesty," he says in a deep, exaggerated voice, "we are honored by your presence."

Maya curtsies beside him. "May your snow never melt!"

I join in, offering the most dramatic bow I can manage without falling face-first into the snow. "Long live Mr. Sledsworth."

Just as we start to pack up—mittens soaked, cheeks flushed, and thermos lids twisting shut—a snowball comes sailing through the crisp winter air and hits Mateo square in the back. He freezes mid-motion, standing straight. Slowly, he turns around.

Maya is standing a few feet away, one mittened hand suspiciously behind her back, the other raised in mock innocence. "It wasn't me." she says, trying and failing to suppress her grin.

Mateo narrows his eyes. "Oh," he says in a deep ominous voice, "it's on."

And just like that, all hell breaks loose.

Maya yelps and takes off running, boots crunching through the snow, her high-pitched laughter echoing through the trees. Mateo scoops up a handful of snow and begins packing it like he's preparing for war.

"I need backup!" he yells, ducking behind a park bench like a soldier in a dramatic war film. "We're under attack! Commander Chula, are you with me?!"

I laugh so hard I nearly drop the thermos. "I'm a civilian!" I call out, hands raised. "Leave me out of this!"

"Too late!" Mateo shouts. "She's compromised. We can't leave witnesses!"

Before I can even run, a snowball hits me square in the shoulder. "Hey!" I shriek, spinning around with wide eyes. "You hit me!"

Maya's peal of laughter rings out from behind a tree. "It was Mateo!" she squeals.

Mateo gasps, scandalized. "Maya! You sold me out!"

I scramble behind a low stone wall, clutching a handful of snow. "I'm choosing violence," I say under my breath. "You two are going down."

The snowball fight that erupts could be written into the town's history books. Maya is agile and quick, darting behind trees and pelting us from every angle. Mateo hams it up to the extreme, ducking dramatically and yelling things like, "Incoming!" and, "Cover me!" as he belly flops into the snow. At one point, he grabs a sled and uses it as a makeshift shield, crawling behind it like he's storming the front lines.

I try to stay out of it, I really do, but Maya's too good at sneak attacks. She pops up behind me and drops a snowball right down the back of my jacket. I shriek like a banshee.

"That's it!" I cry, charging after her with two hastily made snowballs in hand.

She screams and sprints toward Mateo. "Save me!"

He scoops her up mid-run, spinning her into the air like she weighs nothing. "Retreat! Retreat!" he yells, while she shrieks with delight, clinging to his neck.

I take my shot and nail him in the chest.

He stumbles backward, grinning like a fool. "Commander Chula has turned on us!" he bellows.

"Commander Chula is sick of being cold and wet!"

"You'll pay for your treason!"

"I'm not scared of you." I laugh, crouching low and throwing another snowball that goes wide.

He pretends to collapse into the snow, Maya toppling with him in a dramatic heap. "You got me," he groans. "Tell my story."

"Nooooo!" Maya cries, crawling over his chest like she's straight out of a telenovela. "Don't die on me!"

We're all laughing too hard to breathe. My stomach hurts. My face aches. My gloves are soaked through and I'm pretty sure there's snow down my pants, but I don't care. The joy in this moment is blinding.

Mateo suddenly lunges up and tackles Maya gently into the snow, both of them giggling uncontrollably. She flops back, arms wide, making a snow angel around her own laughter. Mateo collapses beside her, out of breath, his dark curls dusted in white.

I drop down beside them, breathless and red cheeked, my hair stuck to the inside of my scarf. All three of us lie there in the snow, staring up at the sky as soft flakes begin to fall again, slow and lazy like confetti at the end of a party.

Maya wiggles closer to me, pulling one of my arms around her, then reaches for Mateo's hand on her other side. He threads his fingers through hers without a word.

"I think I won," Maya says after a moment.

"In your dreams," Mateo teases.

"I definitely won," she says with authority, a smug little grin tugging at her lips.

"You didn't even let me keep score," I argue. "There was no official referee."

"There was no need," Maya says matter-of-factly. "You were both clearly losing."

We laugh again. The sun is starting to dip behind the trees, painting the sky in pale hues of lavender and gold. I can feel the wetness of the snow seeping through my jeans, but I still don't want to move.

Mateo shifts onto his side, propping his head up with one hand as he watches us. "This might've been the best day I've had in years," he says.

I meet his gaze. "Same."

Mateo kisses Maya's cheek, then mine. "Let's go get cocoa," he says, brushing snow from his sleeves.

She lifts her arms up dramatically. "I accept your offer!"

Mateo scoops her into his arms like she's a tiny queen and spins her around again. Her laughter floats into the sky. I follow behind them, framed by the last light of the day, snowflakes catching in their hair, joy trailing behind them like a ribbon.

The sight of them makes my heart feel so full it might burst.

Back home, we peel off wet layers and dump gloves by the heater to dry. Mateo starts a fire in the living room while I warm up cider on the stove.

Maya settles on the couch with a blanket and the marshmallow heavy mug I hand her. "This was the best day ever."

"You say that every snow day," I tease.

"Because they keep getting better."

Mateo comes over and sits beside me, arm wrapping around my shoulders. "We should make this a tradition. First snowstorm of the year, snow chaos and cocoa."

I lean into him. "Deal."

Maya yawns, fighting sleep, but it wins. She drifts off halfway through a movie, curled between us.

Mateo pulls the blanket higher over her shoulders. "She's out."

"Hard day ruling a snowy kingdom."

He smiles. "She's something else."

"She's everything." I glance up at him. "So are you."

His eyes meet mine, and there's something so tender in them it makes my throat tighten.

"I think this," he says softly, nodding at the fire, the sleeping child, the warm house, "is the happiest I've ever been."

I reach for his hand, intertwining our fingers. "Me too."

Outside, snow still falls softly, blanketing the world in peace. But in here, with him, with her, I've never felt more at home.

Chapter Twenty-Four

ANALYSE

I send a message to everyone in our chaotic-as-hell group chat.

ANALYSE

> Family dinner tonight at my house. Be there or die.

MATEO

> That's a lot of aggression for nine in the morning, chula.

ANNA

> I like it. I'm in.

MARI

> You can count Seba and I in as well.

SEB

> What if I didn't want to be counted in?

MARI

> Well then you die. Obviously.

ANALYSE

Yeah, Seb. You'll obviously be subjected to death at my hands.

SEB

Oh, right. Count me in.

NATHAN

Do you need me to bring anything?

ANALYSE

You're the only one to ask! Such a gentleman. But no, no need. Unless....bring the good wine?

NATHAN

You got it.

ANDRES

Hey! I was going to offer too! Cap just didn't give me a chance.

ANNA

Sureeeee. Whatever you say.

MARI

I can bring desserts from The Rolling Pin!

ANDRES

Yes! BRING DESSERTS!

ANALYSE

Thanks for answering for me, Andres.

ANDRES

You're welcome. Just giving your little typing fingers a break.

MATEO

I think it goes without saying...I'll be there, baby.

MARI

Awwww

> **ANNA**
> You guys are so cute it makes me sick.

> **SEB**
> Bro, not while I'm here please.

> **ANALYSE**
> Shut up Seb.

I set the last pair of scissors on the table, step back, and grin. The dining rooms looks like Pinterest and a craft store had a love child. There are magazines everywhere, poster boards propped against mason jars full of markers, glitter glue, and sparkly washi tape.

I glance at the clock. Five minutes until the gang shows up for what they think is just a casual dinner. They have no idea they're walking into a full-blown vision board party.

"Maya!" I call down the hall. "Are you ready?"

She comes racing out of her room in a fuzzy pink sweater, polka-dotted leggings, and her sparkly boots. She's clutching a stack of old kid's magazines and a glue stick in her arms.

"I'm gonna make mine say I want a unicorn and a puppy!" she announces proudly.

"That's right! Dream big, mamita," I say with a laugh, smoothing down one of her wild curls. "That's what tonight's all about."

A knock at the door pulls my attention. Showtime.

I swing it open to find Anna, Mari, Seb, and Andres huddled on the porch, their faces red from the cold. Mari's carrying a bakery box, Andres has a bag of chips, and Seb has nothing but an expression that already screams regret.

And right behind them, cheeks flushed and bottle of wine tucked under one arm, is Nathan.

"Sorry I'm late," he says, stepping in with a grin. "Had to track down the good wine."

"You're forgiven." I laugh. "The good wine earns you instant immunity."

They filter into the house, stomping snow off their boots, and then they see the dining room.

Mari lets out a gasp. "Wait. What is all this?"

Anna drops her coat and bolts over to the table. "No. Freaking. Way. Are we doing vision boards? Analyse, this is GENIUS."

Seb and Andres stop dead in their tracks, exchanging wide-eyed glances.

Andres slowly sets the chips down. "I thought we were having tacos and chisme. This is glitter. Glitter is dangerous. Glitter gets everywhere and then in three months from now I'll still find more of it lingering in my house without any clue as to how it got there."

Seb points at a bottle of sparkly pink glue. "Is this thing loaded?"

I laugh and gesture toward the table. "Surprise! Tonight is about feeding your stomachs *and* your manifestations."

Mari sets the bakery box down and claps. "Honestly, I'm obsessed. And Lyse, this is SO the teacher in you."

Anna's already flipping through a magazine, tongue between her teeth as she tears out a page. "I'm making mine aesthetic. Maybe some dreamy beach vibes with a hot mystery man reading poetry in a hammock."

I raise a brow. "I wonder who that man will be."

"I guess we'll find out if the manifestations come true," Anna quips without looking up.

Nathan leans over and points to her page. "Don't forget to add a dog. No dream guy is complete without a dog named Biscuit."

Anna snorts. "Biscuit?"

He shrugs. "It's a solid name. Trust me."

Just then, another knock sounds. Mateo walks in, snow clinging to his hair, cheeks flushed from the cold. He scans the room, eyebrows lifting at the sight of the chaos.

"Vision board night?" he asks, lips curving into a slow smile.

"You're not even surprised," I say, crossing my arms.

He shrugs, walking toward me and wrapping an arm around my waist. "At this point? You could tell me we're doing interpretive dance in the backyard and I'd still show up."

Maya runs over and tugs on his sleeve. "I'm putting a unicorn and puppy on mine!"

Mateo crouches to her level, eyes wide. "That's amazing. But are you sure you don't want to add a dragon that breathes glitter? Just in case?"

Her mouth drops open. "YES." She darts off again, magazine in hand, and Mateo straightens, chuckling.

"She's so yours," he murmurs, kissing my temple.

We settle into the table, and for the next hour, it's chaotic, colorful magic. Scissors snip. Laughter echoes. Andres pretends to be too cool for it, but I catch him carefully cutting out the word adventure and pasting it under a picture of a mountain.

"I want to hike Machu Picchu," he mumbles.

Mari claps. "YES, manifestation king! Put that right under your little photo of a llama."

"I like llamas," he mutters.

Seb is the last to cave. "Fine," he sighs, grabbing a board.

An hour later, his board says *stability*, *gym gains*, and *less back pain*. There are also photos of pancakes, a house with a wraparound porch, and a bunch of kids.

"Mari, based on his board, you're going to be popping out a bunch of little Sebastians," Anna teases.

He shrugs. "More like little Mariana's."

Mateo's board is surprisingly quiet. He cuts slower than the others, more deliberate. I glance over and see words like *peace*, *home*, *love*. There's a tiny photo of a firefighter's helmet next to a photo of a little girl flying a kite.

I place a hand on his thigh under the table. He covers it with his own and squeezes.

"Yours is beautiful," I whisper.

There's still so much healing to do—for both of us. But this moment feels like a start.

Nathan leans over from the other end of the table and shows me his board. "Mine's a weird mix of fitness, travel, and finally remodeling the damn kitchen I keep pretending I don't have time for."

I grin. "You forgot 'intimidating us with your maturity.'"

He chuckles, low and easy. "Please. I'm just old enough to have made most of the dumb decisions already."

"And now you just make adult ones? Like buying a second air fryer?"

"I'll have you know, the second air fryer is for hosting. Don't knock the setup until you've had my honey garlic wings."

Andres stares at him from across the table. "You cook? Like, *cook* cook?"

Nathan raises a brow. "I meal plan, Andres. I *season*."

Anna fans herself dramatically. "The bar is so low it's underground, but somehow Nathan is just...up there. Floating in the clouds with his spice rack and his emotional stability."

Nathan winks. "What can I say? I'm a man of many talents."

Seb groans. "I suddenly hate him."

Mari pats Seb's arm. "It's okay, baby. You can still learn."

Maya's finished board has sparkles in every corner. "Mine

says I'm gonna be a ninja-clown-vet-scientist," she announces proudly.

"Well then," Mateo says. "Dr. Ninja Clown Maya, I believe in you."

She curtsies. "Thank you, kind sir."

Seb groans. "I can't believe this is how I'm spending my Friday night."

"You love it," Mari says, tossing a pillow at him.

"I love any second that I get to spend with you, mi tesoro," he admits.

Nathan leans back in his chair, sipping cocoa. "Honestly? This is better than most parties I've ever been to."

"See?" I say, beaming. "I told you manifestation night was the move."

We clean up with music playing and cocoa mugs in hand. Anna and Andres dance around the kitchen like idiots while Mateo carries Maya on his back, both of them giggling. Nathan helps Mari gather the scraps and sticky glue sticks, his sleeves rolled up, a smear of glitter on his cheek.

As the night winds down and everyone prepares to leave, I glance around the room. The boards are drying. The house smells like chocolate and cinnamon. The people I love most are here, warm and full and laughing.

My gaze drifts back to Mateo's board. Between the pictures of fire trucks and family dinners, one small square catches my eye—our initials drawn inside a crooked little heart. My breath hitches. It's simple, almost hidden, but I know. That one's about us.

Mateo comes up behind me, sliding his arms around my waist again. "This was perfect."

"Really?"

He nods, pressing a kiss just behind my ear. "Vision boards, glitter bombs, chaotic energy. All of it. I'd do this every night if it meant I got to see you like this."

"Like what?

He tilts his head. "Happy."

I lean back into him, content and full in a way I didn't know I could be. "I am," I whisper.

We watch Maya run to show Seb her board again, and Anna threatening to laminate hers. Andres has glue in his hair, and Mari is laughing so hard she's crying. Nathan's lounging on the couch, shaking his head as he peels glitter off his jeans.

It's messy. Loud. A little ridiculous...or maybe a lot. But it's mine, and I love it.

A knock echoes through the house. We all freeze.

Seb glances around. "Who could that be? We're all right here."

Anna frowns. "Unless someone invited Santa, we're not expecting anyone."

Maya gasps. "Is it the unicorn I manifested?"

I give her a soft smile, ruffling her curls. "Not this time, mamita."

I force my feet to move toward the door. When I open it, a blast of cold air hits me—and so does the sight of Nico. He's standing there, snow clinging to the shoulders of his coat. His jaw is tight, his hands shoved into his pockets.

Mateo is behind me in second. His voice is low and sharp. "What the hell are you doing here?"

Nico's eyes narrow. "I'm here to see my kid, obviously."

I step between them, heart pounding. "You can't just show up here unannounced."

"I just need to talk to you," he says, his tone tight. "Ten minutes. That's it."

Mateo bristles behind me. I can feel the tension radiating from him. "Analyse—"

"It's fine," I say, cutting him off. I turn back to Nico. "Five minutes. Outside."

Nico nods, shoulders relaxing slightly.

Mateo steps closer. "You want me to come with you?"

I shake my head. "No. Just stay with Maya, please."

His eyes search mine, unwilling to let me walk this alone. "You sure?"

I nod. "Yeah." I lean in and kiss him, lingering just a moment. "I'll be okay."

Mateo watches me for a beat longer before stepping back into the warmth of the house. I shut the door behind me, sealing myself into the cold. Snow crunches under our feet as I lead Nico to the edge of the porch. The lights inside spill faintly across the snow-covered yard, but out here, the air bites harder. It's quiet except for the distant hum of wind through the trees.

"What do you want?" I ask, arms wrapped tightly around myself.

He stands there for a second, rocking on his heels. He blows out a breath, fogging the air between us. "I don't even know where to start."

"Try the truth."

His jaw tightens, but then he looks at me with eyes that are softer than I remember. "I've been thinking about you. About Maya. About everything."

I stiffen. "You don't get to think about us now like we're some nostalgic memory you can revisit."

"I know, I know," he says quickly, holding up his hands. "I just...I've changed. I've been changing. I'm not the same guy I was back then. I've been getting my shit together, finally. And I started thinking, maybe there's still a chance."

I blink, confused. "A chance at what?"

He steps closer. "I told you when I came back into town, Lyse. A chance at us. At being a family. I want to be in Maya's life. And I want to try again with you."

"And I told you that I have a boyfriend, Mateo. I'm happy. We are happy. There is no trying again with me."

"Fuck that guy. He's not the guy for you. I've missed you, Analyse. I've missed what we had. I still think about the night we danced on the beach. I still remember how you looked the night you told me you were pregnant. Scared. But strong. I was an idiot for leaving, but I want to be the man you and Maya deserve now."

I stare at him, stunned. "You don't even know her."

"I can. I want to," he says, desperate now. "I want to be a real father. I want to make this right."

I shake my head slowly, trying to absorb the audacity. "You've had seven years, Nico. Seven. Every single day you could've picked up a phone. Written a letter. Shown up. And you didn't. Since you walked your ass back into town, you've had every opportunity to actually get to know her. But you haven't. You've been so caught up in trying to win me back."

"I know I screwed up—"

"No, Nico. You abandoned us. That's not a screw up. That's a choice. And what I don't get is—why now? What changed? What suddenly made you think you can walk back into our lives like nothing happened?"

He shifts, looking down at the snow. "I don't know, Lyse. I was lonely. Everything else in my life was falling apart, and I kept thinking about you. About our baby. About what I missed. I thought maybe if I came back, I could fix it somehow."

"Do you hear yourself? You came back because *your* life fell apart—not because you suddenly grew a conscience, not because you wanted to show up for her. You left me to raise our daughter alone. And now that the hard part's over, now that she's no longer a newborn screaming through the night, you think you can show up and play daddy?"

"I'm trying," he says, voice cracking. "I'm trying to make up for lost time."

"You can't make up for all these years with a fucking apology and a plea to get back together."

His mouth twists, frustration starting to seep through the cracks in his calm. "So what? That's it? You're just going to stay with him?"

I go still. "Mateo?"

He scoffs. "Yeah. Him. The fucking hero. You really think he's going to love her like I can?"

My eyes flash. "He already does. He's been here, Nico. Through all of it. He didn't flinch. He didn't bail. He stayed. And she knows it. She trusts him."

"And you?" he asks, stepping closer. "Do you love him?"

I hesitate for half a second too long. His face hardens.

"Fuck," he mutters, raking a hand through his hair. "All this time...I thought maybe you'd still be waiting. That after everything, I'd come back and we could just pick up where we left off. Guess I was an idiot."

"You were gone for seven years, Nico." My voice cracks. "You don't get to abandon us and expect me to keep a life on ice for you. That's not love. That's selfish. And it sure as hell isn't family."

He snaps then—shouting like a man unraveling. "Fuck! Give me a fucking break, Analyse! I was twenty-goddamn-four! I was young! I wasn't ready to have a kid. I wasn't ready to be a father. I barely knew what I wanted to do with my life —not everyone can be like you and have it all figured out straight out of college. I fucking panicked, okay? I. Panicked. You said you were pregnant, and I freaked the fuck out. All that ran through my mind was that I didn't have my shit together, and I didn't have money to raise a kid, I wasn't good enough and you were supposed to be on birth control—"

"FUCK OFF, NICO." My voice cracks through the cold night like a whip. His eyes widen, but I keep going, heart thudding so hard it hurts.

"I *was* on birth control. But guess what? Sometimes birth control fails. Do you think I was ready? No. But I didn't run. From the moment I saw those two lines on the pregnancy test, I stepped up and got my shit together. You think I had money? I'm a teacher, for God's sake—we're not exactly making a shit ton of money."

I'm shaking now, from the rage and cold and pain.

"But that didn't matter. I was young, too. I was twenty-four, too. And I didn't run. I never ran. I never, not for one damn second, let my daughter down. I was there for every single second. ALL OF IT. While you were being a coward, I was doing whatever I had to do to make sure Maya always knew she was loved and special and the most important thing in the world. She is my whole damn world, Nico. So forgive me if I don't give a shit about your sorry ass excuses."

His jaw works, but I don't stop. Can't.

"Do you have any idea how hard it was for me? I was twenty-four and in one fell swoop not only did I learn I was pregnant, but I became a single mom, too. I went through every second of that pregnancy alone. Every kick, every doctor's appointment, every sleepless night wondering if I'd be enough. I had to be induced early because I had pre-eclampsia and I was so fucking scared." My voice breaks, throat raw.

"And you weren't there. Not for the birth. Not for the late nights. Not for the first smile, the first word, her first steps. But you know who was there? My mom. My dad. Sebastian. Andres. Mateo. Hell, even Nathan."

I point toward the house, toward the glowing windows and the life I built without him.

"They were there. Through all the sleepless nights—and there were many—they rotated shifts to help me. Mateo, God, Mateo, he was there most of all. Maya's had him wrapped around her little finger since she was a newborn." I blink, tears threatening now.

"He was the one who held her when I couldn't even keep my eyes open. He fed her when I was too sick to get out of bed. He sang to her. Changed her. Rocked her to sleep. He never ran. He showed up. Day after day. Week after week. Year after year."

Silence stretches between us. Nico is frozen, lips parted, chest rising and falling.

Finally, he says, voice low, "I'm leaving town."

I nod once, emotion pressing hot behind my eyes. "Exactly."

His brows knit, confused.

"You're leaving. Because that's what you do, Nico. You don't show up for people, you just show up when it's convenient. This was never about Maya. It was about me. About getting me back. And now that you see you can't, now that you realize I'm not yours anymore, you're running. Again."

I shake my head, fury giving way to heartbreak. "It was never about her. Not really. If it was, you'd stay. You'd try. You'd fight. But you're not. You're walking away. Again."

He doesn't deny it. Doesn't say a word. Just stares at me like he's seeing the truth for the first time and hates it. I don't say goodbye. I don't need to.

I walk back inside, the door clicking shut behind me.

The second the door closes behind me, the noise of the house rushes back in—Maya's laughter from down the hall, the low hum of music still playing, the buzz of conversation. But it all feels distant, muffled. Like I'm underwater.

Mateo is waiting in the kitchen, leaning against the counter with his arms crossed, eyes fixed on the door like he was willing it to open the whole time I was gone.

When he sees me, he straightens immediately. "You okay?"

I nod. Then shake my head. Then shrug, because I don't know which one is true. He doesn't press. Just opens his arms, and that's all it takes. I fall into his chest like I'm collapsing.

The second he wraps his arms around me, the tears come. Big, silent ones that soak into his shirt. My shoulders shake. My knees buckle. And he just holds me.

"I'm sorry," I whisper.

"Don't be," he murmurs into my hair. "Let it out."

I don't know how long I cry. But when I finally pull back, my voice is barely there. "He's leaving town."

Mateo's jaw clenches, but he doesn't say anything. Just waits.

"And he never...he never wanted her. He didn't come back for Maya. He came back for me. And now that he knows he can't have me..." I wipe my face with the back of my hand, breath catching. "He's just going. Like she's nothing."

Mateo's eyes soften, heartbreak and fury mixing behind them. "I'm so sorry, baby."

I nod, swallowing hard. "It just...it breaks my heart. For her. For what she deserved and never got. For what she still won't get."

His thumb brushes my cheek, catching another tear. "He doesn't get to come back into her life and choose again. Not like that."

I blink up at him, searching his face. "You've always been there. Always. Since the beginning. When it wasn't your job. When it would've been easier not to. You've shown up every single time."

He leans in and presses a soft kiss to my forehead, lingering there. I take a step back, exhaling shakily.

"Well," I say, managing a wobbly smile, "I guess since he's gone now...we can break up."

Mateo jerks his head back. "What?"

I gesture to the air between us, voice barely holding together. "You were only with me to protect us, right? To be there for me like you always are. To help me while he was around. That was the deal."

The words taste like ash even as they leave my mouth. I don't even know what I'm saying, but I can't seem to stop. Part of me wants to snatch them back, to throw myself into his arms and beg him not to let me go. But the other part—the broken, frightened part—pushes harder, determined to ruin this before I get the chance to lose him for real.

He stares at me, stunned. "Lyse—"

I smile again. Small. Sad. "It's okay. You did your job."

Then I walk past him, leaving him speechless in the kitchen, heart pounding in my ears.

Chapter Twenty-Five

MATEO

I step into the living room as Analyse disappears upstairs with Maya. Her arm was around her daughter, voice soft, careful, nurturing, but I saw the way her shoulders trembled as they climbed the stairs. Whatever happened out on that porch, it fucked with her head. I know it.

The living room is still buzzing with leftover energy. Glitter clings to the floor, cocoa mugs and wine glasses litter the coffee table, and everyone's voices are too damn loud. They don't know, though. They can't tell that everything is falling apart right now. They don't realize that there's a crack in the air.

"Alright," I say, clapping my hands once. "The party's over."

Seb frowns from the arm of the couch, one brow arched. "Is everything okay with Lyse?"

"No," I answer honestly. There's no point in pretending. "But I've got it."

He starts to stand, Mari and Anna right behind him.

"Seriously. She just needs a minute. I'll talk to her."

"She's my sister."

"And she's my girl."

Seb hesitates. "You sure?"

"Yeah." I nod. "I'm sure."

They start gathering their things. Andres is the first to step out the front door, muttering something about glue still being in his hair.

Anna kisses my cheek on her way past and whispers, "Take care of her."

"I always do."

Nathan lingers the longest, arms crossed over his chest. He gives me one of those long, assessing looks. Finally, he nods, murmurs, "Good man," and follows the rest out.

The house quiets. I sit on the edge of the couch, elbows on my knees, watching the stairs, waiting to magically have the answers I need. I don't know exactly what Nico said, but I know Analyse, and I know the look in her eyes well enough to recognize old pain when it's been freshly scraped open.

To no surprise of mine, he fucked up.

The first time I met the guy was when he came rolling back into town like everyone's been waiting on him with bated breath. And I saw right through him. I could see what he was really after by coming back. I was hoping I was wrong. I was hoping that I was just being cynical. Maya deserves so much fucking better. Analyse deserves better.

I don't hate people. I don't usually care enough for anyone to elicit hate in me. But I hate that motherfucker. The urge to run out of this house and wrap my hands around his neck is great, but I know that isn't what's right for Analyse and Maya. That isn't what they need. They need me.

So here I am. Sitting here, waiting. Because I will never turn my back on them. No matter how hard she wants to push me away right now. I will never be him. I will never hurt them.

When she finally comes downstairs, her steps are slower. Controlled. Her face is blank, but not unreadable. Not to me, at least. I see the glimmer in her eyes, the tight set of her jaw. She halts when she sees me.

"You're still here," she says quietly, surprise written all over her face.

"Of course, I'm here."

"I thought maybe..." She gestures vaguely toward the door, not finishing.

"I'm not going anywhere."

Her lips press into a line. She walks into the kitchen and starts stacking mugs. I follow her, leaning against the counter across from her. She won't look at me.

"Lyse."

"Yeah," she says as she continues to clean the mess surrounding us.

"Look at me."

She looks up at me with those big brown eyes, and the pain I see within them tears my heart clean apart.

"He's leaving town," she says after a beat.

I don't say anything. I just wait for her to let it all out.

She sets down the last mug and finally turns toward me, tears beginning to slip from her lashes. She folds in on herself, body curling inward as she breaks down in front of me. I'm there in an instant, pulling her into my arms. Her hands clutch at my hoodie as she sobs into my chest.

"I don't get it," she chokes out. "I don't know how he could walk away from her. From this. From everything."

"I know," I murmur, stroking her hair, holding her close. "I know."

We stay like that until her breathing slows, until the trembling eases just a little. When she finally pulls back, her face is blotchy, eyes red, and still the most beautiful woman in the world.

"Nico's gone," she says again, voice hollow. "So we can

break up now. We'll tell everyone we tried but realized we're better off as friends."

I blink. "Is that what you want, Lyse? To be just friends?"

She hesitates then says, "We were always supposed to end, Mateo. That was the deal."

"That's now what I asked."

Her jaw tightens. "I'm not sure what you want me to say."

"How about the truth?"

"I don't know what the truth is, Mateo. I don't know!" Her voice cracks. "I'm confused, dammit. I thought I had it figured out. I thought I knew what I was doing, and now I don't think I know anything."

I take a step closer. "So how about I give you a truth then, Lyse."

She doesn't move, doesn't speak, she just stands there, staring. She has no idea. I'm not letting her go. Not like this. Not ever. Not unless she really doesn't want me. Not unless she really doesn't want us.

"I remember the first time I ever laid my eyes on you," I say, my voice low. "You were twenty-four. Pregnant. And scared out of your damn mind on how your life was about to change. You walked into the firehouse like a storm—wearing this yellow sundress covered in tiny white daisies, your long curly hair was wild and frizzing from the summer heat."

She blinks fast, her lips parting, like she remembers too.

"You came in with fire in your eyes, demanding that Seb take you to the next town over because you were craving candied apples. You didn't even say hi to the rest of us...you were on a mission." I huff a quiet laugh. "Everyone else thought it was funny. I couldn't stop staring."

I pause, just for a second, my voice catching before I go on.

"You looked...tired. Overwhelmed. But underneath it all, you radiated something I didn't have words for yet. You were scared—anyone could see it—but what I saw first, what hit me like a punch to the chest, was your strength. How sure you were that even if you had to do it all alone, you were still going to do it."

Her arms fold over her chest, holding herself together.

"I didn't know you, not yet, but something about you pulled at me. Like gravity. You were this force, Lyse. A magnet. And I felt it from the jump. I felt it in my gut. That I needed to know you. That I wanted to be near you, even if I didn't understand why."

She looks down, a tear falling before she can swipe it away.

"And from that moment on, I made a choice—even if I didn't realize it then—that I would show up for you in whatever way I could. However you needed. Because even when you were a stranger in a sundress with nothing but fierce words and tired eyes, I knew you mattered. I didn't have all the details. I didn't need them. I just knew."

I take another step, slowly, not wanting to spook her.

"I didn't know what it meant then, but I know now. I know that I was meant to love you. I was meant to love both of you. I've spent every day since getting closer to that truth."

"Mateo..."

"No. Let me finish."

She goes quiet again, tears slipping down her cheeks.

"I don't care how scared you are, how many walls you try to build, or how hard you try to push me away—I'm not going anywhere. You can tell yourself this is temporary, that we were always meant to be some short-lived thing, but you and I both know that's not true. I know you feel the same way I do, even if it terrifies you. Even if saying it out loud makes it more real than you're ready for."

I take a breath, steadying my voice. "What we have, this thing between us, it's not perfect. It's messy. It's layered with history and heartache and baggage neither of us asked for. But it's real. God, Lyse, it's so real. And it's ours. You feel it. I know you do."

I reach out and brush a tear from her cheek.

"I'm not giving up on you. I'm not giving up on us. I'm going to show you that I'm here, that I'm in this for the long haul. Because I love you, Lyse. I love you so damn much."

Her breath hitches.

"I love you so much that if you told me you wanted space, I'd give it to you. If you told me you needed time, I'd wait forever. But if you're standing here trying to convince yourself that you don't love me back? That we were always supposed to end? That this doesn't mean everything?" I shake my head. "Then I'm calling bullshit."

She covers her mouth, shoulders shaking.

"I know you're scared," I say, softer now. "Hell, I am, too. You've been through a lot, and I'd never fault you for protecting your heart. But don't pretend this isn't real just because it's easier to run. Don't lie to yourself because it hurts less than letting someone in."

I move closer, giving her space to pull away...but she doesn't.

"You don't have to say anything. Not tonight. Not tomorrow. But I need you to hear this."

I rest a hand over my heart. "If I really believed, for even a second, that you didn't want me...that you needed me gone to be okay? I'd walk out that door and never come back. Because I love you that much, Lyse. I'd do it in a heartbeat."

A pause. Her breath is shallow, her eyes locked on mine.

"But that's not what you want. I know it. You know it. You're scared, not indifferent. And I can work with scared. I can meet you in the middle of it. I can sit in it with you every damn day until the fear quiets enough for the love to speak louder."

She presses a hand to her chest, like trying to hold something in.

"So go ahead," I say. "Build your walls. Push me away. Slam every door you think you need to. I'll still be here. Every time. I'll keep showing up. Until the day you let yourself believe what I already know."

I step even closer now, until we're just a breath apart.

"I'm gonna go home tonight," I tell her gently. "Give you space so that you can go upstairs, take a hot bath, and listen to one of those podcasts you love so much."

Her lips twitch, almost like a smile.

"Do whatever you need to do to feel like yourself again. I mean it."

I let a beat pass, watching her carefully. "But I'll be back, chula. I'll always come back."

I press a quick kiss to her forehead, then I step back, letting my hand trail down her arm before I turn around and walk toward the door. I walk out into the quiet night, the cold nipping at my skin, and close the door gently behind me.

Hope hums in my chest like a steady flame—because I meant every word. I'll keep showing up. I'll keep loving her through the fear, the silence, the uncertainty. I'll keep choosing her, over and over again...until the day she chooses me too.

Chapter Twenty-Six

ANALYSE

I wake up before Maya this morning. The house is still and quiet, the kind of precious silence that only exists right before the sun comes up. I slip out of bed, careful not to make a sound, and pad to the window.

Pulling back the curtain, I look out across the town. A fresh layer of snow blankets everything—rooftops, trees, streets. The sunrise is just beginning to stretch its light across the horizon, casting everything in soft gold and pale pink. It's the kind of morning that looks like peace. Like possibility.

But inside me? It's the opposite.

My chest feels tight. My thoughts, heavy. I press my forehead against the cool glass, hoping the chill might ground me, wake something up in me. Because no matter how beautiful it looks out there, I can't feel it. Not really.

Outside, it's serene. Magical even. Inside me, everything is gray. Dull. Heavy. Ugly. I wish I could match the beauty outside. I wish I could feel even a fraction of that brightness in my bones. But right now, all I feel is hollow.

The snow outside is pristine. Untouched. Not yet ruined by muddy boots or tire tracks. I wish I could say the same about my heart. I wish I could say the same about Maya's. Because I don't just have to worry about protecting myself. I have to protect her, too. And I'm so fucking scared I'm going to mess this up.

I rest my forehead against the cold window and close my eyes. My breath fogs the glass, and for a second, I pretend I'm somewhere else. Somewhere quiet. Somewhere easy. Somewhere I don't feel this pressure clenching around my chest.

When I found out I was pregnant, I thought the scariest part would be the birth. Or the money. Or the long nights. It wasn't. The scariest part has always been how much I love her. How much she means to me. How much I would give up, walk away from, or burn to the ground if it meant she would be okay.

Nico's goodbye...it wasn't even a real one. It was a tantrum. He never came for Maya. Not really. He came because he thought he still had a shot at me. And when he realized he didn't, when he saw Mateo standing there, in my kitchen, with love in his eyes, he left.

And now I'm left with the aftermath. Left with the broken pieces of a little girl who's going to start asking questions I'm not sure how to answer.

Where's my dad?
Why did he leave?
Did he not want me?
And worst of all: *Was it my fault?*

I wrap my arounds myself tightly, my fingernails digging into the sleeves of my sweater. I've spent Maya's whole life trying to protect her from that kind of pain. From that kind of abandonment. It was easier before she met him; I was all she ever knew. Now she's older. Now she knows who he is. And now I can't stop the pain that comes with his departure.

And then there's Mateo. The truth is, I trust Mateo. I do. I trust him with myself in ways I didn't think I'd ever trust anyone again. But this is bigger than me. It's her, too. I press the heel of my palm into my chest, trying to steady my breath. I think of Mateo's hand, steady on my face.

"So go ahead. Build your walls. Push me away. Slam every door you think you need to. I'll still be here. Every time. I'll keep showing up. Until the day you let yourself believe what I already know.

"I'll be back, chula. I'll always come back."

I want to believe him so badly. But the last time I believed someone's promise, it wasn't just my heart that shattered—it was Maya's future that got rewritten. The consequences of my trust don't fall on just me anymore. And maybe that's what's really breaking me.

Because even though every instinct is telling me to run, to shut it all down, to build walls so high no one can get in...I don't want to. I want Mateo. I want him to keep showing up. But I'm terrified that wanting him will one day hurt Maya. And I don't know if I could survive that kind of regret. I don't know if I could ever forgive myself.

I grab my phone from the nightstand and unlock the screen. I open the group chat and fire off a message.

ANALYSE

Can we met up?

The three dots appear instantly.

MARI

Oh my god, Lyse. I'm so glad you reached out. I hope you're okay. Absolutely, I'm free.

ANNA

Here for you, babe! Name the time and I'll be there.

I swallow the lump in my throat, blinking against the sting

in my eyes. I don't know what I'm going to say. But I need them. I need my girls.

ANALYSE

The Rolling Pin? In an hour? I'll get a sitter for Maya.

MARI

Done. Love you.

ANNA

We've got you. Always.

I walk into The Rolling Pin and immediately inhale the comforting scent of pastelillos, warm sugar, and fresh coffee. Mari looks up from the corner booth, already standing before I can blink. Anna's beside her, both of them bundled in thick winter sweaters. Mari rushes toward me and wraps her arms around me so tightly that my knees nearly buckle.

"I've got you," she whispers into my hair.

My throat burns. I nod, but I can't speak.

Anna joins in seconds later, arms looping around both of us. "We've got you," she says softly.

When we finally pull back, I manage a small smile. "I'm sorry for the dramatic text."

"Stop," Mari says, brushing a strand of hair from my face. "You don't ever have to apologize for needing us."

We slide into the booth, Mari on my left, Anna on my right, our knees bumping under the table. The table already has a plate filled with meat and cheese pastelillos, three cups of café con leche, and flan. I grab a pastelillo and tear off a corner, but the knot in my stomach makes it hard to swallow. The flakiness melts on my tongue, the savory meat and cheese warm and familiar, but nothing quiets the storm churning inside me.

Mari pours more coffee into our mugs from the carafe she brought over and gives me a pointed look. "You look like you haven't slept."

"I haven't." My voice comes out thin, like it's been wrung out overnight. "I can't stop thinking."

Anna places a hand on my leg. "Then think out loud. Let us carry some of it with you."

I blink down at the pastelillo in my hand, the golden crumbs scattered on the plate below. I don't even know where to begin.

"I keep thinking about what Maya's going to ask," I whisper. "What am I supposed to tell her?"

Mari leans forward. "You don't have to tell her everything, Lyse. She's still little."

"She's not stupid," I say. "She's not going to forget he was here. She's not going to forget he asked to see her and then disappeared again. She's going to ask why he left."

Anna frowns. "Then you tell her the truth. That he made a mistake. That he didn't know how to stay. But that you did. You stayed. You always stayed."

"It's not just that," I murmur. "It's not just Nico."

They both go quiet, waiting.

"I'm scared of letting someone else in again," I admit. "Of trusting someone with my heart. Of trusting someone with Maya's."

Mari reaches for my hand, squeezing gently. "Of course, you're scared. You're a mom. You've been through hell and still show up every single day with love to give."

Anna leans in, voice softer now. "But, Lyse...Mateo isn't Nico."

"I know that," I whisper. "I do. It's just—there's something else."

CHAPTER TWENTY-SIX

They both freeze, eyes locking in on mine.

"I need to tell you something. And I need you to not freak out."

Mari raises a brow. "You know that's never worked on us, right?"

Anna folds her arms. "Spill."

I suck in a breath. "Mateo and I...we weren't actually together when we first said we were."

They blink. Simultaneously.

"We started out fake dating."

Mari's mouth drops open. "I'm sorry...what?"

Anna gasps. "Like a Hallmark movie fake dating?"

"Yes," I groan, covering my face with my hands. "Like a damn rom-com. Nico came back. Mateo offered to help me keep him at arm's length, and it just kind of...snowballed."

Mari stares at me like I've grown a second head. "Wait, so that whole thing—pumpkin patch, Christmas mistletoe, movie nights—that was all fake?"

I shake my head. "No. That's the thing. At first, it was just a favor. A setup. But somewhere along the line, it stopped feeling fake. It became...real. Too real. And that's what scares me the most."

Anna exhales, sitting back. "Holy shit. That's why you've been so hesitant. You didn't just fall for him...you weren't supposed to fall for him."

Tears sting my eyes. "It wasn't supposed to happen. I didn't mean for it to. But he was just...there. For everything. For me. For Maya. And he didn't treat it like an act. Not even for a second."

Mari's expression softens. "Because it wasn't. Not for him."

I look down, heart thudding. "I think I'm in love with him."

Anna lets out a choked laugh. "Ya think?"

"I'm serious," I say, voice cracking. "And that's what's breaking me. Because I know how it feels to be left. I know how it feels to be the only standing in the wreckage. And If I left him in and it falls apart...Maya's heart breaks with mine. I'm not just scared for me. I'm scared for her."

Mari nods, brushing a tear from her own cheek. "That's fair, Lyse. It is. But you're not that twenty-four-year-old anymore, trying to survive on your own. You've built a life. You've built a village. And Mateo is part of that village. He chose you long before he ever said it out loud."

Anna places her hand over mine. "So you get to be scared. But don't let that fear keep you from something real. Don't teach Maya that love is something you run from just because it might hurt."

"She's already lost one parent," I whisper. "I just want to protect her."

"You are," Mari says. "Every time you show her what love looks like, you are."

By the time I pull up to Hilda's house, my eyes feel dry and tight from holding in everything I didn't say. I take a deep breath, paste on a soft smile, and walk up the steps. Hilda opens the door before I even knock, Maya already bundled up in her puffy pink coat, hat slightly crooked.

"She's all yours," Hilda says with a warm smile. "And full of cookies."

Maya twirls dramatically on the porch. "I had three!"

I laugh. "I'm shocked you didn't negotiate for five."

"I tried," she says with a grin, wrapping her arms around my waist.

I thank Hilda and promise to bring her some pastelillos from The Rolling Pin later in the week before helping Maya in the car. She climbs into her booster seat, humming to herself until she notices the two large boxes beside her, one covered in a blue snowflake patterned wrapping paper, the other a plain white storage bin.

"What are these for, Mami?" she asks, poking the edge of the wrapping paper curiously.

"They're for the school," I say, buckling her in.

"But it's Sunday," she points out, confusion furrowing her little brows.

I start the engine and glance at her in the rearview mirror. "I know. But I want to redecorate the classroom before my kids come back from winter break. I thought I'd get a head start."

She tilts her head. "Why? Did they not like the decorations before?"

I smile. "It's not that. I just want them to come back to something fresh. Something fun. New year, new energy."

Maya seems to think about that for a second, then nods solemnly. "That makes sense. Can I help?"

"Of course, you can."

She looks out the window for a beat, then her voice softens. "Are we going to see Mateo today?"

The question lands like a soft knock on my chest. I keep my eyes on the road. "Not today, mamita."

"Oh," she says quietly. "Okay."

The silence stretches for a few seconds.

Then she asks, "But maybe soon?"

I swallow. "Maybe," I whisper.

Chapter Twenty-Seven

ANALYSE

I pull into the familiar parking lot, the tires crunching over a thin layer of freshly fallen snow. It's completely empty except for my car, a quiet reminder that it's Sunday and no one else is here. I shift into park, take a deep breath, and glance in the rearview mirror, seeing Maya bundled up like a marshmallow in her oversize pink puff coat.

The cold bites at my cheeks the moment I step out. Snow crunches beneath my boots with every step as I lift the large white storage bin from the backseat. Behind me, Maya struggles to carry a box wrapped in shiny blue snowflake paper, her little arms barely managing to keep it balanced. The box wobbles, but she keeps going, her coat rustling with every determined step.

"Careful with that, mamita," I say gently. "It's mostly paper in there, but I don't want anything to rip."

"I've got it, Mami," she grunts, arms wrapped around the sides. "I'm strong."

I smile. "That you are, sweetheart."

We head for the side entrance, the one closest to my classroom. The building looms quiet and still, the usual weekday buzz replaced by a rare kind of hush that only exists when the world hasn't quite woken up.

Most teachers prefer Saturdays for catching up or setting up their classrooms, but I've always been partial to Sundays. There's something sacred about the silence—the way the hallways feel wider, the fluorescent lights softer, the echo of our footsteps a gentle metronome in the stillness. It's the kind of quiet that helps me think, the kind that settles the noise in my mind and lets me breathe deeper.

We push through the heavy side doors, and a blast of cold air greets us, our breaths rising in soft white puffs that vanish into the dim hallway. The heating hasn't kicked in yet—no surprise there. The ancient system is supposed to activate when the building senses movement, but on weekends, it usually needs a little coaxing. Right now, the air is sharp enough to sting my nose.

The janitor's office is dark, the door shut tight with no flicker of light beneath it. The corridors are half-lit, overhead fluorescents flickering weakly, casting long shadows that stretch across the tile. Only a few bulbs are on, buzzing faintly like they're as reluctant to be awake as the rest of the world.

There's no background noise—no chorus of sneakers squeaking on waxed floors, no lockers slamming, no laughter echoing down the halls. Just the sound of our footsteps, mine steady and Maya's a quick, bouncing rhythm behind me.

I shift the white bin in my arms and fumble for my keys, the metal cold against my fingers as I unlock my classroom door. It sticks slightly before swinging open, and Maya wiggles past me with her box and a puff of determination. She makes it to the first table and sets it down with a sigh of victory then beams up at me, proud of her strength.

The classroom feels like it's been holding its breath over break. The gingerbread cut-outs still cling to the window-panes, faded slightly at the edges. A slightly lopsided *Happy*

Holidays banner is still taped above the whiteboard, and paper snowflakes—some symmetrical, others charmingly crooked—decorate the walls. Each one a reminder of the busy hands and bright energy that filled this space just a few weeks ago. The room smells faintly of peppermint-scented sanitizer and dry erase markers, an odd but oddly comforting mix.

I lower the storage bin to the floor with a soft thud then slip off my coat, the warmth of the movement already starting to ease the chill from my bones.

"This is going to be our little winter refresh," I say as I crouch beside the bin and flip the lid open. "New bulletin board borders, snowman crafts, a cozy rug for the reading corner, and a few new book displays. Fresh start for the new year."

Maya's face lights up with excitement. "Can I do the snowman ones?"

"Absolutely," I say with a smile, handing her a Ziploc bag filled with foam shapes, construction papers, googly eyes, and buttons. "Go sit at the reading table, I'll grab your snack."

She clutches the bag and skips to the reading corner, where the little rug waits. She drops cross-legged onto it with ease and starts pulling out supplies, already humming a tune under her breath—something cheerful and familiar.

I unzip her lunchbox and pull out a juice box and a foil-wrapped sandwich. "Here you go," I say, bringing it to her.

"Thanks, Mami," she says, unwrapping it quickly and taking a bite like she hasn't eaten in hours. My little drama queen.

As she munches, she spreads the snowman pieces out across the rug, arranging them with an intense concentration she surely gets from me. I watch her for a moment—so content, so creative—and feel something warm settle in my chest. This moment is exactly what I needed after the chaos from last night. Just the two of us.

Chapter Twenty-Eight

But somewhere deep in the building—on the opposite end, where the art room sits empty and dark—something flickers.

It started earlier.

A frayed extension cord, plugged into the wall beneath a table full of leftover holiday crafts, sparks once...twice...and then catches.

The paper angels go first.

They curl inward like dying leaves, edges blackening before bursting into flame. The fire eats quietly at first—small, licking, almost gentle. But it's greedy. The art room is a nest of kindling. Cardboard dioramas, dried-out tempera paints, brittle paper mache, stacked boxes of forgotten supplies.

Flames crawl across the floor like fingers, dragging heat in their wake. A glue bottle bubbles. A poster curls. Plastic beads melt into the tile.

The blaze swells, growing louder now—snapping, cracking, feeding on air, on glue, on paper. The room glows with it, pulsing orange against the dark.

Just a few feet away, the janitor's closet ticks with quiet, flammable promise. Bottles of cleaner. Ammonia. Bleach. Industrial chemicals sealed tight...but not tight enough.

The fire finds it all.

There's a hiss. A small pop. Then a bloom of heat like breath exhaled through a dragon's mouth.

And the school is empty.

No alarm blares.

No sprinklers activate.

No one sees it.

Chapter Twenty-Nine
ANALYSE

It's only twenty minutes later, when I'm stapling a *Welcome Back!* banner onto the bulletin board, that I hear it.

A faint creaking above me—metal groaning, shifting. Then a low whooshing from the hallway vents, like a heavy breath being exhaled. Then—

"Mami?"

I turn.

Maya stands in the doorway of the classroom, her sandwich forgotten on the table behind her. Her pink coat hangs off one shoulder, and her voice is small—tight with something she can't name yet.

"It smells funny."

My stomach dips. "What kind of funny?"

She wrinkles her nose, hesitating. "Like...burnt marshmallows. But not good ones."

I cross the room fast, adrenaline already building. I don't wait to question it. The moment I crack the door open, it hits me. Smoke. Thick. Acrid.

It slams into my face like a wall—hot, chemical. Choking.

It doesn't smell like marshmallows. It smells like burning plastic. Melting wires. Panic.

"Maya," I say, sharp and loud now. "Back up. Go to the desk. Now."

Her eyes go wide. She stumbles back, obedient and scared, her little hands clutching at the edge of her coat. She's crying now, silent tears slipping down her cheeks.

I step into the hallway—just enough to look.

The smoke is everywhere, pouring from the east corridor like a living thing. Low to the ground at first, but rising, swirling. I can't see flames, but I can feel them—somewhere close, too close. My classroom is down the far opposite wing, but I can already tell...it's spreading fast.

Too fast.

No alarm.

No flashing lights.

No intercom, no alert, nothing.

Just smoke.

I stumble back inside and shove the door shut, coughing hard, chest already burning. The seal won't hold long, but it's something.

"Maya," I gasp, grabbing the water bottle from her desk and pushing it into her hands. "Small sips. Go sit under the teacher desk, okay? You need to get low. Stay low."

She nods, lips trembling, her breath coming out in shallow hiccups. "I'm scared."

"I know, baby. Me too. But I'm right here."

I turn to grab my phone and keys, heart hammering, hands shaking. I knock over the storage bin. Markers roll across the floor. My phone slips beneath the metal supply shelf. Shit.

I drop to my knees, groping blindly in the shadows, my fingers scraping cold tile, the edges of forgotten pencils, a dust bunny, nothing. My lungs scream as I suck in another breath that tastes like burning plastic and fear.

Behind me, something shifts in the walls. A sudden thud. Then a howl through the ventilation system, a roar that sounds almost a live, like the building itself is exhaling fire.

The heat is coming. Fast.

Chapter Thirty

MATEO

Sundays at the station are usually slow. There's something special about them—the quiet, the routine, the stillness that settles in like a warm blanket. No drills. No sirens. Just coffee, bullshitting, and the occasional grocery run.

Today's one of those days.

Seb and Andres are arguing at the kitchen table...again. Something about how Andres put way too much hot sauce in the breakfast scramble.

"You dumped half the bottle in there," Seb says, jabbing his fork in accusation. "That's sabotage. No one needs that much damn hot sauce. Especially not in their eggs!"

"It's called flavor," Andres fires back. "Sorry your taste buds are basic."

Cap has retreated to his office with a mug and noise-cancelling earbuds, pretending not to hear the chaos. He absolutely can. He just knows better than to get in the middle of it.

I lean back in my chair, stretching. My spine pops. "If it stays this quiet, I might finally finish that book Analyse lent me."

Seb immediately stops chewing and glares at me. "You did not just say that out loud."

"What?" I grin.

"You *never* say that. That's like asking for all hell to break loose."

"Seriously," Andres adds, pointing at me. "You just cursed us, bro. That's Firefighter 101. You never say it's quiet."

"I said *if* it stays quiet," I counter, but even I can feel the shift in the air. It's like the universe just held its breath.

And then it hits.

The station alarm blasts through the walls, and dispatch crackles overhead:

"Structure fire reported. Lake City Elementary School. Flames visible from the east wing."

We're up in an instant.

"The elementary school?" Andres asks, face tightening.

"On a Sunday?" I say, already moving.

Gear on. Boots pounding the floor. Adrenaline slamming through my system. Cap's already at the rig when we hit the bay.

"Confirmed," he says, climbing in. "Smoke's visible from blocks away. This isn't a false alarm."

"Hopefully," Nathan replies, grim.

We're on the road in seconds, sirens slicing through still air. Snow clings to the sidewalks. The sky is dull gray. Everything outside feels undisturbed, like the city hasn't caught up to what we already know...something's burning. Bad.

I tighten my grip on the edge of my seat. My fingers drum against my leg. I don't know why, but something about this one feels off. Wrong in a way I can't quite name.

When we turn onto the school's block, the answer hits like a punch to the chest. The east wing of Lake City Elementary is on fire.

Not just smoke or a small blaze. No. The entire section is

engulfed. Flames ripping out of shattered windows, dancing across the rooftop like they own the place. Black smoke coils into the sky like its job is to block out the sun. The heat is visible from the street, warping the air above the building.

My stomach drops.

We pull up and jump out. The heat slams into us even through our gear, blistering and immediate.

Cap doesn't hesitate. "Engine Three—hydrant hookup. Ladder One, get eyes on the roof. Mateo, take Crew B and flank right. We stop this from crossing into the center corridor. Now."

"Copy that," I say, tightening my straps and yanking my mask into place.

We move fast. The kind of fast that's second nature, muscle memory forged from hours of drills and dozens of calls. I lead the team around the side of the building, where the fire is curling up along the brick like it's trying to claw its way inside.

I pause for just a second, scanning the windows.

Through broken glass, I spot a row of classroom posters curling inward, melting like they're crying. Bright colors—dinosaurs, letters, a crooked calendar—blistering into black. A single paper snowflake tumbles from the top corner and disintegrates before it hits the ground. There's something about it that guts me. Innocence turned to ash.

"Water on!" Seb yells behind me.

We direct the line toward a vent that's hissing smoke. The fire's pushing hard—angry and fast. Seb and I sweep low, hitting the edge of the blaze as it tries to creep along the building's outer wall.

"Pressure coming up!" someone shouts, and the hose line jumps in my hands. Steam explodes where water meets flame, turning the air into a thick, blinding fog.

Still, the fire climbs. Faster. Higher.

The smoke coming out of the vent pulses, like it's being exhaled by something alive. It billows in waves, too heavy, too dark. Inside that smoke, for just a second, I swear I hear something.

A faint clatter? A soft, distant thud? Or maybe I imagined it.

"Cap, fire's in the vents," I radio. "We're keeping it from breaching the corridor, but this things aggressive. Like...it's looking for fuel."

"Copy," Nathan says. "Hold position. Don't breach entry until interior crews give the green light."

"Roger that," I reply, but I can't shake the itch in the back of my neck.

I glance at the lot. Empty. Snow untouched. A perfect sheet of white stretching from the sidewalk to the front doors, still and undisturbed like a painting. Not even the imprint of a bird or the scuff of a tire. Just blank, quiet stillness.

Too quiet. No janitor's car. No delivery truck. No set of footprints leading toward the side entrance where the staff usually sneaks in early. Nothing but ash dancing across the snowbanks like burnt confetti.

And even though it's Sunday, even though I know no one is ever here on a Sunday, that silence sits wrong in my ears. It hums behind the roar of flame and scream of sirens, a silence that doesn't belong.

The building groans, a low, warping sound that vibrates through the ground beneath my boots. Somewhere to my left, glass shatters. The heat pulses outward again like a second heartbeat, like the fire's alive and breathing. Every instinct I have flares, sharp and urgent.

I shift my weight and look up at the jagged window nearest us. Smoke is pouring out of it now in thick, heavy streams.

I blink hard, wipe my glove across the lens of my mask. Nothing but smoke. Still...I can't shake this feeling.

Not with the way the windows are cracked wide like a scream frozen in place. Not with the way the wind carries the fire's heat but not a single sound from inside. Not with this pressure in my chest, tight and crawling like something inside me knows before my brain does.

Because sometimes it's not what you see. It's what you feel. And right now, everything in me is screaming: Something inside that building is wrong.

Chapter Thirty-One

ANALYSE

S tay calm.

That's the only thing repeating in my head, over and over again, even as the smoke thickens and the classroom starts to feel like it's shrinking. The air is no longer just heavy—it's sharp, bitter, invasive. Each breath feels like swallowing splinters. My lungs ache. My eyes sting.

The door is no longer keeping the hallway sealed off. Smoke curls in through the edges, low to the ground, creeping like it has a purpose. Like it knows where we are.

Maya is crouched under the teacher's desk, knees pulled to her chest, hugging her water bottle like it's her last tether to safety. My sweet baby girl. Her face is pale beneath the soot smudges, her eyes wide, too wide for a little girl. But she hasn't screamed. She hasn't panicked. She's just watching me.

"You're doing so good, mamita," I say as gently as I can, forcing steadiness into my voice even as my throat burns. "I promise I'm going to get us out."

She nods, her lower lip trembling. My strong, brave girl.

I drop to my knees, coughing. The smoke's getting worse by the second, clouding my vision and clogging my throat. I squint under the shelf where my phone is, but the haze has swallowed everything.

I can't waste time. I push up, dizzy from the sudden movement.

"Maya," I call out, crossing the room, knees shaking. "Come here, mi amor. We're leaving."

She climbs into my arms without hesitation, trusting me completely. Her little hands clasp around my neck, and I feel her heartbeat pounding against my chest. Too fast. I'm sure mine is no better.

I hoist her higher, pain blooming across my back, and stumble toward the door. The second I crack it open, the hallway answers.

A wall of heat slams into us—fast, wild, suffocating. The hallway is no longer just smoky...it's hell. Orange light pulses through thick haze, and deep above us, something groans. Then cracks. Then gives.

A support beam crashes down without warning. A thunderclap of wood and steal and heat. Instinct takes over. I twist my body, shoving Maya toward the floor and throwing myself after her. Pain explodes through my left leg.

The impact is blinding, a bolt of lightning through bone. The beam slams just below my knee with the force of a truck, crushing everything beneath it. I hear something snap. Maybe me. Maybe the beam. I can't tell.

The pain is too much. My scream stays trapped in my throat. I can't breathe. Can't move.

Maya is sobbing beside me, reaching for me. I hear her voice through the ringing in my ears, but I can't focus on what she's saying.

My vision swims. I blink hard. I need to move. Now.

"Mami?" she whimpers.

"I'm okay," I lie. "I'm okay, mi amor."

I can't put weight on my leg, can barely crawl, but I have

to. My arms lock around her, dragging her back inside with everything I have left. My fingers scrape the tile. I can't feel my left foot. The fire behind us roars louder. The door is wide open. Smoke pours in like it's chasing us.

I spot the bookshelf, wedge my body up against it, and heave. It's heavy, too heavy with my leg screaming in agony, but I shove it into the doorway until it catches the warped frame. It won't close completely. It's not a seal. But it's better than nothing.

Then I collapse.

My body crumples to the floor, breath hitching in broken gasps. My throat is raw. The taste of ash is everywhere. My jeans are soaked with blood. I don't dare look at the wound.

Maya crouches beside me, tears streaking through the soot on her cheeks. Her tiny hand lands on my cheek. "Mami, you're bleeding."

"I know," I rasp. My voice doesn't sound like mine. "But I'm okay. Just need to rest for a second."

The edges of the classroom blur. There's not much light left, just the flickering red orange of the fire pressing against the walls outside. I glance toward the supply shelf, just barely visible through the haze. My phone is stuck under there. No way I'm reaching it now.

I close my eyes for half a second. My head drops back against the wall. My lungs feel like they've shrunk. My whole body trembles. Maya shifts beside me.

"You dropped your phone," she says softly.

"I know, baby," I cough. "I can't get it."

She's quiet. Then asks, "Can I try?"

Every instinct in me screams no. I want to pull her to me and never let her out of my arms. But I can't. We don't have time for giving up. We need help.

"Stay low," I whisper. "Crawl on your belly. Try to reach under the shelf. But only if you can do it quick."

She nods and moves fast, flattening herself to the ground, arms outstretched, her little face set with focus I didn't know such a small child could wear. My heart is pounding so loud I can barely hear anything else. She disappears behind the haze.

"Maya?" I call.

Then her voice cuts through. "Got it!"

She scurries back toward me, coughing, holding the phone tightly. "What do I do?"

"I need you to call 911," I say, wincing as I shift to a half sit. "Tell them where we are. Tell them I'm hurt."

She nods, lips trembling, and presses the emergency button. One ring. Two.

Then a voice. "911, what's your emergency?"

"My name is Maya Garcia," she says, her voice trembling. "I'm at Lake City Elementary School with my mommy. There's a fire, and she's hurt. We're trapped in her classroom. Room twenty-four."

The dispatcher's tone is calm, steady. "Maya, you're doing great. Is your mommy awake?"

"She's awake, but her leg is really hurt and she can't walk. The fire knocked something down and it hit her."

"You're being so brave. Can you tell me if the door is closed?"

"It's kind of closed," she says. "But smoke is still coming in."

"You're doing amazing, Maya. I'm sending help now. I'm going to stay on the phone with you, okay? Can you both stay low to the ground and try to breathe slowly?"

Maya nods and lowers the phone like she's been trained her whole life for this. "She says to stay low. And breathe slowly."

"You did perfect," I whisper, tears burning hot as I pull her into my arms. "You were so brave, mi amor."

She presses her face into my neck, still shaking, still

holding the phone as the dispatcher's voice continues to murmur on speaker. I wrap my arms around her and press my forehead to hers.

We're not out of danger. Not yet. Not even close. But someone knows we're here. And God, I'm hoping that might be enough.

Chapter Thirty-Two

MATEO

The smoke hasn't let up.

It keeps pouring from the east side of the building like the school itself is exhaling its last breath. Every few seconds, there's a new groan, a new crack, a new warning deep inside the structure that it's only a matter of time before something gives.

We've managed to hold the fire back from the central corridor...barely. It's a patchwork of soaked drywall and scorched tile, a barricade of desperate effort and luck that could fail at any second.

I swipe a hand across my brow, adjust my mask. The hallway ahead of us is warped with heat, air shimmering above the floor. It smells like burning paper, plastic, and glue...like a school turning to ash.

The structure's groaning more now. Louder. Closer. Everything sounds strained, like the building is holding its breath for the final blow. One bad shift and this whole damn wing is coming down.

I bark directions to the crew—check the corner duct, reinforce the east pressure line. Everyone moves quickly, in perfect synchronicity. We all know the rhythm. Fire pushes, we push harder.

It's chaos. But it's controlled. We've got this. That's all I think...until I see the look on the firefighter sprinting across the lot toward command. He's young. Pale under the soot. Eyes wide, not just fear, but panic. And not the kind of panic that comes from smoke or flame. This is something else. Something bigger. Something worse.

He doesn't even stop to catch his breath. "Captain...we've got a problem."

Nathan doesn't look up from the incident map he's yelling into. His voice is clipped. "Yeah, I know. The building's falling apart. We've got active flames in three corridors and a roof about to give."

"No," the guy blurts out, cutting him off. "It's worse. Dispatch just called it in. A 911 call came from inside the building. A little girl. She said her mom's hurt. She said they were decorating a classroom and got trapped."

Nathan's head jerks up. The words hit like a hammer. A classroom. A little girl. My stomach drops.

"Was the girl's name Maya?" I ask, but I already know.

The firefighter nods. "Yeah. Maya Garcia."

And that's it. My body moves before I can think. I lunge forward, boots already hitting pavement. The world narrows to a single point: that building. That smoke. That little girl.

"Mateo!" Nathan's voice explodes behind me. "Don't you fucking go in there!"

But I'm already gone. I make it five steps before Seb charges up beside me.

"That's my niece," he pants. "My sister's in there." His voice cracks, panic bleeding through every word. He doesn't even look at me, his eyes are locked on the flames like he's ready to throw himself into them.

I reach for him. "Seb—"

But I don't get a chance to say more. Two firefighters from Ladder One slam in from the side, grabbing Seb before he can take another step.

"Sebastian, no!" one of them yells. "You're not cleared for entry!"

He thrashes in their hold, kicking, twisting, teeth bared like a man possessed. "That's my family in there! Let me go!"

I turn to run, but Andres is suddenly in front of me—arms out, blocking my path. "Bro, no. Just stop a second. Think."

"Move," I snap, trying to shove past, but he grabs me, arms locking around my torso. "Andres, don't—"

"Mateo, please," he says. "Cap gave a direct order—"

"There's no time!" I bark. "She's just a kid, Andres. She's just a kid. Analyse is hurt. And Maya, my Maya, called from inside that fucking fire. We don't have minutes—we barely have seconds!"

Behind us, Seb roars, fighting harder against the fire-fighters holding him back. "Then let him go! You let Mateo go! He can get to them!"

Andres falters, just a beat. His grip slips, the pressure around my chest loosening as he looks between us.

"Please," Seb says, voice breaking. "Get them out."

Andres nods once. Just once. I tear free.

Nathan's voice explodes behind us, "Mateo! STAND DOWN! That's an order!"

I don't turn around. I don't hesitate. The only thing I hear is Seb yelling, "Let me go! Let me fucking go!"

Nathan shouts, "Hold him back! Nobody follows! Mateo made his choice!"

Boots scrape pavement. Radios crackle. Someone curses. But I'm already halfway across the lot. Smoke curls up around my boots, thick and punishing, blurring the edges of the world. The school looms in front of me like a dying beast—cracked, groaning, flame pulsing in its ribs.

I don't stop. I don't think. I just see Analyse's face. I only hear Maya's little laugh.

God. They were here the whole time. And I didn't know.

I slam through the west-side entrance, the heat hitting me like a freight train. The hallway snarls around me—sparking lights, moaning beams, smoke clawing at the seams. My gear feels too heavy, my breath too thin, but I press forward.

Because I don't know what room they're in. I don't know how long they've been trapped. I don't even know if they can still breathe. But I know Maya. I know Analyse. And I know I will not walk out of this building without them. There isn't a single thing in this world that can stop me from getting to them.

I couldn't save my mom when the fire came for our home. Couldn't be there for my dad. And Maribel, I couldn't save her. I lived and they didn't...a truth that's carved into my bones, carried in every alarm bell, every scream through smoke.

But this time...this time, I'm not too late. I am going to save Maya and Analyse. I have to. There's nothing that will stop that.

Not fire. Not steel. Not the weight of this gear or the walls falling down around me. Not even death. If this building takes me, I'll claw through ash and bone to find them. If the flames eat me alive, I'll let them burn through everything but the part of me that loves them. Because no grave, no fire, no force in this world can hold me down if they're still breathing.

I crouch low, sweeping my flashlight side to side, heart slamming in my chest like it's trying to break free.

Eighteen. Twenty. Twenty-two. My gut twists. They have to be here. They have to be. A loud crack echoes above—wood splintering. I duck instinctively as debris rains down from a collapsing air vent.

I keep moving. Smoke curls in every direction, coiling, taunting me like it wants to take something from me. But it won't. Not today. Because Maya called for help. And no one—nothing—is getting to her before I do.

Chapter Thirty-Three

ANALYSE

The room is a furnace.

Heat presses in from all sides, thick and unrelenting, a living thing that gnaws at every inch of exposed skin. My clothes cling to me, soaked in sweat, ash, and fear. It's like the walls are moving inward, each breath tighter than the last. My skin feels too tight, like it's shrinking against my bones. Every inhale tastes like scorched wood and melted plastic. My lungs scream.

I'm slumped against the wall, barely upright, one hand braced against the warped tile floor. My other hand clutches Maya's. It's the only anchor I have left. The only thing tethering me to now, to here, to the reason I can't fall apart.

Her tiny fingers are sticky with sweat and soot, trembling in mine, but she hasn't let go. Not once.

"Mami," she whispers, her voice paper thin, crackling. "Why isn't the fire truck here yet?"

I force my eyes open. They burn, dry and raw, like they've been scrubbed with sandpaper. My vision blurs at the edges, but I find her face.

"They're coming," I rasp. My throat feels torn. "I promise, baby. Help is coming."

She nods, even though I can see the fear tightening every part of her little face. She's trying so hard. Trying to be brave for me.

Her shirt is pulled over her nose, just like I told her. I guide her hand back to the damp cloth I ripped from the bulletin board earlier, some faded decoration with a turkey on it, now barely more than a wet rag.

"Put this over your mouth again," I say gently. "Like we practiced. Breathe through your nose. Slow. Like little sips."

She obeys without question. Because she trusts me. God, that trust. That's the part that undoes me. Please, please, please, don't let her trust in me be wrong. Don't let me fail her.

The bookshelf I shoved in front of the door, my last ditch attempt to block the worst of the smoke, has started to blacken. Thin tongues of flame lick up the sides. It's turning into a torch.

I press my back harder into the wall, leg shrieking in protest. The pain is sharper now, deeper, pulsing with every beat of my heart. I can feel the blood soaking into my jeans, thick, sticky, and far too warm. When I try to move it, something shifts wrong. A grinding sensation, deep and nauseating. Something's not where it should be.

But I can't afford to focus on that.

"I'm so sorry," I whisper, my voice breaking. "I should've told someone we were coming. I just thought...it would be quick. I didn't think—"

Maya's hand tightens around mine. "You didn't know, Mami. You didn't do anything bad."

Tears sting my eyes, but they don't fall. They just sit there, burning uselessly as smoke curls through the air like a curse.

The window in the far corner cracks with a sharp pop, a

spiderweb of fractures splitting the glass. Maya jumps, the cloth falling from her face for just a second. I reach out and tuck it back up.

"Stay down," I say. "You keep that cloth on your face, and you don't move unless I tell you. Okay?"

She nods again, this time harder, like she's working hard on convincing herself too.

The air is thick, now, too thick. It's like breathing molasses. I have to concentrate on each inhale, each exhale. Slow breaths, Lyse. My chest burns, my lungs wheeze. My ears ring, and the edges of the room begin to blur.

I shake my head, trying to stay conscious. I can't fall asleep. I can't. Maya needs me.

Maya scoots closer, resting her head against my shoulder. Her little arms wrap around mine. Her small body trembles against mine, but she doesn't cry this time.

"It's okay, Mami," she whispers, her voice softer than breath. "You don't have to talk. I'll wait. I'll wait for them."

I want to tell her how proud I am. How she's braver than I've ever been. My throat won't work. Time stretches, thick and endless. The bookshelf catches fully, flames crawling up the spine like they've been waiting for the chance. The room glows orange, flickering like a candle at the end of its wick.

Another groan. A loud one, somewhere above. The ceiling is shifting—warped, heavy. The sound makes my stomach drop. I brace myself, shielding Maya with my arm as a beam somewhere outside crashes to the floor with a thunderous slam.

The air rushes in afterward like a vacuum broke. Smoke pours under the door, black and fast. I cough hard, chest splitting open. When it passes, my limbs feel too heavy. I glance down, trying to wiggle my toes. Nothing. Just a deep, numbing throb where there should be movement. Like my leg's gone quiet.

Not paralyzed, I tell myself. Just hurt. Just swollen. Just... not now. Don't panic now. I can't let her see. I can't let her know.

"If anything happens," I whisper, the word barely audible, "You stay low. Crawl if you have to. Call for help. You don't stop until someone finds you."

Maya bolts upright. "No! Don't say that. I'm not leaving you!" Her voice breaks, and for the first time, her fear shows all the way through. She wraps her arms around my waist, as far as they can go, and buries her face in the side.

"You're the bravest girl I've ever known," I whisper. "I love you more than anything."

She lifts her face, smudged with soot, and presses a kiss to my cheek. Her lips are cracked, dry. Her eyes shimmer with unshed tears. I let mine close. Just for a second. Just to rest them.

But a crash snaps them open again. Closer. Louder. A vent? A support beam? Smoke crashes in like a wave. and I lose sight of everything.

"Maya," I gasp.

"I'm here," she cries. "I'm right here."

I reach for her hand. She finds it instantly. And even though I'm shaking, even though I don't know how much longer we have, I hold on. Because we're still here. We're still here.

Chapter Thirty-Four

MATEO

Everything is on fire.

The hallway groans around me, beams cracking like brittle bones, the walls gasping smoke as if the building itself is choking. Sparks rain down from the ceiling tiles, embers skittering like fallen stars across the floor.

I charge forward, ducking beneath a broken beam, my boots slamming into the warped linoleum. My flashlight cuts through the thick air, slicing through plumes of gray like a blade. My lungs are tight. My vision tunnels. Every thought narrows to one thing: Get to them.

I know this wing. Analyse once told me they got stuck with the worst classroom. The one with the drafty vents, busted heater, and cabinets that fell off the hinges if you breathed wrong. Room 24. She said it like a joke, laughing the way only she can. Analyse. She could always turn something broken into something beautiful.

I hold on to that detail like a map etched into my ribs.

A wall of heat slams into me as I round the corner. The air shifts, more violent, more alive. Debris blocks the path ahead —wood, tile, melted plastic—but there's just enough space under the wreckage to drop to my knees and crawl. Smoke churns thick and black, coiling like a living thing. Embers flicker across the rubble like dying stars in reverse.

"Analyse! Maya!" I yell, voice ragged, the smoke clawing at my throat like it wants to take something from me.

Nothing. For one gut punched second, I hear nothing. Then—

"Mateo!"

A small voice, muffled and cracking. But it cuts through everything like a prayer.

"Maya?!"

"We're here! In here!"

My entire body jolts. I surge forward, heart punching against my ribs, trying to claw its way out.

Room 24.

Smoke bleeds from the doorframe, thick and furious. The door is warped from the heat, the handle blackened and missing. I don't think. I just move.

One kick. Two. On the third, the door splinters, groaning open as smoke explodes outward in a wave of heat and ash. Flames snarl along the edges of the wall. Paper peels from the bulletin boards. The air tastes like chemicals and grief.

"Mateo!" Maya throws herself into my arms. She's shaking. Her little face is streaked with soot, her cheeks blotchy with tears. I drop to one knee and wrap my arms around her.

"I've got you," I whisper. "You're okay, baby. I've got you."

She clutches my neck like a lifeline. "Mami...she can't get up. She's hurt."

I swallow hard and set Maya down just outside the door. "Stay right here. Low to the ground. Use your shirt. Cover your mouth, okay? Don't move unless I say."

She nods and does it without hesitation. Because she's brave. Because she's her mother's daughter.

I turn back into the flames. And there she is. Analyse.

Slumped against the supply shelf, one arm limply curled over her stomach, her body folded like she's trying to shield herself. Her head tilts to the side, eyes barely open. Ash clings to her lashes. Her jeans are soaked with blood, her leg bent at a sickening angle that makes my stomach lurch.

"Analyse." Her name slips from my mouth like a vow. I fall to my knees beside her. "I'm here. I've got you, mi amor."

She blinks. "Mateo?"

Her voice is barely a whisper. I lean in, forehead to hers. "Yeah. I'm here, chula. I'm gonna get you out."

She tries to say something more, but coughs instead—deep, rattling. Her whole body trembles.

"I know it hurts," I say, sliding an arm under her knees, the other around her back. "But we've got to go. Just hold on"

The room growls louder. I lift. She screams.

I squeeze my eyes shut. "I'm sorry. I know. I'm so sorry, baby."

The pain is etched across her face, raw and gasping. But her arms cling to me, her face burrowing into my neck. I carry her to the door, each step a war. Maya is right there, eyes wide and shining.

"Grab my coat," I tell her. "We're getting out of here."

She nods and grips the edge of my turnout gear with one soot-streaked hand. We step back into the hallway. Hell waits for us.

The fire has found its roar—full throated and hungry. Ceiling tiles collapse like bombs. The air blisters. Every breath is a fight. My boots splash through puddles that evaporate beneath us.

"Move!" I shout. "Stay with me!"

Maya clings tighter. Analyse whimpers against my chest, her breaths shallow, her skin too hot. I push forward through the smoke, flame, and falling ash. Then—a thunderous crack.

Behind us, the ceiling gives. The hallway caves in. Room 24 disappears in a wall of fire. I don't look back. I run.

The west exit is ahead, blurry though the smoke. But it's there. It's life. I barrel toward it, muscles burning, lungs screaming, everything inside me held together by a thread made of their names.

We break through. Sunlight crashes into my face. I drop to my knees, clutching Analyse like the last thing I'll ever hold. Maya falls beside me, sobbing. Everything explodes.

Seb's voice. Mari. Anna. Captain Nathan shouting orders.

"Maya!" Seb lifts her into his arms. "Oh my God, baby."

But I can't look away from her. "She needs a medic!" I scream. "Now!"

Boots pound across the pavement. Radios crackle. Someone yells for a stretcher.

I brush the soot from her face with shaking hands. "You're okay," I whisper, my voice broken. "You're okay, Lyse. I've got you. You're safe. I love you. I love you. I love you."

Her lashes flutter. She blinks up at me, barely awake. Barely there. But she's alive. I can't believe it. She's alive.

A sob punches out of my chest. I saved her. I saved them.

Chapter Thirty-Five

MATEO

The hospital's waiting room is packed. Shoulder to shoulder. Boots tracking melted snow. Voices low, murmuring their concerns over what is happening with Analyse, what happened to Maya.

Lake City is a small town. And in a small town like ours, when someone gets hurt, the whole damn place shows up. Especially when that someone is Analyse. The entire town loves her and Maya.

Mari is pacing, arms folded tight across her chest. Anna sits beside her, wringing her hands. Hilda hasn't said a word since we got here, sitting in her seat, frozen in shock. Every person is here. Teachers, parents, former students. They're all packed into this fluorescent-lit room that smells too clean and feels too damn cold.

And I'm sitting here with Maya curled into me, her cheek against my chest, wrapped in one of the hospital's scratchy blankets. She hasn't said a word in over twenty minutes. When we walked in, the doctor checked her out right away. She had mild smoke inhalation and a few scrapes. Nothing life threatening. They cleared her after a round of oxygen and a full exam. They said she was lucky. Real lucky.

Her little fingers are still clutched in the fabric of my jacket. I think part of her is scared that if she lets go I'll disappear.

"I'm not going anywhere," I whisper into her hair.

She doesn't answer, but her body softens just slightly.

Seb is sitting across from us, elbows on knees, head bowed. Every so often he glances toward the doors, like he can will them to open faster. Like the next person to walk through might bring news that doesn't hurt.

The fire's nearly out. Andres texted me ten minutes ago. He said the roof held long enough, and Nathan's already starting the damage report. But none of that matters right now. Not to me. Because she's still back there, and I can't touch her. I can't hear her voice. I can't do anything but wait.

A nurse finally walks out. Everyone jerks to attention, the air sucking straight out of the room. Then behind her, the doctor walks in.

"Family of Analyse Garcia?" he asks.

We all rise, but I step forward, Maya still tucked against me.

"She's stable," the doctor says immediately, holding up a hand like he knows we're seconds from unraveling. "She inhaled a significant amount of smoke, and she's severely dehydrated. Her leg took the worst of it from a beam falling on her. She's got a complex fracture of the tibia and fibula. We're prepping for surgery to stabilize it and insert a rod."

Mari lets out a sob. Seb covers his mouth. And I just grip Maya a little tighter.

"She's conscious," the doctor continues. "But in a lot of pain. We've got her on oxygen and fluids. Once we've completed surgery and she's out of recovery, one of you can sit with her. But it'll be a few hours."

"Is she...going to walk again?" Anna's voice cracks.

The doctor nods. "It'll be a long road. But yes. She will."

And with those words, the air shifts. Not joy. Not yet; we're not completely out of the woods. But relief. Because she's alive. Because we didn't lose her. Maya's mom is still here. I glance down at the little girl in my arms and finally feel her exhale, like she's been holding her breath since the moment we left the school.

"Can I see her?" she whispers.

I look to the doctor.

"Not yet," he says gently. "But soon."

Maya nods, curls falling over her eyes. Then she curls tighter into my chest, and I hold her like a lifeline.

Once we got word that Analyse would be okay, I convinced everyone to head home so that she wouldn't wake up overwhelmed by visitors. It took some effort, but Seb and Mari eventually took Maya back to their place for a bath and a real meal. We promised Maya that I'd call them as soon as Analyse woke up—so she could see her mom.

The seconds feel like hours, the hours feel like days. But I'm a man that can't be moved...not until I see Analyse.

The nurse finally calls my name. I'm on my feet before she finishes the sentence. The waiting room hum disappears, muffled by the pounding in my ears. I follow her through the hall, past closed doors and machines that beep in rhythm with someone else's pain.

She stops outside the room and gives me a soft nod. "She's awake. In and out, but coherent. Just a few minutes, okay?"

I nod, but my throat's too tight for words. Then I step inside.

The room is dim, lit only by the low glow of the monitors

and the fading light leaking through the blinds. Analyse is lying in the hospital bed, pale against the white sheets, a nasal cannula under her nose, IVs in both arms, and bandages on her temple and leg. One of her ankles is propped up slightly, and the monitor beside her chirps slowly and steady. It kills me to see her like this. I'd do anything in the world to trade places with her.

But her eyes are open. And my heart soars. I move to her side quietly, pulling the chair close, not trusting myself to speak. She looks at me for a long moment, lids heavy, lashes wet.

"Mateo...I knew you'd come," she whispers, voice rough and paper thin.

I swallow hard. My hands are shaking as I reach for hers—careful, gentle, scared she might break if I hold too tight.

"I will always come running back to you, Lyse. Always. You scared the hell out of me," I say, and my voice cracks.

She gently squeezes my hand. "I'm sorry. I'm so sorry."

"Baby, no, don't say sorry. This isn't your fault. There was no way you could've known that this would happen."

"Where's Maya? Is she okay?" Panic laces her voice.

"She's okay, Lyse. Maya's okay. I promise. She's with Seb and Mari, but they're going to come back as soon as she's fed and showered."

"She's okay?"

"Yeah, baby. You both are okay."

"Mateo...I know we were in a weird place before all this happened—"

"It's okay, Lyse. We don't have to talk about that right now."

"We do, Mateo. We do. Because life is too damn short. I could've died today. Maya could've died." she says, her voice cracking. "And I would've died without ever having told you how I feel about you. How much you mean to me. I love you,

Mateo. I love you so much that it scares me. I thought I knew what love was. I thought I understood what being in love meant. But now I realize that I didn't know real love until you came along. You've changed me, Mateo. You've altered my chemistry in a way that I could've never imagined. In a way that means my body could never be away from yours. My soul, my heart, could never be without you," she says, pressing a soft kiss to my hand. "You asked me to tell you the truth, and this is it. I want you. I need you. You're the missing part of my heart. And I'd be lying if I said that the idea of you having so much control over my heart isn't freaking me out, but one thing I know for certain is I'd give you my heart any day if it meant always feeling the love that you pour into Maya and I every single day."

Tears are streaming down her face, her big brown eyes staring back at me, and I know that this is it. She is it. Her and Maya are it for me.

I lean in and press the softest kiss against her lips, careful to not hurt her. "I love you, too. You and Maya. I love you both so much. I couldn't survive it if I lost either of you. Chula, tu eres mi alma y mi vida. I'd run into that building all over again for you both. Every single damn time, without a question. I know it hurt you that Nico left, trust me, I want to lay that motherfucker out, but I need you to know that you're not alone anymore. Maya isn't alone. I love that little girl like she's my own. She's *our* girl. Our baby girl. And I promise you that I'll be the father she needs, I'll be everything you both need forever, if you'll have me. As soon as you're better, I'm gonna make an honest woman out of you, because you're mine. You always have been."

"Are you asking me to marry you, Mateo?"

"You're damn right I am, chula. I know I don't have the big fancy ring and I'm not on bended knee, but I can't live without you, Analyse. I don't want to go another day knowing that you're not mine for keeps. Hell, I don't wanna go another second. Please make me the happiest man in the world and say yes."

We're both crying now, her fingers threaded through mine.

"Yes."

"Yes?"

"Yeah, Mateo. I'll marry you. I want to be your wife. I want everything."

I jump up in the air, let out a loud whoop, and run to the door and yell, "SHE SAID YES! THIS WOMAN IS GOING TO MARRY ME!"

Everyone begins cheering, and Analyse lets out a small laugh.

"God, I love you," she says.

"Say it again."

"I love you."

"I'll never get sick of hearing you saying that."

"And I'll never get sick of saying it," she says sleepily, eyes growing heavy.

"Okay, time to rest."

"I'm okay. Really."

"Nope. You need your rest. And I'm gonna call Seb to bring our girl so she can see you. I know she's gnawing at the bits right now."

"Okay. Just a small nap before I see Maya."

I lean in and kiss her forehead and turn to walk out the door. The moment I leave the room, I let out a breath. What a fucking day. But we made it. My girls are okay, and I'm going to marry the woman of my dreams. I saved them. I did it. I did what I couldn't for my family. I fucking did it. Then I slide down the wall and begin to cry.

Chapter Thirty-Six

ANALYSE

Something beeps steadily in the background, a soft rhythm tethering me to consciousness. My body feels heavy, like I'm underwater. There's a dull ache in my leg, a pressure in my chest, and the unmistakable sterile scent of antiseptic.

I blink, the ceiling blurry and washed in a haze of overhead light, and then—

"Mami!"

I open my eyes slowly, the room sharpening with every blink, when I see her. Maya. The brightest light in the room. Instantly, tears begin to stream down my face.

"Mami? Are you okay?" she asks anxiously.

I reach my hands toward her, urging her to come closer. "Yes, mamita. I'm okay. I'm just so happy to see you. I'm so happy that you're okay, mi amor."

"I was so scared, Mami."

"I know, baby. I know. It was scary. But you were so brave. My strong girl. I'm sorry you had to be so brave today. But mommy's here, and I'll never let anything happen to you. I love you, baby."

"I love you, too, Mami. When can you come home?"

"It's going to be a while, sweetheart. But I promise, I'll be home as soon as I can. Mateo is going to stay at our house so you can be in your own room, with all your own things. And Tio Seb and Titi Mari will see you every day."

"Okay, Mami," she says, sniffling, trying to hold back her tears.

"Hey," I say, lifting her chin. "You never have to hold your tears back. You are the strongest little kid I've ever met, but strength doesn't mean never showing emotion. And you never, ever, have to hide what you're feeling from me, okay?"

"Yes, Mami. Okay. I thought...I thought maybe it was my fault," she says, barely audible.

My chest caves in.

"No, baby. None of this is your fault. If anything, you saved me. You were so brave to call for help. I'm here because of you."

Her little brow furrows. "But I didn't know what to do."

"You did exactly what you were supposed to. I'm so proud of you. You are my brave, smart, beautiful girl."

I hug her as tightly as I can, any pain made dull the moment I feel her tiny arms wrap around me. I don't know how we made it out. I don't know what miracle let Mateo find us in time. But I do know this—I will spend the rest of my life making sure Maya never doubts how loved and safe she is. We got lucky today, and I'm never going to take a minute of this second chance at life for granted.

After a few hours, Maya goes home with Seb so Mateo can spend tonight with me. The charmer that he is, he was able to talk the nurses into letting him stay. They even brought in a second bed, a pillow, and a blanket.

I glance over at him now, his chest rising and falling slowly in the bed beside mine, and my heart constricts. I love him. I love Mateo. I still can't believe it. But I meant every word I said. He really does have my heart.

A part of me still thinks I imagined his voice calling my name in the fire. That I hallucinated the way he burst through the smoke like a man with nothing to lose. Or maybe he was bursting in like he had everything to lose. Because Maya and I were there. But he's real. He's here. He loves me. He asked me to marry him, and I'm so glad that I can look at him, kiss him, hold him for the rest of our lives.

My fingers twitch at the thought, and I lift my hand to stare at it—even without a ring, I already feel the weight of forever. The warmth of being wanted. The safety of being seen.

Chapter Thirty-Seven

MATEO

I've never been this damn excited to clean. But today? Today, I'm scrubbing baseboards with more passion than I've ever put into a workout.

I don't think I've ever vacuumed this much in my entire life. Maya's been trailing behind me with a duster, her little pink socks sliding across the hardwood floors as she tries to reach the corners I missed.

"Did you fluff the pillows?" she asks, hands on her hips like a mini general.

"Yes, ma'am," I say, laughing as I lift one to prove it. "See? Maximum fluff."

She nods approvingly. "Okay, that's good. We want everything perfect for Mami."

Analyse is coming home. My girl is coming home.

It's been a full week since the hospital called with the update. After her surgery went well and they were sure there weren't any complications, they kept her for monitoring and physical therapy just long enough to make sure she could manage stairs and short walks with assistance.

I swear I've been counting down the minutes since they cleared her for discharge.

Maya skips ahead of me into the kitchen. "Can we put her cookies on a plate?"

"We'll do that last," I say, checking the time. "That way they're still warm when she gets here."

Her eyes light up. "She loves warm cookies."

"I know," I say, tossing her a wink. "We're not half bad at this, huh?"

She beams. It hits me again, like it always does now, how much she looks like Analyse when she smiles. Same warmth. Same light. Same quiet resilience.

I kneel down in front of her. "Hey, princesa. How you holding up?"

She shrugs, tugging at the hem of her shirt. "I'm excited. But also kind of scared. What if Mami's still really hurt?"

"She's healing," I say, brushing her hair behind her ear. "She's gonna need some help, and we're gonna give it to her. That's what we do. We show up. We take care of each other."

She nods, eyes wide and solemn. "Okay. I can do that." Then she suddenly blurts, "Mateo...why wouldn't my dad want me?"

The question knocks the air out of me. I pull in a steady breath and cup her cheek. "Oh, Maya. It was never about you. You are the easiest person in the world to love. Sometimes people don't know how to be what we need—and that's on them, not you. But you? You've got so many people who choose you, every single day."

She blinks up at me. "Like you?"

I smile, throat tight. "Especially me."

She chews on her lip for a second then leans against me with a tiny sigh. "You feel like my dad," she whispers. "I'd be okay if you were."

I press a kiss to the top of her head, my chest aching. "Me too, princesa. Me too."

She smiles faintly against my chest, and I hold on for just a second longer before pulling back.

I stand and ruffle her hair. "Now come on. We've got candles to light and a couch to fluff for the hundredth time."

We move through the rest of the house like we're prepping for royalty. And if I'm being honest, we are.

I open the windows to let in some of the crisp winter air, fresh but not too cold. The living room smells like vanilla and fabuloso. Maya lines up the throw blankets and double-checks the remote is where Analyse likes it—right next to the couch cushion with the best view of the window.

Just as Maya finishes folding the last blanket into a perfect square, there's a knock at the door.

She races to it before I can stop her, yanking it open. "Titi Mari! Tio Seb!"

Sure enough, Seb and Mari step inside with the bags of food and soft voices full of excitement. Right behind them are Anna, Andres, and Nathan, all crowding into the living room.

"Hey, pequeña," Seb says, scooping Maya into a hug. "We heard someone special's coming home today."

"She is!" Maya grins, arms flung around his neck. "We made cookies."

Mari walks over to me and lowers her voice. "Everything okay? You good?"

I nod, wiping my hands on a towel. "Yeah. We're ready. The place is spotless, blankets are folded, candles are lit, and Maya's already taken command."

"She gets that from Analyse," Anna jokes, placing a hand on my shoulder. "Go. We've got her."

I glance at all of them—my people, our people—settling in to keep Maya busy, keep her distracted, make this moment even softer for Analyse when she gets here. And suddenly I'm overwhelmed with gratitude. This town, this family, this life we're building...it's everything.

I press a kiss to Maya's head. "Be good, princesa. I'll be back soon—with Mami."

"You better," she says, arms crossed with a grin.

I laugh, grabbing the keys off the counter, my heart racing. I've waited a long time for this moment. And now, I'm going to bring my girl home.

The drive to the hospital feels like it takes forever, even though I hit every green light on the way. My hands grip the steering wheel tighter than they should, my heart thudding harder the closer I get. I've been picturing this moment all week, walking out those hospital doors with her by my side. No sirens. No smoke. No panic. Just us, headed home.

When I pull into the patient pick-up area, she's already waiting outside in a wheelchair, bundled in a soft gray sweater, a blanket tucked over her lap. A nurse stands beside her, holding a clipboard, but all I see is her. Analyse. Her hair's pulled back in a loose braid, her eyes a little tired but still full of fire. She's biting her bottom lip like she's trying not to cry.

I throw the truck into park and practically leap out.

"Hey, chula," I say softly as I jog up to her.

Her eyes meet mine, and damn, there it is, that look that knocks the wind right out of my chest.

"Hey," she breathes. "You're early."

"I'm on time. Everyone else is late." I crouch beside her and press a kiss to her knuckles. "You ready to go home?"

She nods, lips trembling slightly. "More than ready."

The nurse helps me get her into the passenger seat, carefully lifting the leg with the brace. I buckle her in and adjust the seat a little, trying to make sure she's as comfortable as possible. When I close her door and walk around to the driver's side, I catch her watching me with this soft, awestruck smile, like she can't believe I'm real.

I know the feeling.

The ride home is quiet. Not awkward. Just...full. Her hand finds mine on the center console, and we sit there like that, fingers laced, silence humming between us. Every few minutes, I glance over to check on her, but she always beats me to it, already looking at me with those big brown eyes that say everything without a single word.

When we turn down our street, she inhales sharply. "I missed this."

"You're almost there."

The house is glowing when we pull up. Soft lights in the window, a warm flicker from inside. I swear it looks like something out of a damn movie. And when I open her door and help her out—slowly, carefully—I feel her body shake with a quiet sob.

"Hey, hey. Are you okay?"

She nods against my chest, her hand clinging to mine. "I just...I didn't think I'd get to come back here. Not like this."

I press a kiss to her temple. "You're here. You made it back. And we've got you."

I guide her up the front steps slowly, my arm around her waist, her crutch on the other side. I open the door and call out, "Careful, a queen is incoming!"

There's a collective cheer from the living room.

Maya's the first to come flying down the hall, socks nearly taking her out on the hardwood. "Mami!"

She skids to a stop just in time, eyes wide as she takes in the sight of Analyse.

"Gentle, baby," I remind her.

But Analyse opens her arms. "Come hare, mamita."

Maya buries herself in her mom's side, sniffling and

hugging her tight. Everyone else keeps their distance, watching, smiling.

"I told you we'd make it," I whisper into Analyse's ear as I guide her the rest of the way in.

She looks around, teary eyed, at the folded blankets, the candles, the cookie set on a plate with a little handwritten note from Maya that says, *Welcome home, Mami*.

"Did you do all this?" she asks. She smiles through her tears. "God, I love you."

"I love you more." I grin. "Now come on. Let's get you to the couch."

As I settle her in, Maya curls up beside her and the rest of the crew quietly heads into the kitchen to give us space. For the first time in a long time, everything feels calm. No alarms. No chaos.

Just us. Home. Together.

Chapter Thirty-Eight

ANALYSE

T he second I step through the front door, I feel it...the warmth, that scent, that deep soul sighing feeling of being home.

Everything is familiar, but new. The lights are soft and golden. Candles flicker on the mantle. The pillows on the couch have been fluffed within an inch of their lives. And the smell...vanilla and something sweet. Cookies.

My eyes land on a little note sitting next to a plate of chocolate chip cookies on the coffee table, written in uneven, careful handwriting.

Welcome home, Mami.

I can't stop the tears from welling.

Mateo's arm tightens around me as he helps me over to the couch. "Easy," he murmurs, lowering me gently onto the cushion with the best view of the front window, the one I always sit at when I want to see the sunset.

He props a pillow behind my back and adjusts the blanket over my legs with a tenderness that steals my breath. Before I can even finish exhaling, the rest of the crew spills in from the kitchen.

Mari's the first to rush over, her eyes misty but her smile wide. "There she is," she says, crouching carefully beside me. "You look...exhausted and amazing. And don't argue, I'm taking this as a win."

I snort. "I'm going to tell Seb to take you to get your eyes checked, because clearly your vision is struggling."

Seb is right behind her, carrying what looks like half a bakery box and something that smells suspiciously like pastelón. "We brought food," he says. "And yes, Mari insisted we bring the good Tupperware."

"You only get the good Tupperware for major events," Mari says seriously, and I love her so much in this moment I could cry all over again.

Anna slides in next to them on the floor, crossing her legs and offering me a coffee cup. "Decaf, but at least it tastes like real coffee...mostly."

"Man, I missed you guys."

And I mean it. Even as the pain flares and my body reminds me I'm not anywhere near healed, the ache in my chest has less to do with injury and more to do with how much I've missed this, being surrounded by them. The laughter, the teasing, the way we all show up without being asked.

Nathan settles against the wall near the window, arms crossed, quiet like always but with that watchful glint in his eye. Andres hands off a bag of extra blankets and somehow ends up rearranging the entire linen basket with Mari whispering critique over his shoulder.

"Are you sure you're okay with us crashing here for a while?" Anna asks, her voice dropping low. "We figured it might help Maya feel a little more normal. Keep the energy soft."

"I'm more than okay with it," I say, my voice thick. "I'm... grateful. For all of you."

Mateo sits back down beside me, hand resting gently over mine. "This is what family does."

I lean my head on his shoulder. "Still feels unreal."

"You'll get used to it," he murmurs. "One day at a time."

And as the noise swells again—Seb making proclamations about who makes the best empanadas, Anna and Mari bickering over where to put the extra pillows, and Maya quietly curling up on the floor with her sketchbook—I feel it: the slow but steady return of peace.

It's not perfect. My body still aches, and I've got weeks of recovery ahead. But I'm home. I'm surrounded by love. We're going to be okay.

The house has finally quieted down, in that way it only does when the chaos moves outside. Through the cracked window, I can hear Maya's laughter echo from the backyard, mingling with the low rumble of male voices and the occasional bark of encouragement from Seb.

They're playing tag, or something close to it, and judging by the sound of Nathan yelling, "You can't tackle a kid, Mateo!" it's going well.

Inside, it's just us.

Mari hands me a mug of tea, still steeping, and settles on the edge of the couch. Anna sinks into the armchair across from me, tucking her legs under herself and cradling her own cup of something warm and chamomile scented.

For a few beats, no one says anything.

"Okay," Mari finally says, eyes sweeping over me, "you look better. Still like you got your ass kicked by a haunted staircase, but better."

I laugh, careful not to jostle my leg. "I'll take it. And yes, the haunted staircase won. Don't tell it I said."

"Too late," Anna says, sipping her tea. "I texted the ghost while you were napping."

Mari and I both chuckle, and the sound feels like home. Like normalcy. Like the part of me that wasn't sure I'd get to have this again can finally take a breath.

The laughter fades, replaced by something softer. Heavier.

Anna's staring into her mug. Her brows knit, fingers wrapped too tightly around the ceramic.

Mari notices, too. "Alright," she says, tilting her head, "what's up with you?"

Anna glances between us and then exhales slowly. "I wasn't sure if I wanted to talk about it tonight, but…" She sets her mug on the side table and rubs her palms over her knees. "After everything that happened…the fire, seeing you in the hospital—"

I reach for her hand automatically, and she takes it, her grip strong but shaky.

"I just kept thinking," she says quietly, "what if I never get the chance?"

I blink. "The chance to…?"

"To be a mom."

The words hit like a quiet thud, like a pebble dropped in deep water. It takes a moment to ripple through me.

Mari stills. "Anna…"

She doesn't flinch. "I've been thinking about it for a while. And I kept finding excuses—timing, work, money, dating in this town, which, as you both know, is a flaming dumpster fire." She tries to laugh, but it fades too fast. "But after what happened to you, Analyse…I don't want to keep waiting. I want to do it. IVF. On my own."

My heart stutters. "Are you sure?"

She nods. "I'm not saying it'll be easy. Or that I'm not scared. But something about almost losing one of my best friends flipped a switch. Tomorrow isn't guaranteed. But if I start now...maybe someday, a little person will call me mama."

I feel the tears before I realize they're there. Mari wipes at hers openly, no shame in the way her mascara runs a little.

"Oh, Anna." I squeeze her hand. "That's...beautiful."

Mari leans forward, eyes shining. "You're going to be such a badass mom."

"Really?" Anna asks, voice cracking just a little.

"Hell yes," Mari says. "You already are. Look at the way you show up for Maya. The way you argue with every school board about their outdated library list. You've got the fight in you. And the heart."

Anna lets out a slow breath and gives us a watery smile. "I was afraid you'd try to talk me out of it."

"Talk you out of chasing something you want with your whole heart?" I say. "Never."

She looks down then back up. "I've been researching clinics. There's one an hour away that seems promising. I'm going to schedule a consult."

Mari reaches over to clink her tear cup against Anna's. "To doing brave shit."

Anna clinks back. "To being terrified and doing it anyway."

We all turn to look out the window. Maya's sitting on Mateo's shoulders, arms stretched out like wings as he runs in slow, bouncy circles. Nathan's trying to coach Seb through a cartwheel while Andres films it with the most serious expression I've ever seen.

Warmth rises in my chest, curling around my ribs. These people, this moment...it's all so fragile and so fierce at once.

"You won't be alone in this," I tell Anna. "Whatever you need—appointments, hormone injections, late-night ice cream runs—you've got us."

"And if anyone gives you shit, or even gives you a side-eye," Mari adds, "I'll fight them."

Anna laughs, blinking fast. "Deal."

I look at the two women in front of me—one ready to leap into motherhood on her own, the other fierce, loyal, and hilarious—and I feel a swelling in my heart I didn't know was possible after this week. After everything.

We survived the fire. Now, we get to build something new. Something strong. Together.

I glance down at my hands then back up. "Can I tell you both something?"

Mari narrows her eyes. "Please let it be a good something. My heart cannot take anymore. I'm too emotionally fragile right now."

Anna laughs, leaning forward. "What is it?"

I exhale. "Mateo proposed."

Their jaws drop in perfect sync.

"Shut. Up," Mari says, setting her mug down with dramatic care. "When?"

"In the hospital," I say, cheeks burning. "After I woke up. It wasn't some big elaborate thing, no ring—just him, holding my hand, telling me he didn't want to waste another minute."

Anna lets out a quiet gasp. "Oh my god, Analyse. What did you say?"

"I said yes," I admit. "I really love him and I want to spend the rest of my life with him."

They're both crying. I'm crying. We're all just a bunch of puddles, surrounded by throw pillows, tea, and candles.

Mari wipes her face. "I'm going to need so many details. Not now. But soon."

"And we're absolutely throwing you the most chaotic, over-the-top engagement dinner," Anna says, already plotting. "With a shit ton of champagne and cake."

"I wouldn't expect anything less," I say, laughing through tears. "But actually...how about you skip the engagement dinner and go straight to planning our wedding?"

They both freeze.

"What do you mean?" Anna asks, eyes wide.

"We want to get married," I say, voice soft. "As soon as I'm able to walk again."

Mari launches off the couch like she's been spring loaded. "You didn't think to lead with that?!"

Anna claps her hands together, already half in tears again. "That is the most romantic thing I've ever heard. Are you kidding me? That's a movie."

"I just..." I trail off, blinking fast. "I don't want to wait. This whole thing, the fire, everything—it made me realize how fragile life is. I love him. He loves me. That's enough. I don't need a yearlong engagement or a Pinterest-perfect ceremony. I just want us. Him and me. Maya by our side."

Mari places a hand over her heart. "I'm gonna need someone to sedate me before this wedding or I'm going to ugly cry through the whole damn thing."

Anna leans forward, practically vibrating with energy. "Okay, listen. We can pull this off. I know people. I can get a dress for you easily. And if you want to wear sneakers under it, I fully support that choice."

"Mateo said we could do it in the backyard," I say, smiling. "He wants to build an arbor."

Mari wipes her eyes again. "He's so in love with you. I love you guys together."

We all laugh, and it feels good. So full. My chest aches in the best way—stretched by love and gratitude.

Anna raises her mug. "Another toast! To reckless, beautiful love."

Mari lifts hers, too. "To Mateo and Lyse!"

CHAPTER THIRTY-EIGHT

I smile, lifting my cup with both hands. "To second chances."

I soak this all in—the people I love, the life we're rebuilding, the future we're choosing. And finally, it feels like I'm living.

Chapter Thirty-Nine

ANALYSE

The high school gym looks nothing like it did when I was a student here.

Back then, it always smelled faintly of sweat and floor polish, the bleachers creaked no matter how still you sat, and the banners lining the walls felt impossibly grand when you were fourteen and full of nerves.

Now, the space is unrecognizable in the best way. Streamers in mismatched shades of blue and yellow hang from the rafters, clashing a little with the high school's maroon and silver, but no one seems to care.

Paper stars flutter above the tables, strung on a fishing line and lit from below by string lights tucked around table legs and raffle baskets. Every surface is covered. Handwritten sheets curling at the corners, mason jars full of tickets, Tupperware containers brimming with cookies, brownies, and pastel frosted cupcakes.

It's chaotic. It's crowded. It's beautiful.

Mateo threads his fingers through mine and gives a gentle squeeze, his hand warm and steady against mine.

Seb passes by, carrying a tray of cupcakes like his life

depends on it. "If I drop these, Mariana's going to kill me," he mutters, eyes wide with concentration, disappearing into the crowd before we can respond.

I can't help the laugh that escapes me, and then just as quickly, I wince as the movement tugs at the muscles in my healing leg. The crutches tucked under my arms feel heavy, my arms already sore from relying on them all day. They wobble just slightly, and before I can shift my weight, Mateo is there. One arm wraps around my back, the other steadying the crutch before it slips.

"Easy," he murmurs, voice low, eyes sharp. "Are you okay? Are you sure you want to be here?"

I nod. "I'm okay. I needed to be here. It's more than just a fundraiser...it's a beginning."

And it is. More than a bake sale or a raffle or a few heartfelt speeches. This isn't just about rebuilding the elementary school—it's about reminding everyone that we still have something left. That even in the face of smoke, ashes, and sirens, we showed up. We pulled together. We made something out of the pieces.

It's about the teachers and students who lost their classrooms. About the parents still holding their kids a little tighter at night. About the way this town doesn't just survive...it insists on healing out loud, together.

And maybe, selfishly, it's about me, too. About proving to myself that I'm not broken. That I can show up, even if I'm still a little wobbly. That I'm part of this community, too. Not just someone who needed to be saved, but someone who can stand beside the people doing the saving.

Mateo settles into the chair beside me, his thigh brushing mine, his hand never leaving my own.

"You did good, Lake City," I murmur, eyes sweeping the crowd.

He smiles, eyes soft. "We did good."

The principal of the elementary school takes the stage, her voice cracking as she thanks everyone for coming. She talks about the night of the fire, the courage of the first responders, and the miracle that no lives were lost. And then she talks about the kids—about what they've lost, but most importantly what they still have.

Each other.

By the time she finishes, I'm holding back tears. So is half the gym.

"Alright," the MC calls into the mix, "raffle winners will be announced in ten minutes, and we've still got three pies left for the throwing booth, so if you've ever wanted to smack your favorite firefighter in the face with dessert...now's your chance."

Mateo groans. "Why did I agree to that?"

"Because you love this town," I tease. "And because you look great covered in whipped cream. Too bad I can't lick it up."

He leans in, voice low, and warm against my ear. "Please don't make my dick hard right now, chula. Not when I can't rip off your pants and fuck you the way I want to."

I smirk, cheeks flushed. "Soon enough, baby."

He gives me a look, equal parts heat and affect, then presses a kiss just below my ear, his thumb sweeping over my knuckles.

Before I can respond, Maya's voice rings out from across the gym. "Mami! They're starting the pie booth!"

Mateo groans again, dramatically this time. "Pray for me."

"I thought you liked whipped cream," I call after him as he heads toward the inevitable.

"I like it better in private!" he throws back, and I laugh so hard it almost hurts.

I settle back in my seat, crutches resting against the chair, and watch as Mateo jogs toward the crowd forming near the pie booth. Maya is already there, bouncing on her toes like she's just chugged three Capri Suns, her tiny hands clasped together like she's begging the pie gods for a direct hit.

The gym is buzzing. Kids weaving between tables with sticky fingers, neighbors greeting each other, and volunteers darting around with clipboards and cash boxes. It's chaos, but it's good chaos.

Mari slides into the seat beside me, a cookie in one hand and her phone in the other. "You see Seba almost get decked by that toddler with the juice box?"

I grin. "Only because he stole the last brownie bite."

"Justice was served."

We sit together for a beat, watching the town move in waves of laughter and sugar highs. Then we both turn at the sound of whipped cream splatting and a chorus of gasps and cheers.

Mateo stands frozen, face dripping with pie, Maya doubled over in laughter next to him. He shoots me a mock betrayed look.

"Worth it," I mouth, and he shakes his head with a grin.

He's wiping whipped cream from his eyelashes as he walks back over, Maya tugging on his arm. "Did you see me, Mami? I got him right in the face!"

"You were incredible," I say, pulling her in for a side hug.

Mateo leans down and kisses the tops of both of our heads, his fingers brushing over my shoulder. "You two are dangerous together."

"Get used to it," I tease.

A voice cuts in over the speakers. "And now, the moment you've all been waiting for—our grand total for tonight's fundraiser."

The gym hushes, everyone turning toward the sage.

"We've raised," the MC says, voice rising with emotion, "$18,765. And counting."

The entire room erupts. Applause, cheers, a few people outright crying. My throat tightens, eyes stinging. That's nearly double what we hoped for.

Mateo squeezes my hand again, his lips brushing my temple. "Told you we'd do good."

We did better than good. We did incredible. And we did it together.

≈

We're back home from the fundraiser.

I ease back against the pillows on the couch, my crutches leaning against the side table. Mateo insisted I take the recliner, but I wanted to be here. A throw blanket is draped across my lap, still smelling faintly of lavender from the last wash. A mug of tea rests on the coffee table in front of me, untouched.

The fundraiser was a success. More than a success. It was a reminder of who we are when we come together. This town is made of grit and heart. And tonight proved that again.

Maya's already asleep, curled up on her bed with a belly full of cupcakes. She wore her *Official Volunteer* name tag until she finally passed out, refusing to take it off, even when she changed into pajamas.

Mateo walks in from the kitchen, his hair still damp from the quick shower he took after coming home pie covered and sticky with whipped cream. His T-shirt clings slightly to his chest, and his sweatpants hang low on his hips. He's barefoot, humming something under his breath as he sets a bowl of ice cream down in front of me.

"Dulce de leche," he says. "Don't say I never gave you anything."

I smile. "You spoil me every day."

He flops down beside me, stretching his arm across the

back of the couch. His fingers toy with a strand of my hair. "How's the leg?"

"Sore," I admit. "But manageable."

"Do you want anything else? Extra pillow? Massage? Foot rub? My eternal devotion?"

"You already gave me that last one, remember?"

He leans in, pressing a kiss to my temple. "Still offering it daily."

"I'm proud of you," I say quietly.

He glances over. "For what?"

"For today. For letting people throw pies in your face and smiling through it. For making everyone laugh. For reminding me why I fell in love with you in the first place."

Mateo's eyes flicker, something tender settling in them. "You saying you almost forgot?"

"Never," I quickly respond. Taking a slow breath, I ask, "You know what I kept thinking tonight?"

"Hoping no one accidentally pegged the mayor with a cupcake?"

I laugh. "That, yes. But also, I kept thinking about how much we've already rebuilt."

He tilts his head. "Do you mean the school?"

"No. Us. Our life. Everything. A few weeks ago, I was afraid of letting myself want any of this. And now, I can't imagine a future without you in it."

He doesn't speak right away. He just looks at me like I'm the only one in the room worth looking at. Then he lifts my hand and presses a kiss to the center of my palm. "You've always been it for me, Analyse. Even when we were just pretending. Even when you didn't know it yet. Hell, even when I didn't know it yet."

"I knew," I whisper. "I just didn't trust myself to believe in it."

He tucks a curl behind my ear, his voice low. "Then let me make you believe it, every damn day."

I nod, and he leans in to kiss me slowly. When we part, I rest my forehead against his.

"What happens next?" I ask, more to myself than to him.

"Well," he says, shifting to pull a folded piece of paper from the table. "This happens."

I raise an eyebrow. "What is that?"

"Permit forms," he says, smug. "For the backyard ceremony. You said you wanted to get married as soon as you could walk without the crutches. I figured I'd get ahead on the paperwork."

Tears blur my vision, but I manage a laugh. "You're ridiculous."

"I'm yours," he corrects, then grins. "And I'm ready. We've done the hard part, chula. Now we get to do the fun part."

The clock ticks quietly behind us. Outside the window, the moon is high and silver, casting soft shadows over the quiet neighborhood.

I glance over at the photos on the wall. Me and Maya at the pumpkin patch, Mateo holding her on his shoulders, a candid from the night of Christmas dinner. I see love in every single frame.

"I want to tell Maya tomorrow," I say softly.

He just nods. "We'll do it together."

I reach for my ice cream, which has started to melt, and take a spoonful. "Did you ever think we'd get here?" I ask.

He stretches an arm behind his head and gives me a crooked smile. "Not exactly here. But something like it. I knew I'd fight for it."

I rest my head against his shoulder. "You never gave up."

"And I never will, mi amor."

I smile and reach for my phone. My fingers fly across the

screen before I can second guess myself, sending a text to The Council of Chaos.

Me: Anna, get your planning fingers ready, The wedding is in 10 weeks. Save the date!

I hit send, grinning as three little dots pop up almost instantly.

We sit like that for a while, no rush, no need for anything more than this. And even though my leg aches, and I know we have a hundred things still ahead of us—wedding plans, surgery follow ups, the reality of raising a daughter together— I feel calm.

Because whatever comes next, we'll face it like we always have. Together.

Chapter Forty

MATEO

The morning light spills across the living room in soft, golden streaks, warming the hardwood floors and catching on the specks of glitter Maya somehow still has on her cheek from last night's fundraiser. Andres is right, glitter lasts for fucking ever.

She's curled up on the couch in her unicorn pajamas, a blanket wrapped around her like a little burrito, cartoon playing low in the background. One of her legs bounces absentmindedly, the way it always does when her brain is going a mile a minute.

She doesn't know it yet, but today's going to be big. Not like yesterday's, everyone's covered in whipped cream kind of way. But in a big way that matters.

She's going to learn that her whole world is about to shift —in the best possible way...at least, I hope she feels that way.

I take a deep breath and run my hand over my jaw, nerves buzzing low and steady in my chest. I've fought fires, dragged grown men out of burning buildings, performed CPR under pressure. But telling a six-year-old I want to be her dad? That might be the scariest thing I've ever done.

"Are you okay?"

I turn to find Analyse standing in the hallway, leaning against the wall with her crutches tucked under her arms. She's already dressed—leggings, a loose sweatshirt, her curls still damp from the shower.

"Just...thinking," I say.

She makes her way over slowly, and I meet her halfway. Gently, I reach out and take the crutches from her, steadying her as she shifts her weight to lean against the arm of the couch. My hand rests on her hip without thinking.

"You ready for this?" she asks.

I hesitate. "Am I ready to be her dad? Absolutely. There's nothing I want more. Am I ready to ask her? I don't know. What if she doesn't want—"

"Mateo." Her voice is firm. "She loves you. So much. She already sees you as hers. This just makes it official."

I nod slowly, still staring at the little girl on the couch who changed everything in my world without even trying.

"Okay," I breathe. "Let's do this."

She smiles, leans in, and presses a kiss to my cheek. "I've got you. We've got her."

We settle on the couch with Maya between us, the blanket still wrapped around her little legs. She's halfway through an episode of *Bluey*, but the second I grab the remote, her eyes narrow.

"You better not be turning that off."

Analyse chuckles. "Just for a minute, bebé. We need to talk to you about something important."

Maya crosses her arms. "Is it bad?"

"Nope," I say. "Promise."

She huffs but nods. "Okay. But only if I get chocolate milk after."

"Deal," I say, my throat already tight.

Analyse reaches over and smooths down her wild bedhead.

"You remember last night at the fundraiser? How proud we were of you?"

"I was the best volunteer," she says, sitting taller. "Even Principal Ortiz said so."

"You were," I agree. "And that's one of the reasons we wanted to talk to you today. Because you've been so brave, and kind, and strong. And because...well, we have something really special to tell you."

Her eyes bounce between us, curious now.

I glance at Analyse. She gives me a nod.

I turn back to Maya. "You know I love you, right?"

She tilts her head. "Yeah. You always say that."

"I do. But I want to say it again. I love you so much, Maya. And not just because you're funny, or smart, or because you give the best hugs...though all those things are true."

She giggles.

"I love you because you're you. Because you've made this house feel like home. Because every time I see you, I know that I want to be here, with you and your mom, for the rest of my life."

Maya glances at Analyse, who squeezes her hand.

"Is this about you getting married?" she asks, nose scrunching. "Because I already knew that. You kissed her like a bajillion times at the fundraiser."

Analyse snorts and coughs into her coffee.

I laugh, pressing a hand to my chest. "Okay, yes. We are getting married."

"In ten weeks," Analyse adds, pulling out her phone. She types quickly and then holds it up to show us both the message she sent to the group chat:

Anna, get your planning fingers ready. The wedding is in 10 weeks. Save the date!

Maya's eyes go wide. "Are we going to wear matching dresses?!"

"We'll both be wearing white dresses, mi amor," Analyse says.

"I want to sparkle!"

"You always do," I say, brushing a crumb from her cheek.

She shifts her weight and looks back at me. "So, what's the special part? I already knew you were going to marry Mami. Duh."

I take a deep breath and grab the envelope I tucked into the coffee table drawer last night. I hold it out to her.

"What is it?" she asks, taking it with small fingers.

"Open it."

She tears it open with reckless abandon. Inside is a simple drawing I made—stick figures, because I can't draw for shit. The three of us, holding hands. Above us, in big, blocky letters, it says: The Rodriguez Family.

Maya blinks. "That's us."

"Yeah," I say. "It's us. But I want to make it official."

She looks up, confused. "You already moved in while Mami was in the hospital. You make me snacks, watch movies with me, and check for monsters under my bed."

"I know," I say gently. "But I want to do something bigger. I want to adopt you. Legally. I want to be your dad forever. On paper. In name. In every way there is."

Her mouth opens then closes again. She looks at Analyse. "Like, for real?"

Analyse's eyes are glossy, her voice soft. "For real, mi amor. He wants to be your daddy."

"Maya, I want you to know, I don't want to adopt you so that you can feel like you're my daughter. You already are my daughter. I want to adopt you because I love you very much, and it would make me happy for us to have the same last name. So, what do you say, kid? Can I adopt you?"

Tears spill before she even answers. She jumps into my lap, blanket and all, and buries her face in my chest. She nods so hard it shakes both of us. "Yes. I want that. I want you to be my daddy forever."

My own tears break free. I kiss the top of her head, then her forehead, then her glitter-streaked cheek. "Thank you for letting me love you, Maya. I'll never stop."

"Can I still call you Mateo sometimes?" she mumbles.

I laugh, my heart cracking open wider than I knew it could. "You can call me anything you want, bebesita. I'm yours either way."

She pulls back, eyes shining. Then she squints, serious. "Even if I call you Mr. Poopy Pants?"

Analyse loses it. Laughter spills from her like a wave, and I can't help but follow.

"Maybe not that one," I say through a grin.

Maya wraps her arms around my neck. "You're gonna be the best daddy ever."

And just like that, my nerves are gone. All that's left is this girl—my baby girl—wrapped around me, warm and loved and safe. Analyse leans in and kisses my cheek, her eyes never leaving the two of us.

"I told you," she whispers. "You've got this."

She was right. I did. *We* do.

Maya hasn't let go of me in ten full minutes, and honestly, I'm not mad at it. I hope she never does.

She's curled up against my chest, her cheek pressed right over my heart, arms tucked tightly around my neck. I hold her just as close, my hand running slowly through her curls, the steady rise and fall of her little body grounding me.

Across from me, Analyse wipes her cheeks for the third time. We're all a mess, but it's a mess I'd live in forever if it meant I get to keep this feeling. This family.

"Are you okay, Mateo?" she asks softly.

I glance at her, eyes burning, but my chest feels light. Full. "Yeah. I think I've never been more okay in my life."

Maya shifts a little and looks up at her mom. "Can I tell people?"

Analyse nods immediately, reaching over to tuck a loose curl behind Maya's ear. "Of course, mamita. Tell the whole town if you want."

Maya squeals, throws off the blanket, and darts toward her bedroom like she's on a mission—still wearing her unicorn pajamas and trailing the blanket like a cape.

I blink after her, stunned. "Where's she going?"

Analyse leans her head back, grinning. "Probably to get her glittery tiara. The one she calls her important announcement crown."

Sure enough, two seconds later, Maya storms back into the room like royalty. Crown askew, cheeks glowing, eyes wild with joy.

She climbs up on the couch and plants her feet. I'm calling it now, this kid is the next US President. "I have an announcement!" she shouts, arms spread wide. "I'm getting a new daddy and we're gonna be the Rodriguez Family!"

I let out a strangled sound and clutch my chest like she's just straight up slayed me. "You're gonna kill me, princesa."

"No dying," she says with a stern finger pointed at me. "You have to be my daddy forever now."

I give her a mock salute. "Yes, ma'am. Forever."

Analyse chokes back a laugh, dabbing at the corners of her eyes again. "How about we make that chocolate milk now? We've got a lot to celebrate."

Maya's already halfway to the kitchen. I stand and grab her mom's crutches from where they're leaning near the counter, bringing them over. I steady her as she walks, my hand at her back, and when our eyes meet, she gives me this soft, knowing look that sends something warm rippling through my chest.

We're really doing this. A family. A real one.

Maya scrambles onto a stool at the kitchen island, her tiara slipping slightly as she props her elbows on the counter. I grab the chocolate milk while Analyse reaches for glasses.

"Whipped cream?" I ask.

Analyse arches a brow. "Seriously?"

"Special occasion," I say, already pulling it from the fridge.

"Sprinkles?" Maya asks, eyes wide.

I open the cabinet with flair. "Pink and rainbow. Dealer's choice."

As I decorate her drink, I glance at Analyse leaning against the counter. Her smile is soft, eyes still misty. This isn't just about me and Maya. It's all of us. Every quiet night and early morning. Every inside joke and burnt pancake. Every time Maya curls up in my lap like she's always belonged there.

This is what I've wanted. I didn't realize before, but this is everything I needed.

I hand Maya her drink with a bow.

She gasps like it's the most magical thing she's ever seen. "It's perfect," she whispers.

A beat of silence stretches between us.

Then Analyse asks, "What do you think about a movie marathon day?"

"With pancakes for lunch?" Maya says through a mouthful of whipped cream.

"Pancakes, popcorn, and pajamas all long," I say. "The perfect day of rotting."

Maya cheers, already sliding off her stool. In no time, we're dragging every blanket and pillow we own into the living room. Maya builds a fort, Analyse supervising from the couch. Meanwhile, I'm flipping pancakes in the kitchen while Maya heckles me like a pint-sized Gordon Ramsay.

"That one's burnt!"

"It's called caramelized!"

"Chef's banned," she declares, arms crossed.

"Chef's underpaid," I mutter, grinning as I plate the stack.

We eat on the floor inside the fort, maple syrup dripping onto paper towels. When the sugar crash hits, we all end up in a pile—Maya between us, head on my shoulder, blanket tucked up to her chin.

Maya reaches for my hand without looking, just this tiny, instinctive move like she knows that I'll always be there to hold it. And she's right. I will. Forever.

Chapter Forty-One

ANALYSE

Today's finally the day. I get to marry the love of my life.

The last ten weeks have been a whirlwind. Between wedding planning and physical therapy, there were days I wasn't sure we'd make it to the finish line with our sanity intact—but here we are. Anna and Mari helped with everything. From picking florals to making a custom playlist that included both Daddy Yankee and Adele—because we all know that's my vibe—we made it happen. I still can't believe we pulled it off.

And after weeks of stretching, strengthening, and more tears than I'll admit out loud, I can finally walk without crutches. I get to walk down the aisle today on my own two feet. It may not seem like a big deal to anyone else, but to me? It's everything. I fought for this. Every ache, every step, every "just one more rep" led to this moment. And I'm going to soak in every second of it.

In the middle of wedding madness, we also finalized Mateo adopting Maya.

To no one's surprise, Nico didn't even put up a fight. I

don't know if that makes me feel sad or relieved. There's a part of me that still grieves the version of him I once hoped he'd become. But when the papers came through and Mateo held them in his hands, I knew—without a doubt—we were exactly where we were meant to be.

Mateo is over the moon. And today...today I get to marry him. Today I get to become Analyse Rodriguez.

The dress fits perfectly. Creamy white, off the shoulder, with little lace details that Mariana insisted on adding "because you deserve to feel like a princesa." My hair is curled and pinned loosely, a few strands framing my face. There's a single white daisy tucked behind my ear—a nod to the dress I wore the first time Mateo ever saw me.

I smooth my hands down the front of my dress, nerves and joy tangled together in a knot somewhere beneath my ribs.

Anna pokes her head into the room. "Are you ready, bride?"

I look and smile, eyes already glassy. "As I'll ever be."

She steps inside and holds out a small envelope. "This is from Mateo. He said to read it before you walked down the aisle."

My heart does a full somersault as I take it. The envelope is simple. No name, just a little heart drawn in the corner with a Sharpie. Very him.

Inside is a note, scrawled in his blocky, slightly tilted handwriting:

You once told me you weren't sure if forever was meant for you.

Today is the first day of our forever. I'm going to spend the rest of my life proving it to you.

I'll carry your heart in every step, in every breath.

See you at the altar, chula. Te quiero mucho.

—M

I press the paper to my heart and let out a breath that shakes loose every last nerve. This is real. It's happening.

"Okay," I whisper. "Let's do this."

The hum of music floats through our backyard, soft and golden like the fairy lights strung from the trees. It's warm tonight. The sun is beginning to set, painting the sky in warm amber and gold. It feels like magic.

Laughter ripples through the air, mingling with the faint clinking of glasses and the smell of fresh florals and food.

I stand just out of sight, heart thudding in my chest, fingers curled loosely around my bouquet. Through the fluttering white curtain draped over the archway, I catch a glimpse of Mateo—he's wearing a dark navy suit, pacing in place near the altar with a nervous smile on his face.

People are already seated, Mari is handing Maya her basket of rose petals, and the soft melody of "Moon River" is playing on a speaker nearby. And then the music changes. The soft strum of a Spanish guitar blends with the first chords of a ballad version of "Tu Amor Me Hace Bien," and I know—it's time.

The doors open.

Maya goes first, her little white dress sparkling with every step. She throws petals to the ground, pausing halfway to wave dramatically at the crowd. Everyone laughs.

And then it's just me.

Mateo is standing under the arch, hands folded, eyes locked on mine like the rest of the world has disappeared. I feel it instantly—the grounding weight of his gaze, the love that pulses steady and deep between us. Every step I take feels like a vow in itself. Like a promise I've already been living.

When I finally reach him, he takes my hand, brings it to his lips, and whispers, "Hi."

"Hi," I breathe back.

His hands tremble slightly as they hold mine, and I realize he's just as wrecked as I am. Hilda officiates—somehow managing to sound both gracious and slightly inappropriate, which makes the whole crowd laugh at least twice. But when she talks about love, real lasting love, she goes soft.

"I've known Analyse since she was just a girl," she says, glancing at me, eyes glistening. "And I've never seen her like this. I've never seen her lit up from the inside out."

My eyes sting.

She turns to Mateo. "And I've known Mateo long enough to know he didn't believe he deserved this kind of happiness. But here he is. Shining like someone who finally realized he was worthy of everything. And you are, Mateo."

Mateo swallows hard, and I reach for his hand again. We say our vows. His are unrehearsed, rough edged, and beautiful. Mine are scribbled on a notecard I rewrote six times, but when I say them, they come out clear and unwavering.

We talk about choosing each other. About being safe places. About laughter in the hard times and dancing in the kitchen at midnight. About Maya. Always about Maya.

When Hilda finally says, "You may now kiss your wife," Mateo doesn't hesitate.

His hands are on my waist in an instant, and his lips find mine in a kiss that feels like everything—past, present, and future all wrapped into one.

The crowd cheers. Someone whoops loudly (probably Andres), and Maya throws more petals in the air while shouting, "They're married now!"

We turn to face everyone, hands raised in triumph, and Mateo leans down to whisper, "You're stuck with me now."

"Good," I whisper back, "because I've never felt more sure of anything."

~

The house is quiet now. The music from the reception has faded, the last of the guests have gone, and Maya is tucked in at Seb and Mari's for the night.

I stand barefoot in the middle of our bedroom, heart still fluttering from the high of the day, from the way Mateo looked at me like I hung the moon and then some. I run my hand over the soft lace of my dress one last time before I slip the zipper down and let it fall to the floor.

Ten weeks ago, I could barely walk without pain. And now, I'm standing tall, on my own two feet, about to have sex with my husband. God, I can't believe we got married—my husband, my husband, my husband, I'll never get tired of saying that.

My entire body hums. Mateo appears in the doorway to the bathroom, one hand braced on the frame, that crooked grin already tugging at his mouth. "I have a surprise for you," he says, voice low and full of something wicked.

I raise a brow. "Oh yeah? What is it?"

He laughs, dark and warm. "You'll see."

I bite my lip, heartbeat kicking up a notch. "Bring it on, Mr. Rodriguez."

The door creaks shut behind him. When it opens again, I turn, and nearly lose my breath. Mateo steps out shirtless, wearing nothing but black boxer briefs...and a Ghostface mask.

"Are you serious?" I ask, already breathless.

He leans against the doorframe, voice low and full of mischief. "You said it was a fantasy. And I did promise you a wedding night gift."

CHAPTER FORTY-ONE

I laugh, nervous and turned the hell on. "You're ridiculous."

He tilts his head, the mask making the motion both eerie and stupidly hot. "And you married me anyway."

"Because you're hot," I tease, backing toward the bed.

"I think you want me to chase you," he says, taking slow, deliberate steps forward.

I swallow, my thighs pressing together. "I want you to ruin me."

That's all it takes.

He's on me in seconds, dragging me to the bed, pinning me beneath him with a growl that goes straight to my pussy. The cool plastic of the mask presses against my cheek as his mouth finds the curve of my neck.

"You've been teasing me in that dress all night," he mutters. "Looking like a fucking angel. And now you're mine, Mrs. Rodriguez."

"Say it again," I breathe, my nails digging into his shoulders.

"Mrs. Rodriguez. My wife. My filthy, perfect wife."

He pulls back just enough to rip the mask off and toss it aside. His mouth crashes onto mine, and the heat between us explodes like it's been waiting all this time. Because it has. Since the fire. Since the pain. Since the fear. But now? Now, there's only this.

He kisses me until I can't think, then trails his mouth down my body, over the valley between my breasts, my stomach, the dip of my hips, leaving a trail of open-mouthed kisses and soft bites that make my legs shake.

"Still okay?" he murmurs, glancing up.

"Yes," I gasp. "God, yes."

He slides my panties down slowly, groaning when he sees just how ready I am. "You're so fucking wet already."

"You in that mask kind of did it for me," I pant.

He grins, wicked. "Noted."

He dips his head and licks a long stripe through my folds, and I arch off the bed, a broken sound ripping from my throat.

"Fuck, Mateo—"

His tongue works me over with slow, deliberate strokes. He teases me, torments me, sucks my clit into his mouth until I'm begging. Then he slides two fingers inside, curling them just right.

"I missed this," he growls. "Missed how you fall apart for me."

I come hard, sobbing his name as my legs shake. He doesn't stop—not right away. He kisses my thigh, my stomach, working his way back up until he's hovering over me again, eyes dark with want.

"Still good?" he whispers, brushing hair from my face.

I nod, pulling him in for a kiss. "I need you inside me. Now."

He lines himself up, eyes locked with mine. "I've thought about this every night. You have no idea how badly I've wanted you."

"Show me," I whisper, wrapping my legs around his waist.

He pushes in slowly, stretching me, filling me inch by inch. The sensation is overwhelming after so long, and tears spring to my eyes, not from pain but from the pure relief of having him inside me again. Of being whole.

"Fuck," he hisses, trembling with the effort to go slow. "You feel like heaven."

I dig my nails into his back, urging him deeper. "Don't hold back. Not tonight."

Something feral flashes in his eyes. He grabs the Ghostface mask from beside us and slips it back on, the juxtaposition of the sinister mask and his loving eyes sending a thrill through me.

"What if I want to make my new bride scream?" he whispers, voice muffled behind the plastic.

I shiver, spreading my legs wider. "Then do it."

He pulls out almost completely before slamming back into me with a force that makes the headboard hit the wall. I cry out, my body arching off the bed.

"Is this okay?" he asks, stilling momentarily, eyes searching mine through the mask's openings.

"God, yes. More. Please, more."

His hips snap forward again and again, each thrust deeper than the last. The mask should be ridiculous, but it's not...it's making me wetter, my fantasy coming to life in the most unexpected way. My husband knows my darkest desires and loves me for them.

"You're so fucking tight," he groans, gripping my hips hard enough to bruise. "So perfect for me," he continues, voice ragged behind the mask. "Look at you taking me so well after all this time."

I clench around him, savoring the fullness, the delicious stretch that I've missed for too long. My body remembers him even after weeks of healing, welcomes him home like he belongs there.

"Harder," I demand, hooking my ankles behind his back. "I won't break."

His laugh is dark, filtered through the mask. "No, you won't. You're the strongest woman I know."

He shifts his angle, hitting that spot deep inside that makes stars burst behind my eyelids. My back arches off the bed as he pounds into me, the slick sounds of our bodies meeting filling the room alongside my desperate moans.

"That's it," he encourages, one hand sliding between us to circle my clit. "Let me hear how good it feels. Let me hear my wife."

My wife. The words send another wave of heat through

me. I'm his and he's mine. Legally, fully, in every way that matters.

"Take it off," I gasp, tugging at the mask. "I want to see your face when you come."

He yanks the mask away, revealing flushed cheeks and wild eyes. His hair is damp with sweat, curling against his forehead. Beautiful. Mine.

"I love you," he groans, thrusting deeper. "Fuck, Analyse, I love you so much."

My body tightens around him as another orgasm builds. I've missed this. Not just the sex, but the connection. The way he looks at me like I'm his everything.

"Come with me," I beg, feeling my second orgasm building. "Please, baby, I need you with me."

His rhythm falters, hips jerking as he drives deeper. "Fuck, chula. I'm close."

I reach up to touch his face, my thumb tracing his bottom lip. The contrast between this tender gesture and the raw, animalistic way he's fucking me makes everything more intense.

"Look at me," I whisper. "Look at me when you fill me up."

His eyes lock with mine, pupils blown wide with desire. The connection between us is electric, transcending physical pleasure. This is what I've missed most during those long weeks of recovery—this profound intimacy that makes me feel seen in ways no one else ever has.

"Mine," he growls, and I feel him swell inside me. "All fucking mine."

The pressure of his fingers increases on my clit as he pounds into me with renewed desperation. His eyes never leave mine, even as his body tenses, ready to fall over the edge.

"Come for me, Analyse. One more time," he commands, his voice raw and broken.

When the wave hits, it's devastating. My entire body convulses around him, muscles clenching so hard I see white. I cry out his name—a prayer, a plea, a promise—as my nails leave half-moon indents in his shoulders.

"Fuck," he groans, burying himself to the hilt. "I'm coming, baby. I'm—"

He pulses deep inside me, a hot rush that fills every inch and sets my nerves on fire. I feel him unravel, hips stuttering, his fingers digging into my thighs so hard I know I'll have bruises in the morning.

The sensation of him spilling inside me is overwhelming— slick heat, the rhythmic clench of his cock feeding another wave of pleasure that builds and builds until there's nothing left but raw, pure sensation. I shudder, trembling around him, and the force of my orgasm sharpens, stretches. It's not just pleasure, it's something else—like I'm coming undone in layers, peeling back years of fear and pain, until I'm nothing but feeling.

He gasps my name, voice ragged and reverent, and the sound pushes me higher. My body locks up, toes curling, and I sob, literally sob, from the intensity of it. Mateo holds me through it, his hands never leaving my skin, his body pressed flush against mine as if he could fuse us together with the heat alone.

The aftershocks are endless. I convulse around him, every spasm squeezing out another gasp, another tear. The room blurs and spins and spins, then narrows to the two of us, chest to chest, still joined and shaking and desperate to hold each other closer.

When the last tremor fades, we collapse together in a tangled heap. He's still inside me, still impossibly hard, but the urgency has softened into something sweeter, something that feels like coming home after a long, hard journey.

We cling to each other, breathless and sweaty and stunned.

315

My cheek is pressed to his chest, where his heart pounds steady and strong beneath my ear. His arms stay locked around me, and I tilt my face to look up at him.

His Ghostface mask is somewhere on the floor, discarded in the heat of everything, and what's left is just Mateo—bare, flushed, and looking at me like I'm the beginning and the end of every dream he's ever had.

"Holy, shit," I whisper.

He laughs, low and hoarse, pressing a kiss to my temple. "You good, chula?"

I nod against his skin, still dazed. "Better than good. I'm married to the ultimate fantasy."

He groans softly and buries his face in my neck. "You saying I'm your fantasy?"

I drag my nails light down his back. "You in that mask? Definitely."

His laugh rumbles through me, and for a second, everything slows...just the two of us tangled in sheets, wrapped in love, sweat, and everything we've survived to get here.

"I love you," I whisper.

He shifts just enough to cup my cheek. "I love you, too. Forever, mi vida. Forever."

I wake up the next morning with a sense of bliss washing over me.

Mateo is asleep beside me, one arm flung over my waist, his chest rising and falling in a steady rhythm that calms every corner of me. I should be asleep, too, but my mind is wide awake, tracing over every moment that led us here.

I used to lie awake and feel a different kind of quiet. One that echoed with uncertainty. With grief. With the ache of everything I'd lost, everything I thought I'd never have again.

There were nights I couldn't imagine a version of myself that wasn't crawling through the wreckage—of Nico, of heart-break, of loneliness.

Now I'm lying here with my husband. With a new name. With a heart stitched back together by the very same hands that helped pull me from the fire...figurately and literally.

I didn't just survive. I lived. I laughed again. I kissed again. I let myself fall, even though it scared me. Even when I didn't know if my legs could hold the weight of it. And somehow, we built a home in the middle of the mess. A home with Sunday pancakes, silly playlists, Ghostface masks, and glitter crowns.

A home with love etched in every corner. Mateo did that.

He shifts slightly, bringing me closer to his body.

I run my fingers through his hair and whisper, "I'm not going anywhere."

Because I'm not. We made it. Something I thought was not for keeps became my forever. It wasn't a perfect journey, and it wasn't always painless—but we did it. Boldly. Together.

And now, until my very last breath, I get to wake up as a Rodriguez. As someone who finally stopped running from the fire and decided to build something beautiful in its place.

Epilogue

I t's been nine months since the fire. Nine months since I nearly lost the two people I love most in this world. Six months since I married Analyse and adopted Maya—since we finally made official what had already been written in our hearts.

And now we're here.

It's hard to believe that a year ago, Analyse asked me to be her fake boyfriend. Just for show, just to keep Nico at bay. At the time, I said yes without hesitation, not knowing that her request would change the entire course of my life. That pretending to be hers would feel more real than anything I'd ever known. That somewhere between the fake kisses and made-up stories, I'd fall harder than I ever thought possible—for both of them.

Back then, I didn't realize how deeply I craved a family. How badly I wanted to be someone's home. Analyse and Maya gave me that. They gave me purpose, laughter, and love. They gave me everything I needed.

The rental car is quiet, save for the soft hum of music playing from the speakers—something acoustic that Analyse picked, because she said the moment felt like it deserved something soft. California sunlight streams through the windows, warming my forearms as I drive, one hand on the wheel, the other laced with hers.

Her fingers squeeze mine gently, and I glance over. She's looking out the window, but I can tell she feels it too. The weight of it.

This trip wasn't easy to agree to. I haven't been back since the funeral. I couldn't. Not when the pain still felt like it might choke me in my sleep. But it's time. Analyse said as much one night, curled up beside me in bed, her hand on my chest.

"I think they'd be proud of you," she whispered. "And I think they'd want to meet us. All of us."

So I booked the flights. Took the time off. Packed Maya's little pink suitcase and steeled myself for a moment I'd avoided for far too long.

Now, as the cemetery comes into view, my pulse kicks up. My chest tightens. But I keep driving. Because this time, I'm not alone.

We pull up the hill and park under the shade of a jacaranda tree, its purple blossoms scattered across the ground like confetti.

"Are we here, daddy?"

Daddy. I still haven't gotten used to how easily it falls from her mouth, or how right it feels.

"We're here, princesa," I say, lifting her out of her booster seat and offering her my hand.

She grabs it and holds tight as we walk up the path, Analyse on my other side, her arm looped through mine. It doesn't take long to find the headstones. I know exactly where they are. Even after all this time.

There's a quiet kind of peace up here. Wind rustling the

trees. Distant waves crashing below. The ocean was always my mom's favorite.

I stop in front of the three gravestones—Mom, Dad, and Maribel. My baby sister. The ache in my chest roars to life. I kneel, my fingers brushing over the engraved letters.

"Hi," I whisper. "It's been a while."

Analyse doesn't say anything. Just kneels beside me, her hand on my back, grounding me. Maya settles on the grass and starts picking up a little bouquet of wildflowers.

I clear my throat. "I'm sorry it took me so long to come back. I couldn't...I wasn't ready. But I am now. And I wanted to introduce you to someone."

My voice shakes, but I push through.

"This is my wife. Analyse. She's...God, she's everything. She's strong, brilliant, and fiery as hell, and she loves me like she sees every broken part and wants it anyway."

Analyse lets out a soft laugh. "High praise, Rodriguez."

I squeeze her hand.

"And this," I say, turning to Maya. "Is Maya. My daughter. She's seven and smarter than I ever was. She loves glitter, pancakes, and asking a million questions at bedtime."

Maya beams and runs over, wildflowers in hand. "Hi, Grandma and Grandpa, and Titi Maribel. I brought you these."

She lays the flowers across the headstones, one for each, then settles between me and Analyse.

"I used to not have a daddy," she says solemnly. "But now I do."

My throat tightens. I don't know how I got this lucky.

Analyse leans into me slightly, her voice soft. "They'd be so proud of you, Mateo."

I nod, not trusting my voice. And then, like she planned it perfectly—which, knowing her, she probably did—she shifts, pulling a small envelope from her purse.

"I, uh, have something too," she says, cheeks a little flushed.

I look at her, confused. "What's that?"

She hands it to me without a word. I open it slowly, careful not to crease whatever's inside—and stop cold. My breath catches in my throat. Inside is a black-and-white ultrasound printout. Grainy and small, but unmistakable. For a second, I just stare. My mind blank, the world narrowing to the tiny curve of life on that paper. A flicker of something brand new. Hope. A heartbeat. A beginning.

"Are you serious?" I whisper, voice cracked and hoarse.

Analyse nods, her eyes glistening. "Surprise, Papa."

She laughs softly, a little breathless. "I didn't think it'd happen so fast. We only took out my IUD a month ago—I wasn't expecting this yet. But...here we are."

I blink down at the print again. My hands are shaking. There are no words for this kind of feeling, the way joy can barrel through you like a freight train and still feel like flying.

Maya's eyes go wide as she peeks at the photo. "Is that a baby?"

Analyse smiles at her. "Yep. In my belly."

Maya squeals and claps her hands. "I'm gonna be a big sister!"

I let out a shaky laugh, tears slipping down my cheeks before I can stop them. I wrap my arms around them both, pulling them into me, kissing the top of Maya's head, then cupping Analyse's face in my hands as I kiss her.

"You have no idea how happy I am," I murmur, forehead pressed to hers. "No idea."

"I think I do," she says, voice thick with emotion.

I stare at her, completely undone. "You've already given me the world, and somehow...you keep finding ways to make it more beautiful. I don't know how I got this lucky."

Analyse leans in, pressing a kiss to my cheek. "You didn't get lucky, Mateo. This is what you were always meant for."

I lean back and turn toward the headstones again, lifting the ultrasound so they can see.

"This is your grandchild," I say. "And I'm gonna do this right. I swear to protect them. I'll protect them with everything I've got."

We sit there for a while—just the three of us, and the memory of three more. The air is quiet except for the rustle of wind through the trees and the distant sound of birds settling in for the night. The cemetery is bathed in golden light, the sun beginning its slow descent behind the California hills, casting long shadows across the grass.

Maya curls into my side, her little hand slipping into mine. Analyse leans her head on my shoulder, the curve of her body fitting perfectly against me, like we were always meant to end up here—like everything before this, the heartache, the fear, the waiting, was just a winding road that led us to this peace.

I glance down at the headstones, and for the first time in years, the weight in my chest isn't unbearable. It's still there, but it's quieter now. Softer. I feel them here. I feel their love in the breeze, their presence in the way the sunlight catches Maya's hair, in the way Analyse squeezes my hand without needing to say a word.

We stay there until the sky turns lavender and the stars start to peek through. Until the chill of the night nudges us back to the car. But even as we walk away, I don't feel like I'm leaving them behind.

They're with me—in every breath, every heartbeat, every step forward. And as I look at my wife, my daughter, and the tiny flicker of life we've yet to meet, I know one thing for sure. This is home. This is forever. This is the happiest ending I never saw coming.

The End.

Acknowledgments

Thank you so much for reading *Not For Keeps*! Writing these stories for you is a privilege I am so grateful for, one that I will never take for granted.

Amir, you make all this possible. Thank you for always supporting me and encouraging me to write. You're a great dad and phenomenal husband. Love you, Sweetface.

To my alpha and beta readers, Catherine and Jo, your insights were so valuable and I'm thankful that I was able to work with you both on this one.

To my family for the constant support and my best friend Jenny for letting me drone on about these characters (and all my random ideas). I love you.

And finally, to the readers, to the BookTok and Bookstagram community, to everyone that was willing to take a chance on me, THANK YOU. You have no idea how much your support means to me. Sorry for making y'all cry, it might keep happening.

About the Author

Jasmine Ahmad is a romance author who writes heart-wrenching, emotional love stories filled with depth and swoon-worthy moments. She loves exploring the messy, beautiful complexities of relationships, and personal growth. A proud Latinx writer, Jasmine's holds a Bachelor's in Psychology, which gives her a deep appreciation for human emotions and the way people connect.

Originally from Queens, NY, she now resides in Southern California with her husband, children, and two cats.

Connect with Jasmine:

Instagram: @AuthorJasmineAhmad
TikTok: @AuthorJasmineAhmad
Website: www.authorjasmineahmad.com

Also by Jasmine Ahmad

Back To You